Adrian Bell was born on 4 October 1901, the ▩▩▩▩ ▩▩rt Bell, a Scottish journalist. He grew up in London (whe▩ ▩isitors to the family home included such figures as G. K. Chesterton) and was educated at Uppingham School. On leaving school, he decided that he would like to work in the open air, and in 1920 he was apprenticed to a West Suffolk farmer, Vic Savage (the John Colville of *Corduroy*). Later he acquired a small farm of his own. His first book about his farming experiences, *Corduroy*, appeared in 1930 and won critical and popular acclaim. It was soon followed by *Silver Ley* and *The Cherry Tree*, making up a trilogy. Adrian Bell married Marjorie Gibson in 1931, and in 1938 they moved to East Suffolk, where he ran a ninety-acre mixed farm for many years. *Apple Acre*, a picture of village life during the Second World War, was his other great success. Adrian Bell was also the compiler of the first crossword puzzle to appear in *The Times*, in 1930, and went on providing *Times* crosswords regularly for fifty years, including the Golden Jubilee puzzle of 1980. Even after giving up his farm, he wrote a number of books placed by literary critics in the rural tradition of Richard Jeffries and Mary Mitford, and he contributed weekly articles to the *Eastern Daily Press* for thirty years under the heading of 'A Countryman's Notebook'. He died on 5 September 1980. The first paperback edition of *Corduroy*, one of the early Penguins, was published in 1940.

Martin Bell has been the independent MP for Tatton since 1997. Previously, he was a broadcast journalist at the BBC. He joined the staff of BBC TV news in 1965, and worked on assignments in eighty countries, including eleven wars: Vietnam; Middle East (1967 and 1973); Angola; Rhodesia; Biafra; Nicaragua; El Salvador; the Gulf; Croatia; and Bosnia; and held the posts of, variously, Chief Washington Correspondent, Berlin Correspondent, Eastern European Correspondent, Foreign Affairs Correspondent and Special Correspondent, BBC Nine O'Clock News.

Martin Bell was awarded an OBE in 1992. He was voted Royal Television Society Reporter of the Year in 1977 and again in 1993 for his work in Bosnia, and has received several honorary degrees. His book *In Harm's Way* was published in Penguin in 1996.

Corduroy

ADRIAN BELL

PENGUIN BOOKS

PENGUIN BOOKS

Published by the Penguin Group
Penguin Books Ltd, 27 Wrights Lane, London w8 5tz, England
Penguin Putnam Inc., 375 Hudson Street, New York, New York 10014, USA
Penguin Books Australia Ltd, Ringwood, Victoria, Australia
Penguin Books Canada Ltd, 10 Alcorn Avenue, Toronto, Ontario, Canada m4v 3b2
Penguin Books (NZ) Ltd, Private Bag 102902, NSMC, Auckland, New Zealand

Penguin Books Ltd, Registered Offices: Harmondsworth, Middlesex, England

First published in Great Britain by Penguin Books 1930
This edition published in Penguin Books 2000
1 3 5 7 9 10 8 6 4 2

Set in 12/14pt Monotype Dante
Typeset by Rowland Phototypesetting Ltd,
Bury St Edmunds, Suffolk
Printed in England by Clays Ltd, St Ives plc

Introduction

Corduroy was originally published in 1930. It was my father's first and best-known book, in a writing career that lasted for half a century and also yielded thousands of newspaper columns and crossword puzzles. It became established very quickly as a countryside classic, and earned him a special place in the history as well as the literature of the Suffolk that he caressed with his words for sixty years.

It was not his native Suffolk. *Corduroy* begins as an escape story about a rather Bohemian young-man-about-Battersea fleeing from the threat of an office life in London. His education had ended at Uppingham School, which he hated and which had been selected by his mother on the advice of the Army and Navy Stores, of all places, which was where she did her shopping for everything, including schools. His father, who was a republican and socialist as well as the news editor of the *Observer*, refused to entertain the idea of sending him to a university, on the grounds that universities were the citadels of privilege and the playgrounds of the rich. His father also convinced him that his professed desire to write was but a manifestation of adolescence, and it was time to go out and do something else with his life. That something would be done in the open air, for he had heard the call of the land, and heeded it. The twenty-year-old dreamy and loitering youth (his own description) mounted his newly acquired motorcycle, which had seen wartime service in France, and headed east. In Weston Colville near Bury St Edmunds he was apprenticed to Vic Savage, a yeoman farmer of the old school who taught him all he knew in the best agricultural college of all, a well-run working farm. The fame of Vic Savage endures, as it deserves to even to this day, in Mr Colville of *Corduroy* – the story of my father's arduous apprenticeship.

The farmer and his apprentice did not know it at the time, but these were the last years of the inherited order of things in agriculture, in which the old ways and rhythms of the land prevailed. Hedging and ditching were done by hand, fox-hunting was not a political issue and fields were farmed by the concerted muscle-power of men and horses. The supporting past of *Corduroy* includes the Suffolk Punches. This was the world before the Great Depression, before the mechanical revolution which drove so many farm-workers from the land – and long before the farms of Suffolk were threatened by the sinister advance of agribusiness. My father, who went on for the next twenty years to own his own small farms in west and east Suffolk, and to write about them in his other masterpieces – *Silver Ley*, *The Cherry Tree* and *Apple Acre* – clung tenaciously to the old ways of doing things, whether or not they were economical, just for the sake of doing them as he had learned them. He was still ploughing with horses in the late 1940s. My twin sister Sylvia and I used the backs of his old and original manuscripts to draw pictures of his venerable farm horses, Kitty and Boxer. We were thus responsible for the loss of some real collectors' items.

There was something about the world he was writing about – mainly because by the mid-1930s it was already seen to be vanishing – and something about the way he wrote about it, that had a most extraordinary impact on readers at that time and in the cataclysmic war that followed. These were not necessarily country people, except in the special and privileged sense that they somehow became so by reading what he wrote. His work, for which *Corduroy* set the standard, had an elegiac quality. It spoke of calmer times and saner values. Its distinguishing feature was a sort of rooted and practical mysticism, seeing its visions and dreaming its dreams in the fields and furrows of a working Suffolk farm. He wrote somewhere, 'I felt I was being used by a power beyond myself for its own purposes.'

Corduroy ran into many editions, together with its sequels, *Silver Ley* and *The Cherry Tree*, throughout the 1930s and 1940s. The most elaborate was the full trilogy, published by The Bodley Head in 1948, and illustrated by Harry Becker. The writer and the artist never met (Becker died in 1928), but they surely knew their Suffolk. The words and pictures match and illuminate each other to perfection. A full set is a rare and treasured possession, much in demand among members of the flourishing Adrian Bell Society.

The most influential edition, without doubt, was Penguin's. It was published in 1940 in a small format and on paper of distinctly wartime quality. It could fit into a soldier's pocket or his kitbag, and often did. It thus found a place wherever British forces served, by land, sea and air, in the war zones of the Second World War.

It was only after his death, in 1980, that I became fully aware of the effect he had had on so many people's lives. At the bottom of a drawer we found a collection of letters sent to him from servicemen who had read his books in their bivouacs and tank turrets, and drawn from them a measure of comfort and hope in the hardest times of their lives. He opened a window on another world, a world of peace and sanity, of enduring values and seasonal rhythms remote from the war's destruction. I also discovered, having visited some of the planet's unquiet corners, that his books held within them an extra resonance for someone who had endured such bleak experiences. It was not nostalgia that he offered, but an alternative vision of England. A Lieutenant in the Royal Artillery wrote to him in November 1943 from North Africa to thank him for having written *The Cherry Tree*, and to urge him to write more:

You will no doubt realise that to us who have not seen green grass, trees and country lanes bounded with hedgerows for a long time, such a book which carries one back to the English countryside so easily is very much appreciated.

In a now half-forgotten magazine, *Everybody's*, he wrote an open letter to one of his far-flung constituents, an RAF fighter pilot serving in the Mediterranean – a pilot who must have faced the prospect of death whenever he took to the skies. It is hard for us who take so much for granted to imagine such an ordeal. But my father understood:

You wrote to me from Malta, from a Malta pounded by air from Italy, from Sicily, from North Africa, ringed by U-Boats, all but cut off. You wrote to me (heaven knows how the letter got through) that when the war was finished, you and your girl wanted to marry and have a little farm in England. You have a vision of England. Wherever you are, it has been your consolation and hope. Keep that vision, because it's true. It may be the key to your life. I am anxious that you should know this; because if you follow your impulses and lead your farming life, with all its ups and downs, at the end of it you will sit back and recall that first vision of it that you had in the desert or the jungle. And you will know then that it was all in all a true vision.

Adrian Bell was born in 1901. He was mercifully just too young for active service in the First World War, and too old for it in the second – even if his health had allowed, which it did not. But he did the state some service, in sharing and communicating his vision of England through the conscripted paperback edition of *Corduroy*. Through the words of writers such as my father, the faith and fortitude of men who had lost touch with friends and family, and the country for which they were fighting, were sustained. Knowing warfare as I now do, I am convinced that in many cases it must have helped to save their sanity. When the war was over and the survivors returned, it is my opinion that the author and the publisher should have been decorated with the DPM (Distinguished Publications Medal), or some such. They had surely earned it.

Adrian Bell's books, with *Corduroy* at the head of the list, were especially prized among prisoners of war. I have in front of me a postcard marked 'Kriegsgefangenenpost'. It was written on 25 May 1943 by Philip Forsyth, POW number 1156, from Stammlager IX C, somewhere in Germany. He wrote to my father:

It's so good to read of simple things still going on in my lovely Suffolk. Three Mays ago I took *Corduroy* to re-read in France. Alas, I lost it unread at Dunkirk. But I found another at Cerniers. Later, on the march in, I abandoned book after book till it remained alone. Then I read each page slowly, twice, for I didn't know when I'd see a book again.

Sergeant G. W. Risdon wrote on 17 March 1943 from Stalag XVIII A:

With anything like luck I hope to be reading *Apple Acre* in England soon. But no matter what the place may be, it will ever be good to absorb the story of England's farms and fieldworkers written by someone who appreciates them for themselves.

And a South African, Coombe Arnold Walter, sent a letter on 10 June 1943 from a prison camp in Italy:

The charm, the homeliness, the peace even in turmoil, the deep satisfying joy of your day to day experiences, come to me and many others in like circumstances as a delight that refreshes and abides, and makes more bearable our own strange life here.

Never mind the critics – and even the critics were impressed – no author could ask for better reviews than those. They show how the words he wrote, most often by lamplight on the kitchen table when the farming day was done, touched the hearts of men in extraordinary circumstances and with extraordinary force. The Suffolk of Adrian Bell has changed beyond recognition, not all for the better, and no one mourned its passing more eloquently than he did. *Corduroy* stands as a living record of it, and is as fresh on the page today as on the day it was written.

This new Penguin edition of *Corduroy*, exactly sixty years after the old one, will bring pleasure to my father's old friends, and I do not doubt that it will win him many new ones. It is also a most fitting way in which to celebrate the approaching centenary of his birth. There are writers, quite celebrated in their day, whose books slide headlong into oblivion as soon as the fashion changes. There are others, like the author of *Corduroy*, whose appeal is timeless. The reprinting of his work and the revival of his popularity are a source of great satisfaction to the family. My sisters Anthea and Sylvia and I take it as a tribute not just to him but to our mother Marjorie, a never wavering source of strength and love. She alone could read his handwriting, which looked as if insects had died on the page, and she even helped with the crossword puzzles. She also lit his fires and milked his goats. He could not have achieved all that he did without her.

His was not just a rare talent, but a unique one. There is a distinction to be made, both in literature and in politics, between things that endure and things that merely happen. My own life's work has been on the happening side, in one profession or another, and will accordingly fade and pass. His was in the category of things that endure. He could find more of interest to write compellingly about in the pond life in his back garden than I could find in the war zones of the world, or for that matter the House of Commons.

There is nothing in my life in which I take more pride than in being the son of the author of *Corduroy*.

Martin Bell

I was upon the fringe of Suffolk, a country rich in agricultural detail, missed by my untutored eye. It was but scenery to me: nor had I an inkling of what more it might become. Farming, to my mind, was as yet the townsman's glib catalogue of creatures and a symbol of escape. The true friendliness of the scene before me lay beneath ardours of which I knew nothing.

I was flying from the threat of an office life. I was twenty years old, and the year was 1920.

There had been a country walk with my father on which he had suggested it was time I should 'do' something. I had replied naïvely that I wanted to write. To which he had made an answer that the desire to write in the young was but a manifestation of the sexual impulse. This had confirmed my worst fears – that there was nothing 'in me' after all save the natural disturbances, as my few scrappy and turbulent compositions seemed to attest. So I had bowed to his implication that my dreams and visitations were one with the spots on my face, and only pleaded that my life should be something in the open air.

My father, perhaps, spoke better than he knew. At any rate, by certain combinations of chance we came into touch with one Mr Colville, an established farmer of Suffolk, who agreed, for the usual premium, to teach me agriculture.

Thus it was that the dreamy and loitering youth, who would have worn a drooping bow-tie had he been able to withstand the jeers of street urchins, set forth upon a motor-cycle (war model, late from France), clad in breeches (war surplus) and boots which the assistant at the Army and Navy Stores had said were their heaviest quality, sold for mountaineering and tramping holidays.

I had allowed half a day for the journey, reckoning on getting lost as well as on mechanical difficulty, my few trial runs having dispelled the illusion that a motor-cycle was any kind of infallible or magic transport. I was about half-way when I paused for lunch, but I did not stay to muse upon the promised land, as I must now leave the main road for circuitous country byways. I feared the dark, knowing my acetylene lamp for an affair of much stink and little light. So I pushed on, a map between my knees. I had made the novice's mistake of choosing the route that looked the shortest on the map, and so lost my way once or twice, and was further confused by asking guidance of the deaf or the witless, as strangers chance to do.

About four-thirty I arrived in the dust of a dry October at Farley Hall, Benfield St George. The farm premises looked deserted, and only the faint chirrup of sparrows broke the silence on the cessation of my engine. A single rustic of Neanderthal aspect eyed me from afar. I left my motor-cycle and knocked at the side door which was nearest and had evidence of familiar use. I had already fallen into a local practice. It is generally a laugh against country folk that they do not use their front doors. The chief reason for this is that, on a farm, garden gates must be kept closed against straying animals, and no ordinary person will go through the fatigue of opening and closing gates for the sole purpose of arriving at the front door when he may drive up to the side entrance, which opens to the farm, without hindrance.

I was admitted by a young servant with flashing spectacles, and Mrs Colville met me in the hall. She was a dark, slender woman in her thirties. She explained to me over a cup of tea that a shooting-party was being held that day, and most of the farm hands were acting as beaters.

After tea I set forth, on her suggestion, to join the guns. As I passed out of the house, a rich and complex smell of cooking was wafted from the kitchen, whither Mrs Colville had hurried. I asked the grizzled rustic who appeared to be in sole occupation of the farm buildings, and who was, in fact, the yardman, if he knew whereabouts I should find the party. He said something I did not understand, but I followed his pointing arm.

I passed through the stack-yard, noting implements whose toothed and clawed shapes suggested mediaeval violence, and wondering vaguely what the purpose of this or that could be. Their rusty, nettle-buried appearance led me to believe that they were worn out and abandoned. But this was not so, as I found later. Each, when its season of usefulness arrived, would be dragged from the grappling growth, perform its particular earth-tearing function, and be returned to some out-of-the-way corner, to be a sleeping Gulliver for the grass again. The yard itself was a small township of stacks. They were set out neatly in streets, with here and there a round stack like a citadel. On the top of the highest the shape of a cockerel roughly carved in wood had been set like a weather-vane.

I heard a sound of distant gunfire, and proceeded towards it, striking across stubble, fallow, and meadow. The noise grew louder and nearer, was interspersed with shoutings to dogs. Once a shower of shot rattled in a tree beside me, after which I approached with circumspection. I came upon them paused in a group beside a thicket, tobacco-smoke floating among them, and gun-barrels shining in the last rays. These were the inhabitants of my new world. Mr

Colville came forward and shook me by the hand. He was a man of kindly yet commanding presence. He introduced me to the others – his father, an old man still denying old age; his brother Arnold, downright and sudden in manner, rather like an overgrown schoolboy; Mr Phipps, the clergyman, lean and brown, wearing a soft collar and looking like a Colonial pioneer. There was Horace Colville, a half-brother, the mouthpiece of whose pipe was bound with string, a comfortable-looking man; Mr Bartlett, a dark man with a large sinuous moustache. He wore a green breeches suit of stiff quality, and from time to time uttered cynicisms in a chanting style. There was a Mr Crawley, a neighbour, of eagle countenance and restless eye, and one or two others whose names I did not catch.

There were certain characteristics common to the members of the Colville family – an inclination to portliness, small features upon full faces, fair hair, and blue eyes. There was also a readiness among them all to speak out and speak their minds. Their alacrity to dispute led me to believe at first that they were on the verge of a family quarrel, but nothing was further from the case. I never heard a single quarrel all the years I knew them.

The sun had almost set, and the party was discussing the possibility of a last drive, while their dogs – retrievers and spaniels – lay tired, with lolling tongues.

Mr Colville (the one I was staying with – John), who seemed to be in command of the proceedings, settled the question by saying, 'We'll walk that field of roots on the way home. It'll be too dark to do more to-day.'

Thereupon the men lined out, a beater between each gun, to cover the field, and, when all were in position, started slowly through the roots. I walked beside Mr Colville. As we came near the other side, a rabbit ran out and turned along the hedge. I was a pace or two ahead of Mr Colville, and his gun seemed to go off in my ear. The rabbit turned a somersault and lay still.

'Got him,' I cried, unaware then that for John Colville not to hit a rabbit travelling clearly across his field of vision would mean that something was very wrong with him.

He said nothing save, 'Take it, will you?' as the dog returned with the dead rabbit in its mouth. The dog refused to yield its prize to me, a stranger, till Mr Colville shouted, 'Dead!' Then I caused a smile by holding the rabbit by its ears, the result of a memory of rabbit-keeping as a child. I was told to hold it by its hind legs, whither I transferred my fingers, already sticky with its blood. Then my leggings received a dabbling, and a spot or two stained my breeches. By these marks and the dead creature, correctly carried now, in my hands, already I felt initiated, and only wished that certain Chelsea friends could see me.

Then we returned to the house, and the smell of dinner there caused a sudden burst of joviality among the party, tired though they were. Their voices sounded doubly loud within doors as they took off their cartridge-belts and laid their guns aside. Though I understood little of what they said, it was interesting to listen to them. Outside in the darkness lanterns floated to and fro, and through the open door Mr Colville's voice could be heard shouting instructions for the hanging of the game and the tying up and feeding of the dogs.

Arnold Colville, with the round, boyish face, approached me and said, 'You came on a motor-bike, didn't you?'

I said that was so, and he asked what make of cycle it was, and I told him. He then enquired as to speed and horse-power, but interrupted my answer with, 'Let's see it.'

I followed him out into the darkness. He took a lantern

from the yardman's hand, leaving the man standing helpless. Mr Colville, seeing us, shouted, 'Where are you off to? Supper's ready.'

His brother replied, 'Just going to have a look at his motor-cycle.'

'You don't want to be messing about after that now. Come on in.'

'Shan't be a minute,' said Arnold.

Then I heard Mr Colville's voice to the yardman. 'Go and hang them pheasants in the shed! What are you waiting for?' And the yardman's grumbling reply, 'Mr Arnold's gone and took the lantern, sir.'

Arnold opened the coach-house door, and the yellow gleam fell upon my dusty motor-cycle. He looked at it in silence, and I felt apologetic about it, fearing I had brought him out on false pretences.

'It's not much of a one,' I murmured. 'I got it second hand.'

But actually I was playing the right part, for I soon discovered that the object of the excursion was not to see my motor-cycle, but that he might show me his, housed in a neighbouring shed. It was a combination, with substantial mudguards, glistening in the light – certainly vastly superior to mine. He was proud of it, and I saw that my praise pleased him. He told me how he had bought it cheap from a man who had had to dispose of it almost as soon as he had bought it, for financial reasons. Later I learned that it was Arnold's pleasure to get better value for money than anyone else, and demonstrate the fact. He enjoyed the harmless supremacy of the schoolboy whose penknife has a blade more than his fellow's.

We returned to the house as steaming dishes were passing through the hall.

Entering the dining-room, I found that some ladies had been added to the company – Arnold's buxom wife; old Mrs Colville, an erect, sweetly smiling lady, the mother of these robust brothers; and the slender, sharply beautiful wife of the eagle-nosed Mr Crawley.

A boiled batter pudding stood on a dish before Mrs Colville. She put a slice upon each plate and poured a brown gravy over it. This we ate first alone. Then a dish of roast pheasants was placed before Mr Colville at the other end of the table, which he carved with skill and rapidity. This was a complex course, with potatoes, greens, stuffings, sauces. Twice I had started upon mine when some new sauce or accessory came round to me. Beer foamed into my glass. Already I felt hearty, and life was a robust vista of vast skies, blown trees, ploughs going up against the dawn, and evenings of luxurious quiet after toil.

I cleared my plate, and passed it up again with the rest. Not for years had I met such food with such an appetite.

When I had finished that, and the plates were being cleared, I was almost surprised, seeing myself in the wide looking-glass of the sideboard, that I was not large and rosy like the rest – I felt so full-fed and glowing – but pale and thin, sitting like a ghost among them.

'You ain't very strong, are you?' said a neighbour with sympathetic intent, and 'You don't have very good health, I expect?' asked another. Mr Colville said, 'He do look wholly pale, that's a fact.'

The word 'wholly' thus used puzzled me for some time. In Suffolk it is used for 'very' or 'really', and crops up in almost every sentence. But at first I thought Mr Colville was ascribing to me an air of sanctity.

'You're tired after your journey, I expect,' Arnold remarked.

I assured them I never felt better in my life, and was looking forward to its new aspect. I asked questions about farming; I forget what they were, but they must have been elementary and laughable. Not wishing, in politeness, to treat me as a joke, they put me off with mumbled replies, each person I asked feeling self-conscious at dealing with such elementary matters in public. Any kind of enlightenment as to what I was 'in for' I soon found was impossible, as the answer to the simplest question brought in technical terms that meant nothing to me; so I desisted.

They, however, when the first strangeness wore off, questioned me as regards the life that was symbolised by London. When they learned that my father held a responsible position on a well-known newspaper, they referred to me on questions of a public or political nature, and listened with a respectful attention that was embarrassing, treating my youthful opinions as inside knowledge.

As for Mr Phipps, the clergyman, he was intimate with their language and its agricultural foundations, and seemed to have identified himself wholly with them. He succoured me with no suggestion of familiarity with the outer world, as though to lift himself for a moment out of their sphere would have been a slight upon their bluff hospitality. I think he was right, for I ever found them sensitive to the slightest hint of 'superiority', before which they felt, not resentful, but abashed.

Only once, as I was playing the unwilling oracle on some affair of journalistic prominence, I seemed to catch an ironical glint in his eye as he listened with the rest.

After the ragged skeletons of the pheasants, with their many attendant dishes, had been cleared away, a mountain of cream horns was borne in and dispensed by Mr Colville. Mr Crawley, being intent on some vehement statement to

8

his neighbour, seized his in his fingers, without thinking, and essayed a bite encompassing the wide end bulging with cream. The pastry crust, of course, collapsed, and mingled cream and jam oozed forth. Mr Crawley, dropping the sticky wreck, was left with lips of white foam, a white 'imperial' on his chin, and a white tip to his nose, which caused a general laugh. They were very good cream horns; I ate two, and even then did not deny myself the cheese finale.

The ladies rose and retired. Cigarettes and cigars were handed round. The day's sport was discussed. Old Mr Colville, blue-eyed, side-whiskered, cloth-gaitered, remarked, 'I've never seen so few rabbits in my life.'

'A good thing too, in a way,' said John. 'They do a lot more damage than they are worth.'

'Why, we saw more foxes than rabbits,' the old man exclaimed. 'I've never known such a thing on a day's shooting all the years I've been about.'

The saying that there is nothing new under the sun must be reversed to be applied to agriculture, for many a time I have heard old Mr Colville, for all his seventy years, remark of some circumstance of crops or weather that he had never known such a thing in his life before.

A sweepstake was held on the nearest estimate of the day's bag, and I caused a laugh by my wildly erroneous guess.

Under cover of the general agricultural conversation, Mr Crawley approached me and started a political subject. He searched me with his eager, restless eyes, and before we had talked long said, 'I have a scheme for agricultural reform. I have been trying to get it taken up for a long time,' and in a trice had brought out of his pocket a pamphlet of his own composition.

I observed John Colville's eye on us. At the first pause in the conversation he said, 'Well, we'd better go and see how the ladies are getting on.'

All rose and tramped towards the drawing-room. I was in the rear of the group, and I felt a touch on my arm. Mr Colville drew me aside.

'I shouldn't take too much notice of Jim Crawley's schemes, if I were you,' he said in a low voice. 'He'd craze the Devil when he gets on politics. He gets wonderful excited, he does.'

I looked at Mr Colville questioningly, but there was no time just then for more on the subject.

The drawing-room was a room of large windows, fringed furnishings, and elaborately delicate tables. A maid brought in coffee – very white coffee in small cups. There was an incongruity in the sight of those men sitting round the fire, booted and gaitered, their large hands encompassing the thimble-like cups. First tentative sips were taken with soup-noises, for the coffee was very hot. When it had cooled, each drained his at a gulp, tipping his head far back, as the designer of those cups had not considered the nose as an impediment, nor imagined anything in the nature of Mr Bartlett's magnificent moustache.

I noticed that, although we had entered the drawing-room, no mingling of the sexes had taken place, for the ladies were in a group on one side of the hearth, and the men on the other. They sat leaning forward to one another and continuing their agricultural conversations, only in undertones now, the feminine atmosphere of the drawing-room seeming to have an abashing effect. I was chatting brightly to the ladies when I noticed this, and feared that in the eyes of those yeomen I appeared effeminate.

Whereas my opinion was considered by the men to be

of consequence on political questions, I now found I was regarded by the ladies as a young man of fashion, whose proposed sojourn in the country was a 'health' whim, undertaken as another might resort to mud baths or unpleasant tonic springs. They questioned me eagerly as to the shops in London. Did they look gay? And what was the fashionable colour? Whether it was on account of my appearance or manner, I cannot say; but they obviously visualised an abandoned bevy of smart friends to whom I should in due course return.

Later, however, we had a little music, which melted the sex barrier, and we became one company again. Mr Crawley played one or two pieces on the violin, unsteadily, but with ardour. Mrs Colville played 'The Maiden's Prayer' on the piano, followed by 'Robin's Return', and then accompanied a song or two for Mrs Crawley.

John Colville suggested half-penny nap, and we went and sat round the dining-room table. The excitement of the game relaxed that remnant of Victorian drawing-room formality that this society at times seemed to impose on itself, and we ended the evening in high hilarity, the men with pipes and whisky, the ladies with glasses of dark port. It was 'nap or nothing' for a finish, and, after the pool had been swollen with repeated failures, John Colville collared the booty by a spectacular exhibition of luck and skill amid applause.

The night was frosty and moonlit. The yardman, with his lantern, was helping to back ponies into traps. Motor-engines murmured. John Colville bustled to and fro with presents of game to each member of the party. They all shook me heartily by the hand, and hoped I should like farming.

I stood by Mr Colville's side as he gave orders to the man for the morrow's work, listening to the last horse's hoofs clattering down the road. Then we returned to the house and bed.

I looked out of my bedroom window. The stillness of trees and buildings in the moonlight was like a consciousness of age. 'That is the hunter's moon,' Mr Colville had told me. Here, indeed, she was a presence and a personality, that had been but one light among a myriad in the city's midnight day.

There was the rustling of beasts in straw, the cough of a horse, the splash of a rat in the pond. Life here seemed awed, but not sleeping.

2

At cock-crow came the sound of feet and voices outside; gruff 'Morning, Bills' and 'Morning, Berts.' Then, after a silence, the tramp of horses, with chains rhythmically jingling, fading in the distance. Pails rattled. Somebody whistled a tune to which I had danced a year ago, and broke off to cry, 'Goo on then, old cow!'

There was a tap on my door, and Mr Colville's voice said, 'Awake, young fellow?'

I jumped out of bed, splashed in some cold water, and dressed. I found Mr Colville in the kitchen, pouring out a cup of tea. He poured out one for me also, dark and hot. I had no more than sipped mine when he had finished his and was reaching for his cap. I drank the rest hurriedly from the saucer, and followed him out. As I passed along the side of the house a mat came hurtling down from an upper window, narrowly missing my head. I caught just a glimpse of busy bare arms and flashing spectacles up there before another followed the first. As I looked back, I saw a boy gathering them up and putting them across a line to be beaten. Millicent, the maid, was no respecter of persons when the tornado of work was in her, I was to learn.

Mr Colville showed me the autumn work in full swing on the farm – the ploughing of stubbles, the carting of mangolds, the drilling of corn. I had arrived at the beginning of the farm year, he explained to me. This year's harvest was already forgotten, next year's being prepared for. Our walk was accompanied by audible musings on his part as to what crop this or that field should be set to grow next. I returned to breakfast with an inkling of the complexity of farming, and a burdening consciousness of my own ignorance.

After breakfast I helped Midden, the yardman, to pack the game in hampers for London. I endeavoured, too, to be of some help in putting the pony into the trap. In such a slight matter as buckling a strap, affixing a trace to a hock, my fingers were vague and fumbling. Midden had finished on his side before I had much more than begun, and was round beside me altering what I had done wrong, undoing the trace I had at last fastened to untwist it. I felt as clumsy as the oaf that he seemed, with his squat shape and receding brow and chin, while his fingers worked with the deft, unhurried speed that should have belonged to mine.

When all was ready, he went into the harness-room and put on a black corduroy coat over his sleeved waistcoat in which he ordinarily worked, and perched a flat black cap on his head, which gave him a funereal look. He planted a whip in the socket at the side of the trap. I mounted first, and held the reins while he got in. The pony started off eagerly, and he bumped into his seat. We rounded a corner of the buildings with an inch to spare. The wheels crackled on the flints. There was a thrill of speed in our fifteen miles an hour.

'The pony goes well,' I remarked.

'Yes, she's a good pony,' Midden replied. 'She'll trot from here to Stambury in an hour – that's twelve miles. But the road ain't no place for a horse nowadays.'

Then he told me how in the old days, before the coming of motors, the farmers of the neighbourhood used to race one another to market in gigs, and race home again at night without any lamps.

I asked him how that could have been, since on a dark night it must have been impossible to see a vehicle coming in the opposite direction. But he replied that horses could see in the dark, and used to get out of each other's way.

'Sometimes you never knew you was passing anyone till they was right by you, nearly cutting your wheel off, and you felt the wind in your face or heard the chap holler "Good night."'

And the farmers were often half boozed, in any case, Midden added, and that in those days it did not matter, as a horse could be trusted to take a chap home right to the door as long as it wasn't interfered with, whereas now, with a motor, you have to be as sober as a judge or you are soon into something.

Midden sighed for those days.

'Why, anybody then would give a fellow a pint of beer for the asking – beer like what you can't get for sixpence a pint to-day.' He shook his head. 'It ain't right. Chaps what work on the land need beer. It puts a heart into them.'

I noticed the sign of an inn ahead. It was called 'Woodman Spare the Tree'. And the tree had been spared to be a summer blessing to many generations of beer-drinkers, for it stood, an oak, on a triangle of grass before the inn, with a bench beneath. A loaded wagon was already drawn up there, and a man was sitting, mug in hand, under the yellowing foliage.

Whether Midden's remarks had been timed for the moment of the appearance of the inn on the road I did not know, but, taking them as a delicate hint, I suggested he should pause and have a drink at my expense.

'Well, thank you, sir, kindly,' he said, and drew up at the door.

We went into the bar, where a pretty girl of fifteen or

so came to take our order. I asked Midden what he would like, my knowledge of beer being as limited as my knowledge of farming. He said he would like a pint of 'old and mild'. Not to appear finicky, I, too, ordered a pint of old and mild, though what kind of drink that might be I did not know, and I wondered however I should be able to drain the vast mug that the girl was taking down for it.

She told Midden that her father had gone to Stambury to the market. Though she tended the bar in her father's absence, she had none of the brazen qualities of the traditional barmaid, but spoke shyly, and her face had a delicate beauty in the gloomed air. She retired into the tap-room, and, stooping gracefully in a kind of natural curtsey, drew our beer from two of a noble row of barrels. One, I gathered, contained old beer and the other mild – a favourite mixture in these parts.

She bore the brimming mugs to us, for which I paid.

In the bar parlour were skittles and a machine that promised music for a penny. I placed a penny in the slot, and it went rattling away into the innards of the machine. The depths were stirred. Like a lion roused by a tickling straw it gave out a jangling tune. The first ended, another started with hardly a pause, and then another. The suddenness and loudness of the noise caused Midden to glance out to see that the pony had not been startled. He and the young lady gazed at each other and then at me. I felt apologetic.

'You're fond of music, I expect?' said Midden.

I nodded, and smiled at the publican's daughter through the din, who gave me a ghost of an answer and disappeared inwards.

Midden and I took our mugs, and went out and sat on the bench under the oak-tree. Still the machine could be heard pounding out its inevitable music like a robot run amok. It ceased at last. Never had there been such a pennyworth.

Midden exchanged a greeting with the man on the bench. In the blessed silence we gazed up into the foliage.

'I should like to have as many sovereigns as there's been pints of beer drunk under this tree,' Midden remarked thoughtfully.

'I reckon it would take you all your life a'carting of them home,' said the other.

Midden put back his head and drank. The sight startled and fascinated me, for he literally poured the beer into him without swallowing. I had never seen it done before, but it seemed to me a waste of beer, for how could he possibly taste it? I was making slow progress with my mugful, though I drank with all my might. As I put my head into the pot the beer seemed like a brown lake before my eyes, never to be drained.

'It ain't too hot, sir, is it?' Midden asked, smiling.

'Hot? No, of course not. Why?'

'Well, you drink it as though it were.' At which they both laughed.

Another man drove up to the inn with a wagonette. He wore an antique bowler, green on top, as though the nap had turned into moss. He had small keen eyes and a brilliant smile. He brought a mug out under the tree, and lost no time in getting into conversation with me. He spoke very fast, and much of what he said was lost to me. I learnt that he was a carrier and dealer of the neighbourhood. He was full of wonders of the farming world – a marvellously good crop here, an incredibly meagre one there – and of market information. Pigs, chickens, bullocks, eggs, potatoes – he knew the current values of all. Village women entrusted him with their shopping orders (his pockets were full of little lists), so the town shopkeepers sought his custom, and gave him a bonus on the trade he brought them. He paid cash for the goods, and gave the village people credit, which was an inducement to the villagers.

'There's plenty of people set up against me in the carrying trade, but they can't stick it; no, sir, they can't stick it. They start all of a bustle, and say, "I'll make it hot for you, Stebling." "All right, so you may," says I, and in a little while they are broke. But old Stebling, he keeps on, sir; yes, he keeps on. I've never missed a market-day once in all these years. How old do you think I am?'

I looked at him, and judged by the brown hair under his hat and the smooth rosy face that he was forty-five.

He laughed heartily. 'I am sixty to-day. I've been carrying for nigh forty years. And I shall go on, sir. I shan't stop till I die. It would wholly craze me to sit afore the fire all day. Yes, sir, I am sixty years old, and I've never had an ache or pain in my life.'

'What do you eat?' I asked, seeking the secret, journalist fashion.

'I eat pork, sir.'

'What else?'

'Nothing else, sir, except bread and 'taters.'

'You mean to say you eat pork every day?'

'Four times a day, winter and summer, except when I go to market. Then I often bring some kippers back; I usually eat one on the way home.'

'But how do you cook it?'

'Bless you, sir, I don't trouble a-cooking it. I eat it raw, bones and all. It's rare tasty so.'

'But it must be like leather.'

'What I can't chew I swallow.' He snapped his small

white teeth at me. 'I can tear anything with my teeth. I've never had the toothache in my life, nor the bellyache. Why, I can lift a pail of water in my teeth.'

I appeared incredulous.

'Will you bet me a shilling I can't?' Stebling asked.

'Done.'

The next minute he was filling a bucket at the pump. He brought it to me, as full as it could hold, then bent down and, fastening on the handle with his teeth, raised the bucket three feet from the ground with his hands behind him. He grinned at me victoriously.

I gave him the shilling. He span it, caught it, and put it in his pocket. He finished his beer and said, 'Well, I mustn't stop about. I'll wish you gentlemen good morning.'

Midden and the other man were standing by the trace-horse of the wagon, a long-maned chestnut, while Midden ran his hand down one of its forelegs. Then they stood back and surveyed it together. I had still nearly half a mug of beer to dispose of, but I paused and forgot it, for the scene before me had the tranced quality of a picture, with all its significance of attitude. I found it difficult for the moment to rid myself of the fancy that I had sat down on a seat in a picture-gallery, and if I turned my head aside I should see the fashionable crowd of a private-view day – the wagon of faded red and blue with its piled load of sacks, the horses, the two men conferring in a whiff of tobacco-smoke, our own gig, and the inn behind with the welcoming gloom of its open doorway, the sun shining mistily upon all, and the litter of autumn on the grass.

Finding my hand grasping a mug and not a catalogue, however, I experienced the happy strangeness of waking into the scene. The mug was tilting; the men's backs were towards me. I let it tilt, and surreptitiously gave the rest of my beer to the roots of the tree. I looked up to find a face peeping at me from behind the curtains of a window. I was a stranger, an object of secret scrutiny by the young lady whose eyes fled mine in public. I was filled with confusion, feeling that my action would be taken as a slight upon the beer; nor could it possibly have been construed as an accident.

The men were standing by a corner of the wagon. I joined them, and found them with their heads together over a handful of wheat which the wagoner had extracted from a hole in the corner of a sack. They discussed it, moving the grains about, Midden admitting that it was good big-bodied wheat, but that his master had some just as good. They exchanged statistics of coombs and acres, each seeming to have a wonder to relate of rich-yielding harvest, and their chanted figures had a poetic value.

I was surprised to find them so interested in these things. The wagoner was as pleased with Midden's appreciation of the trace-horse as though it were his own animal, and they discussed another man's wheat with professional zeal.

We mounted the gig and moved on. I caught a glimpse of the face at the window watching us away.

Having despatched the hampers of game at the station, we called at the yard of a man who designated himself 'Agricultural Engineer', and took in some ploughshares. We arrived back at the farm just at lunch-time.

After lunch, Mr Colville put me into the charge of a youth who was passing out towards the fields with a horse to do some harrowing. There arose some doubt as to my boots. Mr Colville looked dubiously at them.

'You'll spoil them boots on the clods; they are market boots. You want some rough ones for the land.'

I assured him that they were as supplied for mountaineering and tramping holidays, and I had bought them specially for hard work. But he was not convinced. I, too, had some misgiving, observing my feet. In town they had seemed symbolic of my robust intention, but here, where all was work-worn, they had an elegant look. The youth, too, when we were in the fields, said, 'They are gentleman's boots.'

The stigma of gentleman rankled.

I threw myself whole-heartedly into the business of harrowing. The boy, whose name was Jack, explained to me how easy it was, if one turned the horse about too sharply at the end of the field, to turn the harrows over. That, I was given to understand, was the beginner's invariable mistake. I assured him I would be particularly careful in this respect, and I rather prided myself, after the first few bouts, on showing my capacity for learning from the experience of other people. But in an unguarded moment I allowed the horse to turn in too small a circle, and the harrows with a wild clatter piled themselves on top of one another.

I was angry with myself, angry with Jack for his grin as he came across the field to me, angry with the horse. I was already beginning to feel that I could not touch anything without making an ass of myself.

'That's all right. You'll soon get into the way of it,' said the boy encouragingly, as he wrestled with the harrows. Teeth and chains had become closely tangled in an instant as by the waving of the confuser's wand. At length all was straightened out again, and I continued my journeys across the field. Jack left me to it, and busied or amused himself by burning the dead grass in heaps that the harrows had pulled out.

I remembered then a poem of Hardy's:

Only a man harrowing clods
  In a slow, silent walk,
With an old horse that stumbles and nods
  Half asleep as they stalk.
Only thin smoke without flame
  From the heaps of couch-grass.
But this will go onward the same
  Though Dynasties pass.

I had become that traditional figure.

Apt as these meditations were, they were not good for harrowing, for, while my mind had wandered, so had my horse. Half asleep or not, it had left an ever-widening portion unharrowed, and I had to pull it back sharply to the true course. Then I found a fault in the poem, in the light of my new experience.

Only a man harrowing clods . . .

Why the belittlement of that word 'only'? Had Hardy ever done any harrowing he would not have written a stanza suggesting that man and horse alike were half asleep and vacant, that they just walked on and on, no matter how or where. He would have found, as I found, that, despite appearances, one's mind is kept fully occupied seeing that none of the work is missed, that one does not overturn the harrows, that none of them is clogged or caught up in one another. Stumble, yes; but that has nothing to do with drowsiness, but the unevenness of the ground: in fact, one has to be particularly nimble-footed to keep one's balance.

Hardy, I saw, despite the legend of his rural understanding, had the non-ruralist's attitude – that of one who had not gone to the heart of the matter, the attitude of 'only'.

Only a man harrowing, only a man ploughing, only a man guiding a manure-cart through a gate. And if the stranger tried he would overturn the harrows, knock down the gate-post, and smash the plough. The labourer, with the respect born of knowledge, does not regard these affairs as semi-automatic – given in, as it were, with the landscape – but has an eye to the manner of the job.

So I was beginning to understand; and I was as busy as I had ever been in my life as I moved across the field with my horse, looking no doubt as drowsy as could be to any nature poet who happened to be passing on the road.

I did not even look about me; my eyes were kept noting deviations on the horse's part, and my hands checking them. For I found that a horse moving slowly responds only gradually to the rein, and a slight gap in the work must widen before it can close again, even if the rein is pulled the moment the harrow-lines part from one another. Only at the headlands, after I had turned and made ready for the next bout, did my eyes take a holiday in the brown landscape and its purple distances.

About a quarter past four we returned to the farm, as Jack had pigs to feed, and needed the horse, he said, for the litter-cart. Now, neither Mr nor Mrs Colville had mentioned the matter of meal times to me, and, as I had been given afternoon tea at about four-fifteen the day before when I arrived, which had been followed by dinner at seven o'clock, I naturally concluded that this was the usual regime.

I went into the house, but found no sign of tea in any room, nor was there any stirring saving the ticking of a clock. I wandered out again, and watched Jack feeding the pigs, helped him by carrying slopping pails of barley-meal, which gave my boots a less genteel appearance. At the first rattle of a pail the pigs set up a pathetic squealing, and, when one pen was temporarily lulled with a pailful, the laments of the others rose to a hysteria of anxiety at the sight of their brothers being fed before them. By the time we had brought the refilled buckets to the second pen, the first had finished theirs, and were wailing for more. Thus the chorus went on, in strophe and antistrophe, till all were filled and slept.

I returned to the house. It was now nearly five o'clock, and I saw that the table was laid in the dining-room. I waited awhile, and presently Mrs Colville came in from the drawing-room with a young woman of about twenty-five, pale, dressed in a fluttering frock. Not by any means did she look the robust country-woman, yet I learned that her father and brothers were farmers. The teapot arrived in the hands of the vigorous maid, capped and cuffed, now, and generally starched into a semblance of restraint.

It was not my habit to eat much for tea, and I took only a piece of bread and butter, remembering the large seven o'clock dinner of the previous evening and not wishing to spoil my appetite by eating my fill at five. Mrs Colville urged jam and cakes upon me, but I refused, saying I was not in the habit of eating much for tea.

'What a town appetite you have,' said Mrs Colville, and the young lady remarked that farming would soon alter that, no doubt. They ate heartily, and regarded me curiously as I sat sipping my single cup of tea. Mr Colville was out, and had not yet returned.

After tea, Miss Jarvis (that was the young lady's name), upon being pressed, took her seat at the piano and played some Chopin, followed by Bach. This was a pleasant surprise, and I noted her more closely. Her features just missed being beautiful. From her wrist trailed a loose sleeve. Mrs Colville apologised for the piano. 'It is not played on half enough, and some of the notes stick.'

I complimented Miss Jarvis on her playing, and spoke of the beauty of Chopin, who was, as luck would have it, one of the few composers I had any knowledge of then, and that was thanks to the gramophone.

Then I approached the subject of books. Miss Jarvis asked me if I had read *Vanished Pomps of Yesterday*.

'Some of it,' I replied.

Whitman was at that period my gospel, as was natural, but I had the tact not to bring him to light on the present occasion. Miss Jarvis had just read *Cranford*, and enjoyed it greatly, and was hungry for more Mrs Gaskell. I was just then lapping up the romances of Wells, but tried desperately to recollect a novel of Jane Austen's I had once read as a school holiday task. However, another holiday book came to mind. 'Scott . . .' I began. We discovered common ground in the Waverley novels.

It was with surprise that I learnt from Mrs Colville later that, despite her delicate air, Miss Jarvis had helped her old father to carry on the farm when her brothers had been at the war, ploughing from morning to night in all weathers.

'And once I saw her at the station,' said Mrs Colville, 'with a horse and tumbril after a load of coal. Black as a tinker she was, and laughing too.'

Our conversation was everything that a drawing-room could desire, and Mrs Colville, though a little out of it, seemed pleased enough. Then Miss Jarvis drew her hostess in by informing me that she had an artistic talent, and indicated the pictures on the wall. Entering the room the night before, I had noticed oil-paintings that had the unassumingly reproductive aspect of a feminine pastime rather than of a mode of expression. On learning they were Mrs Colville's own, I immediately rose and examined them, speaking flatteringly of each. There was a stiff impression of Italian mountain scenery, and others, more successful to my view, of the Suffolk countryside.

They gave me an inkling of Mrs Colville's girlhood. I had always imagined that a farmer's wife was buxom, blue-aproned, and with sleeves rolled up, according to tradition. But I was discovering that when a farmer reached a certain stage of prosperity it was his pride to have a wife with delicate tastes, and daughters with a sheen of drawing-room accomplishment upon them, though not at the expense of domesticity.

It was now seven o'clock, and I was growing hungry. Miss Jarvis took her leave. Seven-thirty arrived, but still no sign of dinner. At eight o'clock Mr Colville came in. Now, I thought, we shall have a meal. But no; nor did either of them mention the subject of food. I began to wish that I had eaten the hearty tea I had been offered. A bird in the hand, I reflected, is worth two in the bush. At eight-thirty I was ravenous. I could neither talk nor read, but only sit aching for food. Towards nine Mr Colville folded up *The East Anglian Daily Times* and, glancing at the clock, said, 'We might have supper in now.' He rang the bell, and the maid brought in a tray on which was bread and cheese and cocoa. I ate a great deal of bread and cheese, drank two cups of rich cocoa, and spent a sleepless night.

I discovered that the seven o'clock dinner occurred only after a shooting-party or some entertainment of friends. On ordinary occasions tea is the evening meal in Suffolk – not high tea necessarily, but just bread and butter, jam, and cakes. Bread and cheese and cocoa come at nine as a nightcap – an astonishing one, I thought, more inclined to banish sleep than to encourage it. Mr Colville, however, seemed to feel no ill-effects, though his wife often complained of biliousness. Yet she regarded it as a natural affliction, and did not consider her diet unusual. The only things she forbade herself were raw onions and cucumber.

In future I made a good tea, and was sparing of the nine o'clock tray.

The second morning after my arrival Mr Colville was up and out before me. I wandered about by myself, observing the men at their various work in the fields uncomprehendingly. I met Mr Colville on my return. He had been riding, and had handed his horse to Midden. I went with him into the pig-yard.

'Those are good pigs,' he said, 'aren't they?'

If he had said they were bad pigs I should have agreed with him equally. Their shape meant nothing to me.

'Good length,' he explained, 'broad in the back and not too much head.'

I strove to see it, but no person can appreciate the points of a pig till he has dwelt long with them. Looking back, I cannot tell at what point I began to know a good pig from a bad one. The farmer's eye is as subtle as the artist's.

The pigs were clamorous, though their troughs bore evidence of recent food.

'These pigs are hungry,' said Mr Colville indignantly. 'Where's that boy?' He strode to the gate and shouted, 'Boy! Boy!' in a voice of thunder. No boy appeared. 'Gone to his breakfast, I'll be bound.' He turned to me. 'Ain't it a wonderful thing he can't see that these pigs are hungry? That's it, you always have to be on to 'em.'

He marched to the swill-house and filled buckets from the tubs of soaked meal. Together we carried them to the still hungering pigs. Mr Colville leaped the hurdles with the agility of anger, for all his portliness. I handed a pail across to him. The pigs swarmed round him, buffeting him this way and that; he waded knee-deep in a sea of snouts.

'Wait a minute,' he said, and laid about him with his stick. The dog, seeing sport in progress, leaped the hurdles and sought to lend his aid. He received a whack and a malediction which sent him scuttling back, tail down.

The pigs were quietened and put at a distance. Then he took the pails and filled the troughs. I entered the next pen. Having no stick and carrying the heavy pail, I was almost thrown over. These were black pigs. They put their heads into the trough in anticipation, and I could not avoid pouring the barley-meal over them. The white paste dried on their heads, and they went about looking like clowns for the rest of the day.

At breakfast I was introduced to the Suffolk ham. I found it delicious, and a justification of all the labour of pig-feeding. It was cured in old beer, Mr Colville told me, and then smoked in oak sawdust. It had been hanging in his mother's kitchen for a year, and was now in ripe condition.

After breakfast, Mr Colville sent me, with a knife, to help with the mangold carting. On my way to the field I saw Jack, and told him of the incident of the pigs. He grinned.

'Master be like that,' he said. 'One day he'll say, "These pigs are hungry," and then the next day, if I give 'em more and they leave a little in the trough, he'll say, "Boy, these pigs have got too much food by half." So I ain't ever right like that. But he don't mean nothing by it, only to show he's master.'

I arrived in the mangold field and took out my knife. The men greeted me with grins, saying: 'So you have come to give us a hand, sir! That's good; we shan't be long now.' They evidently anticipated entertainment; nor were they disappointed.

The carts went up the rows. Three men went with a cart, one behind to deal with the two rows that the wheels spanned, and one on either side. The method employed was this: you grasped the leaves of the mangold with the left hand with much the same motion as a cow's tongue makes encompassing a bite of grass. You pulled the mangold out of the ground, swung it upwards, and at the right moment slipped your knife-blade through the leaves where they joined the root. Then, if you had judged correctly, the mangold flew into the cart, and you were left with the leaves in your hand. You dropped them, and stooped to pull another. The whole process took the labourer one second.

The men showed me by example how to do it. I took up my position at the side of the tumbril. But my first mangold flew right over the tumbril and hit the man on the other side.

'You are too strong, sir,' he smiled.

The next mangold hit the wheel, and the next the shaft. For five minutes I bombarded the tumbril in vain. It shook and rattled. I could not judge the right moment at which to sever the leaves from the root. Sometimes the globe fell at my feet, sometimes even it hit the horse, who did not seem to mind, but stood unmoved. I grovelled about picking up my misses and putting them in the tumbril. My hands were muddy. The men were highly amused. I felt hot and impotent, as though the whole thing were a practical joke at my expense.

At last I got one in, and there was a cry of, 'Well done, sir; now another.' By a stroke of luck the next one went in also. I began to smile. I discovered that the whole thing was a matter of rhythm, and by lunch-time I was getting four out of six into the tumbril.

As I was very slow, the man at the back gave me a hand with my two rows besides pulling his own. This hurt my pride, and by the time we knocked off at one I managed to keep up with the tumbril unaided by working twice as hard as they.

At lunch Mr Colville asked me how I was getting on.

'Mind you don't cut your hand,' he warned me. 'That is what everybody does the first time they pull mangolds.' He showed me a scar on his finger. But I smiled, for I was beginning to feel expert, and said I should be particularly careful.

However, the afternoon was not far advanced before the knife slipped and my finger bled. It was, luckily, only a scratch; I bound my handkerchief round it and continued. I was beginning to enjoy the work. The rhythm was restful after my early struggles. It was pleasant to feel the mangold's weight vanish at the jerk of the knife, and see the globe, rosier for the sinking sun, go bounding into the cart. The big ones thundered in, the small ones pattered.

Near the gateway of the field the clamp was set, and thither the loads were taken. A man was stationed there, building up the clamp, and every now and then there would be a deep rumble as he tipped a load down and the mangolds rolled out. Then he arranged them and covered them with straw, so that the clamp was as steep and smooth as a cottage roof.

Sometimes, between loads, the men would slice a mangold, exposing the juicy saffron flesh, and eat it. They found it refreshing. I tasted a slice, it was sweet and cold and crisp. The mangolds in this field were of a kind called 'Golden Tankard', one of the men told me.

There was a glow upon us all. The sun grew large and red, became the king of mangolds there on the horizon. The air turned frosty, the coarse leaves crackled in our hands, and, trampled, gave up their odour. Twilight came on, and horse and tumbril moving clampwards became a silhouette of toil.

We stretched. That was all for to-day. Matches were struck, illuminating faces, and pipes glowed. A minute's contemplation of the sky.

'Rain? No, bor, it won't rain.' A word to me. 'You done wonderful well, sir, considerin'.' And the group toiled homeward over the fields.

I have carted mangolds many times since then, and it is an occasion that always marks for me the beginning of winter. I recall those twilights, the gaunt yet tender-coloured sky, the still air, pheasants calling in the distance, or a hunting-horn sounding for home. The last of summer's wealth is housed, and ahead lies frost and early dark, shooting, hunting, firelight; ploughing and cross-ploughing, the breaking of ice for the creatures' drink, the carting of straw for their warmth.

Mr and Mrs Colville were out that evening, so I had my tea alone. I was sitting before the fire afterwards, reading, and smoking a large cherry-wood pipe which I thought suited my new rusticity, when I became aware of a disturbance outside. The window of the room where I sat looked towards the farm-buildings, and lights were moving there. I put my head outside. The air resounded with deep groans. I hurried towards a group clustered in the moonlight, and was met by the maid Millicent, who said that Midden had fallen, and, they thought, broken his rib. He had been standing on the top rail of a fence, trying to get some turkeys down from a tree where they had roosted, when the rail had broken and he had landed on his side on the second rail.

'I'll go for the doctor,' I said.

Millicent passed it on to the group – 'He says he'll go

fetch a doctor' – and a woman's voice (Midden's wife) cried, 'Oh, yes, sir, please!'

The man's groans increased the sense of urgency, and I ran to my motor-cycle and next moment was bumping down the road. I had not stopped to light my lamp, by which time the man might have been dead, it seemed to me; but the moon shone brightly and showed me my road. The air cut into me, for I had omitted any kind of overcoat in my haste; it was so cold that it stung me to warmth. The country was hazy and mysterious under the moon. A few days ago I had been lounging in orange-coloured interiors, and now here I was rushing along a road I hardly knew, lampless, hatless, in the moonlight.

By luck or instinct I found my way to the little town of Share where the doctor lived. The first houses glimmered. Some men stood outside an inn.

'Which way to the doctor?' I cried.

'You go straight on to the four-a-lete,' said one.

'The what?'

'The four-a-lete – the four crossways – and then turn to the right, and it's a big white house on your left.'

There was no mistaking the one. I rang loudly, and was shown into the consulting-room. The urbane doctor entered, napkin in hand, eating. I panted out my story. It did not stir him. On the contrary, seeing my excitement, he interrupted me, saying, 'Have a cigarette?' and proffered a box. Then, after giving me a light, he asked, 'Was he groaning much?'

'Yes, loudly,' I answered.

'Then there's probably not much wrong with him. If these chaps groan they usually aren't seriously hurt. But I'll be along shortly.'

He gave orders for his car to be brought to the door. In

the meantime he returned to the dining-room, giving me 'Good night' as the maid showed me out.

When Mr Colville came in, I told him the news and he at once went to enquire as to Midden's condition (his cottage was only two hundred yards from the house). He returned saying all was well. The doctor had been, and the rib was not broken after all. He was only severely bruised.

The next morning, as we took our early tea in the kitchen, Mr Colville said, 'We must do some milking this morning, seeing that Midden is laid up.' He took a pail out of the dairy and gave me one, saying, 'We'll have a try. Whether we shall get any milk or not, that's another thing.' He shouted to a rosy youngster who was standing near (somehow there was nearly always a boy within his call), 'Go and fetch the cows up, boy.'

The cows arrived; we tied them in their stalls. I sat upon my stool, gripped the pail between my knees, and, pressing my head against the cow's flank, attempted to persuade the milk from its udder. My fingers squeezed and pulled in vain. Occasionally a spurt of milk would make the pail ring like a bell, but it was only momentarily.

'When I was a boy my father made me milk ten cows every morning for six months,' said Mr Colville. All the same, I heard none of the hissing and frothing of plenty from his direction, but only grumbles of, 'Stand still, old cow.'

My cow gazed round at me mildly, chewing its cud, and, seeing my head conveniently against its flank, added to its comfort by leaning on me. I became aware that my head was no longer supported against the cow, but the cow was supported against my head. It seemed as though the cow would fall and crush me if I withdrew my weight. Then there was a volcanic upheaval of the cow's side which displaced me. The cow had coughed. At the end of twenty minutes my result was a film of milk at the bottom of the pail. I persevered. I confess I was nervous; the cow's leg looked dangerous, and my futile meddling with its udder seemed almost indecent. Every moment I awaited the breaking of its patience.

At length Mr Colville said, 'Phew!' And then, 'I'm too fat, I can't bend rightly. If I was as thin as you, young fellow, I'd jump over the moon.'

I was pleased to see that he had not been much more successful than myself in getting milk from the cow.

'We are strange, that's what it is; they won't let the milk come. It's wonderful how they can hold it back,' he said. Then he called to the urchin, who had been peeping and grinning all the time. 'Go and fetch Luke. He's hedging in Black Pit field.'

Luke came – a man whom I had only seen in the distance, and noted for a big black beard that looked Russian and revolutionary. But at close quarters I found he was really an old man, and his eyes were mild and unworldly. Age adds a tremor to the Suffolk intonation, and mutes it to a musical softness; and this man's voice was pleasant to hear.

'You can milk, Luke, can't you?' said Mr Colville.

Luke was cautious and non-committal.

'Well, sir, in a manner of speaking. I have milked in my time, but –' He looked at his hands, as if doubting whether the old cunning were there.

'That's all right.' Mr Colville cut him short. 'Midden's laid up. You might see after the cows till he's better.'

He strode out into the sun, and Luke meekly took up a pail and set himself before the first cow of the five, the one I must have already exasperated. His task seemed to me herculean, but on our return he was bearing a full and foaming pail to the dairy, where the separator already hummed busily.

'Well, how did you get on, Luke?' I asked.

'Oh, I coaxed it out of 'em, sir, in time. I sung to 'em.'

'A good old-fashioned sort,' Mr Colville designated him as we sat down to the welcome ham. 'They ain't content like that nowadays. You never hear him grumble about anything. If you tell him to do a job, he goes at it, and does the best he can. Some of these young 'uns start complaining as soon as things ain't just right and handy. It wholly gets my goat to hear a man always grumbling.'

I would note here, in regard to Luke's first hesitation, that the rustic will hardly ever admit right out that he can do a job. It is usually an attitude of 'I'll try.' I think this is because nature is a variable element in all he puts his hand to, and no job is ever exactly as it was before. Besides that, he is often reluctant to admit he can milk, as it entails Sunday work.

There was no sitting long after breakfast. It was a matter of a glance at the newspaper and then up and out. Millicent came and cleared away as soon as the meal was over, and if I lingered too long before the fire I was soon made to know of it by a shower of crumbs from the cloth aimed apparently at the grate, or by the nudgings of a broom that seemed to wish to sweep up my feet. Never have I known a person who could so clearly tell me I was in the way by mere attitude as the efficient Millicent. From the first flash of her spectacles I was awed. I always felt she held me in secret contempt. The situation was quite Strindbergian.

But I never had any ill-feeling towards her. Being by nature a dreamer, I admire efficiency. She was always something of a vortex, a whirlwind. She entered a dishevelled room, a cloud of dust arose, and when it cleared the room stood tidied and still. That was the effect. Had she been 'of my class' I had probably been sucked into the vortex and married to her, according to the Nietzschean principle. As it is, I expect I shall marry somebody as efficient.

During Midden's absence I helped fill the gap. Luke managed the cows, but slowly, as in the gentle stupor of old age. So Jack, the pig-boy (the term swineherd seems out of date), and I looked after the bullocks between us. Many an hour, and pleasant too, I spent with him in the chaff-barn preparing their bulky rations. It was an occupation that left the mind free for speech or thought. I would sit scraping swedes and then vigorously grind them in the pulper, while he, with a long-handled tool, would undermine a crumbling cliff of chaff and make a heap in the middle of the floor. Over this the pulped swedes were thrown and bean-meal sprinkled, and all mixed together with a shovel. Then I would fill a rush skep, and trail through the deep straw with it on my back, and tip it into the manger, dodging the horns of the crowding cattle. If I raised my hand against one to drive him away he would close his eyes, flinching from the expected blow in almost human fashion. There was always one bullock that was weaker than the rest; he was continually hustled, and had to snatch mouthfuls where he could.

Yet, even in a seemingly straightforward matter such as the feeding of bullocks, I found that dangerous errors were possible. One day, for instance, I was pulling down the chaff while Jack ground the swedes. I made a good heap, but Jack said it would not do.

'You have pulled down all clover chaff; if I was to give them that it would blow them.'

'Blow them?'

'It would make them swell up with the wind and perhaps die.'

The chaff, packed into the whole bay of the barn, was in strata, and, the clover-chaff happening to be on a level with my natural reach, I had pulled only that down, whereas I should have mixed it with barley, wheat, and oat chaff. In the matter of bean-meal, also, a double handful each was the safe quantity; more would have made them ill.

There were similar prohibitions in regard to pigs, I came to learn, and even more intricate ones for horses. If by chance horses should gain access to peas, it is fatal to let them drink directly after; they will fall into quite shallow holes and be unable to rise again; oats are their food, but oat-flights blind them; cut wheat-chaff is dangerous.

A hundred similar things the peasant carries in his mind, not only in the matter of livestock either, but of crops and their cultivation – wheat may be sown almost anyhow, but oats must be well covered and barley needs a fine seed-bed. Oats, though, are best among clods, as they protect them from frost – all such knowledge is his. And he knows the psychology of animals, when they may be put together and when they must be kept apart.

Accordingly, I found myself transgressing in some respect at every turn. At first my ignorance was so complete that this did not worry me, but later, when I began to know a little and thought I knew a lot, these mistakes irritated me greatly and caused fits of despair. I seemed as though I should never rise beyond the position of novice, so complex were the rules of this game with nature.

3

After the disconnected impressions of the first few days I now began to have some idea of my surroundings as a whole.

The village of Benfield lay in a hollow, surrounded by slopes of stubble and fallow, but with meadows along the valley. The farms of the district were usually arranged with grassland near the buildings and arable land beyond. The hedges were cut to the ground between the cornfields to allow sun and wind to dry the crops at harvest. This gave the higher ground an open aspect, with trees trimmed and pollarded but not cut down, since the pollarded trunks, sprouting, afforded good straight poles every few years. The country did not look bare, as oak woods and plantations stood here and there, cherished mostly for their sporting value by the yeomen. The few smallholders were the only real enemies of trees. These men had a stubborn and sad existence, earning no more than day labourers, yet lacking their irresponsibility, nor allowing themselves the diversions of farmers. They bartered the pleasures of life for an illusory independence.

Farley Hall was a farm of five hundred acres standing on the high ground above the village, some of the land sloping down to the valley. The soil was heavy, with clay below the surface. But the fields varied; towards the village a more friable, or, as the people said, 'a tenderer dirt' was encountered. The farm was considered the best in the district.

The house was T-shaped, with large rooms, cellar, and attics, the kitchen being the largest room of all, with a cheese-room above and dairy adjoining. The house had been built to a social standard also. The drawing-room was, as I have hinted, a room of style. The dining-room, too, was one of which a squire might have been proud, with its massive moulded beam (varnished, unfortunately, to a chocolate hue). The breakfast-room was the business headquarters, the farmer's citadel. It looked upon the yard and buildings. Mr Colville liked this room, and always sat at table facing the window, 'so that I can see what is going on outside,' he told me.

The brick floor was covered with linoleum, and the furnishings were of horsehair, so that rough clothes could spoil nothing. Mr Colville's desk stood there, and every Friday evening the men came to the window to be paid.

The house stood in the middle of the land, and two private roads of half a mile each connected it with the public thoroughfares. There was a second window in the breakfast-room which looked upon one of these roads, so it was possible to see people approaching from either direction.

Before Mr Colville was married, he told me, he used to live almost entirely in this room; the drawing-room remained unfurnished. This is a general practice. In his early days, while he is a bachelor and working for a secure position, the farmer lives in his house almost like a caretaker. (One farmer I knew used to store wheat in his drawing-room.) But when he gets married life takes shape: the workaday picture is completed by gentler touches added by his wife; she furnishes the drawing-room.

From the high land of Farley Hall one looked down to the village within its fortress of trees. I had been told I could buy the right boots for land work there, from Mr Jolman, the shopkeeper. In all else I was complete: my breeches had lost their starchy look, and were settling comfortably about my thighs; my coat was one which I had laid aside a year ago as done for, but which now looked like serving me for another year. (I wondered at what stage a coat became definitely unwearable in my new surroundings: that was another respect in which my values had to be readjusted.) My hat I should have thrown into a Chelsea dustbin long ago but for the fact that it had been easier to leave it lying in a cupboard. My boots, though, betrayed me, even after tramping over clods. The men's boots seemed to absorb earth like second nature, incorporating it into their colour and character, but mine looked outraged by it. Verily they were for 'mountaineering and tramping holidays'; for picnic lunches on green plateaux, for those walks recommended in the week-end pages of the newspapers, but for this lowly occupation of stumbling to and fro over a fallow behind harrows they were quite unfitted.

So one morning I walked over the fields to Mr Jolman's: but not as when I went to find the shooting-party on the day of my arrival. For then I had made my way in a beeline, plunging into the ditches and scrambling out as best I might, through thorn and hazel. I had learned since then that every ditch had a crossing-place, used by others before me, usually at a corner, and already had an instinct for noting that spot and making towards it. Then there were gateways from one arable field to another, though devoid of any gate – earthen bridges over the ditches with pipes carrying the water through underneath.

Mr Colville had said, 'There are some traps set by the wellums: you might see if they've caught anything as you go down.'

'Wellums?' I echoed, at a loss.

'Yes, you'll see,' he said; then, suddenly recollecting that of course I didn't know what he was talking about, explained that the wellum was the waterway beneath these gateways.

This continual need for asking for an explanation of every term made me feel very much out of it all.

Coming to these wellums, I peered in, but saw only mud and water, so decided to report that the traps had so far caught nothing.

I passed the spot where Luke had been hedging when he was called to milk the cows. The hedge was half cut, as he had left it: his gauntlet was tucked into a rabbit-hole. He had been twisting a withe for binding a faggot when he was called, for there it lay, half done, beside the crooked stick he used for holding the grass against his sickle as he trimmed it from the ditch. The ashes of a fire lay on the headland, and the remains of the old man's breakfast – cheese rind and onion skins.

I crossed some meadows. That was smooth walking, so I let my eyes rest on the view of the village. A windmill turned on the opposite slope of the valley. Chiefly the new thatch of corn-stacks shone out down here, and the pale grey church tower. 'This is my bread,' the village seemed to say, 'and this is my belief.' Stack roof and cottage roof were the same except for a chimney floating its blue pennon of life.

'Go by the river, that's your best way,' Mr Colville had said. It was the first intimation I had had that there was a river in the vicinity. I looked out for it, but saw no trace. I asked a hedger, and he said, 'It's just at the bottom of the hill.'

'"Hill," you call this,' thought I. It was only a slope. Coming to the bottom of it, though, I came to no river, so asked another hedger, saying, 'I was told the best way to Benfield was along the river.'

'Why, yes,' answered the man, pointing with his bill along a ditch that held a gurgling flow of water, 'if you follow the river you'll come right into Benfield.'

So I learned that hereabouts a wide ditch was termed a river, just as, in this country of no hills, a gradual slope was called a hill. I might have sought that river over many an acre had I not met the hedger. The 'river' divided the Farley Hall and from Jim Crawley's. His house and buildings stood higher than Farley Hall.

I came to Mr Jolman's shop in the middle of the village. He was an ugly, unscrutably placid man. He said, 'Good morning,' as though I came into his shop every day, though two children buying sweets from his wife were bewitched from the business in hand by my entry, and stared round at me with wondering moon-eyes, as though I had dropped from the sky.

I asked for the kind of boots I wanted, and Mr Jolman hitched down a bunch from the ceiling with a pole. He selected a pair.

'These will fit you, I think.' He pressed his thumbs into them at the instep, and murmured something about 'welt.' I took them and pressed them critically in the same way. Mr Jolman must have had a superhuman thumb: mine could not dent them anywhere.

But there was no doubt about them being the kind I sought. I was impressed by their constellations of nails, and heel-pieces like horseshoes. I tried one on.

'How does it feel?' Mr Jolman asked, having laced it up.

My big toe touched the end, so I supposed the length was all right. By shifting my foot inside I could feel each side alternately, but not both at once, for mine is a long and narrow foot. My instep touched, also each ankle-bone. Yes, I supposed they would do, I said, dubiously, clumping forward a step or two.

Mr Jolman regarded the boot and my leg thoughtfully. My leg looked unusually spindly on account of that boot. Like a pendulum, I thought. I swung it. The weight of the boot shifted on my foot from one tender pivot to another.

Mr Jolman hitched down another bunch.

'These are more – er – pliable.' His thumb went a long way into one of those. He handed it to me. Mine went in a little way.

My fingers, I thought, looked incongruously pink and tapering upon the sturdy leather. (Often at other times, grappling muddy cart-wheels and the like, I observed what a weak shape my hand had against those rugged things, as though it were thinking of the cigarette-holder and the teacup all the time.) I realised then that this putting on of country clothes deceived nobody, not even the wide-eyed children, but made me look even less of a countryman by contrast. I was 'dressed up'.

But Mr Jolman treated me quite seriously in the character I had thought my clothes gave me, although he knew well enough who I was, as, I discovered later, the whole parish did after my first day there.

'No,' I said, handing back the more pliable boots; 'I will take the others.' I was for no half-measures to-day: my feet must learn to go rough-shod.

'Of course, they will "give" a bit with use,' Mr Jolman explained.

Those boots. Only the other day I picked them out of a dark cupboard, rusty ruins now, toes turned up, split at heel, all but nailless. They were a memory of many ardours; having stood on steamy dunghills in January dawns, on

fragrant haystacks in June, slithered on wheat kernels at
the bottom of the harvest-wagon, been soaked, frozen,
scorched, gilded with pollen and whitened with snow.
They did their bit; though they lamed me with blisters at
first.

Before I left Mr Jolman's shop I satisfied both my practical
and colour-loving selves by buying a red spotted handkerchief. It was a thing I had secretly envied the labourer since
childhood, and now I was in a position not only to own
one, but to wear it.

I turned to go out, and for a moment was opposite a face
I knew. It was the publican's daughter who had seen me
pour away the beer. But she immediately averted her eyes,
and continued examining some ribbon as though she had
never glanced in my direction. She forgot about her basket,
which was full of oranges and was tilting in her hand. One
of them fell on the floor, and rolled to my feet, where it
received a dab of mud from my boot. I picked it up, wiped
it with my gay new handkerchief, and returned it to her
basket, for which I received a breathless 'Thank you,' and
next moment she was gone.

Next morning, a little before dawn, I stood with Mr Colville
in the stables, while the ploughmen harnessed their horses
by the light of lanterns hung from the beams. My position
on the farm these days was mostly to be aide-de-camp to
Mr Colville, going about with him and taking orders to
men at work in distant fields. This morning one of the
horses was left in the stable, and a man said, as he led out
his team, 'Captain wants to go to the blacksmith: he's got
a hind shoe off; but there ain't anyone about the yards this
morning to send with him.'

All the men were at hedging far away, so Mr Colville

said to me, 'You could take him down, couldn't you? You know the way?'

'Yes,' I said, and Mr Colville put a bridle on Captain and led him out. He gave me a leg up on to his bare back (I found his backbone unexpectedly sharp), then went back to extinguish the last lantern. I rode out across a twenty-acre field in the moonlight, through a gateway, and down a lane. I knew the way vaguely: Captain knew it well. We were slow and solitary as the last survivor of Flodden Field as we plodded down to the village, close under a wood, and past a pond where a moorhen flew from us, scarring the calm surface with its trailing feet. I had not an inkling then of how many an hour of cockcrow and waning moonlight I should see on those uplands of stubble and corn.

The smithy was silent as the grave and black, though the village windows were aglow. But a little boy came peeping, and another beside him. I asked, 'Isn't your father up yet?' presuming them to be the blacksmith's sons, which they were. The first answered faintly, 'Father's at plough.'

'Where is he to be found?' I asked.

'In Wynd Field.'

'And where's Wynd Field?'

The boy pointed. The direction seemed vague. I said, 'Will you go and tell him there's a horse of Mr Colville's to be shod.'

He ran off, and presently the blacksmith came.

'No, I weren't a-bed,' he said; 'I've got a bit of land over the way, and, if there aren't any horses sent down, I go and farm it. A man can't afford to stand idle these days, master.'

He lit a bunch of straw, thrust it under the embers of the forge, worked the bellows, and in a minute sparks and flame shot up.

'You are about in good time, sir,' the blacksmith said. 'I

45

thought you London folks never got up before breakfast.'
(Breakfast being the very latest hour at which anyone, to his mind, would think of rising, who intended getting up that day at all.)

'You know I am from London?'

'You are the young gentleman what's come to stay along o' Mr Colville at Farley Hall, ain't you?'

So everyone knew me by sight, even those I was not aware of having seen before.

I stood holding Captain's bridle in the shoeing-shed. The forge was through an open doorway. The back of the smithy was a kind of agricultural treasury, the walls hung with chains and wheels, the corners heaped with parts of old machines. One or two ploughmen came while I was there, and hunted about for some small thing they were needing – a tooth for a harrow, a pin for an axle. Children gathered here also, and gazed upon the wonder of fire, awed into silence as the sparks flew high, and an occasional passer-by paused and warmed his hands, exchanging some item of local news with the blacksmith. For in winter the forge was a meeting-place second only to the inn, I discovered.

'I suppose those have made a difference to your trade,' I said, as a motor went by.

'Yes, they don't need the kind of shoes I make,' he replied. 'There's no hackneys kept to-day, no carriage horses; that's how we're hit. And tractors; they ruin the heavy land, and ruin us too. Besides, horses at plough don't wear shoes up like horses on the road. Now, in the days of Squire Lindley – '

Several times I had heard this regretful 'in the days of Squire Lindley', though I had been in the district only a short while. He had been the last to inhabit the Manor House, and that was before the war. Since then it had stood empty. The drives grew green, and in the coppices of the park there were many leaning trees.

'. . . Ah, he was a gentleman, now. It's a pity such as he should ever come to die. What with his hackneys and hunters, why, there was half a living for a man like myself from the Manor alone.'

Mr Colville had told me about Squire Lindley one day when we drove past the Manor. Those had been proud days for Benfield St George. He used to keep a pack of hounds there, and hunted five days a week – twice with his own, and the rest with neighbouring packs. He always slept with the head of his bed by the window, so that he could hear if any of his horses ailed during the night. On frosty mornings he had been seen walking out to a fallow in his shirt-sleeves; as he put on his stock, kicking the clods, impatient to know whether it would be possible to hunt before midday, cursing if the frost were hard. Towards the end of his life his fingers became permanently bent with holding the reins. His heart weakened, and the doctor warned him that if he would prolong his days he must give up hunting. 'But you know, Colville, I could never do that,' he said. One fine hunting morning he was found dead in his bed.

These past inhabitants had become the legends of Benfield, their doings the conversations of old men. I was soon told of them. Jim Crawley's father, for instance, who had such a voice that he could be heard, they said, from the village, giving orders to his men up on the hill. He too had been a great huntsman. Towards the end of his life he suffered from illusions, and used to wake up in the night and take horse and gallop miles in the moonlight, believing himself to be hunting, letting forth terrific 'Tally-ho's' and taking hedges and ditches as they came.

The blacksmith had heated a shoe red-hot, hammered fiery flakes from it on the anvil, and now brought it impaled on a pointed iron. Captain lifted his leg obediently. The blacksmith laid the hoof on his leather-aproned lap and burnt the shoe on. Dense smoke rose, and for a hissing and stinking minute the blacksmith was invisible. The horse blinked mildly at me, as though the business had no connection with him. Then the blacksmith shifted and muttered angrily. I did not understand what was the matter at first, but then saw that the horse was imitating the cow's trick on me and leaning on him.

'Stand up!' thundered the smith's voice like the wrath of God out of a cloud. 'Stand up!' I echoed more privately at the horse's head.

The blacksmith withdrew the shoe, and Captain stood on four legs again. It was heated again, shaped, and cooled in water, then nailed on.

Just then the postman descended from a parcel-hung bicycle and handed out some letters.

'Morning, Sam,' said the blacksmith.

'Morning, Joe,' Sam replied.

Having glanced at the envelopes, the blacksmith said, 'Have you threshed that little wheat stack of yours? I should like some of that for seed.'

'Yes, it ran eleven coomb an acre.'

'Ah, I said to my missis, "I reckon it'll run over ten coomb." It was a rare sight harvest-time,' said the blacksmith.

'I've got a bit of winter oats up now, showing well,' said Sam.

But, I thought this was the postman, I said to myself.

So he was, but in Benfield the primitive mystery of making things grow out of the earth was deep-rooted in the people, and what I didn't know then and do know now is that everybody, be he publican, postman, blacksmith, or miller, practised farming as well as his usual trade. (Excepting only Mr Jolman.)

Thus I found that, if a horse was taken to be shod, it was first necessary to seek the blacksmith in his fields. The miller would be guiding his plough when not grinding corn. The postman would comment on your young wheat as he left a parcel at the door, and you, if you wanted to please him, would ask after his own. Maybe he had only an acre, but there it was, a corn-crop, a theme of discussion, a candidate for harvest honours, by which he could rank as agriculturalist along with the Colvilles.

Mr Jolman alone had no desire to farm. He was a man apart, and a man of power, though passive. It seemed to me, in the light of later knowledge of the village, that he was really top-dog in this little community, the financier. He gave credit where he thought fit; he even lent money. (He had just sent his son to one of the lesser public schools.)

To begin with, he was not a native of the place, but one who had bought the business. His trade was the only one there that was definitely apart from agriculture, and not understood by the people. There is a tendency among country folk to regard anyone whose business they know nothing of as unlimited in resources. There are no half-measures in the rustic mind: one is either poor or wealthy. Besides, it was a known fact that Mr Jolman had more than once cashed a cheque for £30 for Mr Colville when he had been unable for some reason to get to the bank for the farm wages.

He was a Sphinx-like figure in his shop. Children's garments, coloured handkerchiefs, hung down above him: tins and packets formed an escarpment on the counter in front.

There he dwelt as in a lair; behind him a mysterious gloom. If the sun shone, he said, 'A beautiful day'; or, if the rain fell, he remarked that the weather was wretched. His was grocer's weather. He did not take account of the fact that the rain was perhaps at that moment the best weather of all, just what the barleys needed. He was never timely in his enquiries as to crops; they were merely made for politeness. He tended his rose-trees, mowed his little lawn, bedded out begonias. His vegetable region was screened away. The countryman, on the other hand, was as proud of his vegetables as of his flowers; in fact, more so. The countryman used flowers like trimming to set off his vegetable beds. A plot of potatoes would be edged with marigolds: sweet peas and eating peas grew side by side. But Mr Jolman's garden was suburban.

One day I went down to the village for Mr Colville to see his father about some rabbiting, for the season was now approaching and Mr Colville's young corn was already being eaten off near certain hedges. Mr Colville had a cousin Horace who worked for his father, and kept down the rabbits on the estate. His father had a house in the middle of the village. It had been a farmhouse, but the land was now worked from his other farms, and he used the house only as a dwelling. I was sent to ask that Horace might be spared for a day or two to clear off the rabbits round the cornfields of Farley Hall, or, if not, whether we might borrow his ferrets.

As I passed through the churchyard thither the last leaves were falling from the chestnut-trees which surrounded it like pillars; except on one side, which was walled by cottages. They seemed to be huddling close to the tower for comfort no less than the dead. The churchyard was next to a ploughed field: a mangold clamp was set right against the wall, and looked like a giant's grave.

But in the middle of the burial-ground I saw an open grave to-day, and a service was going on in the church. I happened to meet old Mr Colville at the gate, who told me that a certain Sam Spute was being buried; a hard-fisted reprobate of a fellow, it seemed, who had fought, drunk, sworn, driven untamable horses, and, in spite of all, lived to a great age.

'Twice, to my knowledge,' said old Mr Colville, 'he's been tipped out of gigs, and hurt himself so that they thought he couldn't recover. It seemed nothing couldn't kill him. However, he's dead now, poor fellow.'

The organ pealed within, and we listened. The choir was singing 'Nearer, my God, to Thee.'

Presently the mourners came out of the church with the coffin. Among the men bearing it I recognised one of the ploughmen of Farley Hall, a black cap in his hand, looking unfamiliar bareheaded. The group gathered round the grave with Mr Phipps. Old Mr Colville and I removed our hats, and stood a little apart watching them lower the coffin containing the dead victor of a hundred brawls into the earth. Death, said the attitudes of the mourners, must be terrible indeed if it could kill that man.

Whispers of the hymn still seemed to haunt among the dead leaves. It might not, after all, have been altogether inappropriate, for later I learnt from Mr Colville's wife who had visited him that the old bruiser, as though fearing his life had not been in godly pattern, expressed the hope, when seized with his last illness, that he might 'lie a bit': not die at once, but have days for meditation in his bed.

Afterwards I walked with old Mr Colville into his fields, telling him of my errand. In one field he stopped and said,

'I remember as though it were yesterday working with my father harvesting my first crop in this field.' It was as though he had not been listening to my message, but that the funeral we had just witnessed had turned his thoughts to the fleeting of time. Then, as we stood on that rising ground with silver-dewed clover smothering our boots, he told me of his life, turning to gaze on the village and his house as though the story were written there. He told me of his father, who had been a maltster. He, however, had desired to be a farmer, and had persuaded his father to take a hundred acres of land for him.

'You see the thatched part of the house,' said old Mr Colville. 'That was as big as it used to be when I first came to live there; the rest was added later.'

The thatched portion was a third of the whole; the rest was tiled.

'And this field, and that and two over yonder, and one behind there, that was all the land I had then. And now –'

We climbed higher till we could see his whole thousand acres spread out before us; for, though the slopes were gradual, the views were wide in that country. He pointed out to me how farm had been added to farm, till most of the vale was his, while his sons farmed the slopes around.

'It makes me feel old,' he said, 'when I think of the little I started from. Yet it seems like yesterday.'

I saw then how the Colvilles had risen and flourished in the land from small beginnings, and how in time ('Ah, well, we come and go,' he said) they would die away here, and another peasant's seed hold sway.

'There are things you've known so long you feel they'll never change,' he said. 'And people, too; you don't seem to notice them getting older round you, till they begin to fail. There's our servant, who's been with us nearly from the first; and Kelp, my coachman. But you'd never believe how upset they get if I tell them they must have someone to help them. Well, well, I don't know why I should be talking like this. Yes, you had better go and see Horace about the rabbiting. You know where he lives? Gaymer's Hall; you can strike across the fields.'

So I set out to find Horace Colville, passing, on my way, the low-lying farm of Jim Crawley's brother, George. George I had met, and found him as quiet and ruminative as Jim was restless. He was a bachelor and it was always a joke among the Colvilles if a woman was rumoured to have looked his way. He fell in love with a girl in his youth, Mr Colville told me, but her father regarded George as a bit 'queer', and forbade him to come to the house when he knew how things were between them. Her father was dead now, and the girl still unmarried, yet George Crawley had not approached her again. His springtime was past. So there he sat alone in his finely timbered house (Mr Colville and I, peeping once through his uncurtained window, saw him), smoking and staring at the fire, with carved faces laughing down at him.

I came to Gaymer's Hall, and, knocking at a half-open door, was confronted by a bare-armed woman churning, who told me that Horace was in the fields. So I sought hither and thither, and at last saw him, standing stock-still with a gun in his hands gazing over a low hedge. He gave me one glance when I was yet at a distance, but did not look round again, only as I came beside him said, 'Keep still'. So there we stood, two petrified figures, gazing, as far as I could see, at dew-hung thorns.

Then all at once I became aware of a rabbit sitting in the stubble in the next field. I suppose it had been there all the time, really. It jumped forward a few feet, and sat again. It squealed.

"There's a stoat after it,' Horace whispered.

Again it jumped a little way. Then I saw the stoat with eyes like two sparks and flicking tail. The rabbit was free, yet paralysed with fright. Suddenly the stoat sprang on its neck. It squealed piercingly and rolled over, the stoat with it. The stoat was on the rabbit's back, which was towards us. Horace fired, and both lay dead.

'I've been trying to get him for a week,' he said.

I gave my message, and he told me he would come on Monday afternoon. As we walked we put up a covey of partridges. He followed their flight. 'I know that covey,' he said; 'there's one with a dropped leg among them; they mostly keep about these fields.' He had an acute observation for such details.

Horace was a curious man, I discovered later, quite without ambition. He had not risen with the rest of the Colvilles, but was content to be foreman for old Mr Colville at Gaymer's Hall, and receive a foreman's wage. All the same, the Colvilles treated him as one of themselves, though banteringly. It was a joke of which they never tired, when drinking strong beer in the fields, rabbiting, to cry, 'This'll make your hair curl, Horace.' I did not appreciate it till one day he took his hat off. He had no hair at all.

Horace was a kind of Will Wimble; his interest was in observing the wild life of the fields. He knew where the foxes had their lairs, what coverts the pheasants haunted, and which way the partridges in any particular field were apt to fly when driven. Though no horseman, he was an invaluable help to the huntsmen when the hounds ran that way. At the sound of a horn he was immediately on the alert, and it was likely that he saw the fox and noted its line. Many a time he had hallooed the hunt from a check and put them on to the scent again. He was popular among them, for when they drew the coverts of the neighbourhood they were nearly always sure of an immediate find, since Horace knew where the fox lay close. He might have forsaken his lair in the sandpit: Horace had found him, in a hollow tree.

I had another errand that day; to order two tons of middlings from the mill. So next I made my way there, leaving Horace re-setting a sprung trap. The mill was at work. Each sail in its circuit passed close to the ground like the sweep of a giant sword, so swift and shadowy that one really did get the impression that the mill was something monstrous and alive, and Don Quixote's seemed not so wild an illusion. I nearly came within range of the sails without realising my danger. The miller's assistant, standing near, said, 'I've known strangers who would have walked right into them and been killed if I had not stopped them in time.'

The miller, he said, was at the top of the mill, so thither I climbed, gingerly, up many narrow steps. There were three storeys to the mill, and in the floor between each were holes, through which ran chains, and larger openings for sacks. The chains were polished brighter than household silver by friction with the wood, and the edges of the holes were lustrous, rubbed, and rounded. The mill interior was something like that of an old ship. It was built round a tree, a stout, straight trunk which was covered with carved initials and dates. Reckonings in coombs and bushels were scrawled upon the curving walls. The top storey was a small chamber with a casement window. A wooden spindle went across it, to which the sails were fixed outside. The mill creaked and trembled as they revolved.

The miller was a small, rosy man with a powder of meal on his face, which gave him the complexion of a débutante.

He was as unemotional as a dumpling, despite his stirring trade. I was looking about me, all curiosity.

'I expect such things as this seem strange to you,' he said. 'I am afraid we are quite behind the times here.'

'It is so interesting to find a windmill still at work,' I said. 'I expect you are very fond of it.' I remembered the miller of Tennyson's poem.

'It's a queer thing,' he replied; 'folks from town always seem to think that. There seems to be something about the old mill that takes their fancy. I don't know what; it's quite out of date.'

'That's just it; because it's old and still at work.'

He shook his head. 'Can't say as I see any good in a thing that's out of date.'

The mill to him was just an inefficient means of grinding. When next a sail broke he would not have it repaired, he said.

'Why not?' I asked.

'A new sail costs a hundred pounds, and for that I could get an oil engine which would grind all day and every day, whether the wind blew or not.'

So I pondered this paradox that the wind, which costs nothing, is more expensive than engine power to-day.

I caught sight of what looked like a bunch of white sausages. 'What are they?'

He laughed. 'You don't see many of them in London now, I'll be bound. They are tallow candles.'

Here I found them employed in their last use – greasing the works of the mill. Oil would have run and fouled the meal.

This man's father, from what he told me, was more a miller of the traditional kind. He used to enjoy being up in the mill in a storm, and would let the sails revolve in dangerously high winds. He sang, he laughed, he loved wild weather. His son said, 'It seemed to get into his blood.' One January night a storm of unusual violence woke everybody up. The old miller was getting on in years then. He had been in bed for several days, but his son, looking out of the window, saw the mill-sails racing and his father in his nightshirt standing at the window in the mill-top in a gleam of moonlight, shouting and singing. When they reached him he had fallen down in a fit, and that was the end of him.

In the past the mill had been an efficient piece of mechanism: now it was a museum piece. As the miller had to get his living out of it, his lack of affection was understandable.

The next day was Saturday, and we motored into the town of Stambury, as Mrs Colville had an appointment with the dentist there. To while away the time, Mr Colville and I walked into the cinema, where a drama of Society life was showing, according to the placards, on which, for the benefit of those to whom facial expression was no guide, the villain was distinguished by a green complexion. Seated within, assailed by the heavy perfume which the proprietor had disseminated into the air to induce a sense of luxury, I was lulled far from the mangold field, the stubble, the moated farms. Here was a fragment of that other life, Cosmopolis, flung into the market square, and winking at us like a wicked jewel, all temptation. I enjoyed that film.

Coming out in the usual dazed state, it was something of a shock to find the massive farmer at my side, and Giles, unmistakable in face and figure, trooping out to right and left of me, behind and before.

It was among these peasants that I found the division between the generations sharpest as I lived in Benfield my first country year. While their fathers sat relishing the past

('You remember how old Noaky came a tippler off that load of straw,' etc.), the sons trimmed their acetylene lamps and mounted hire-purchased bicycles for town. There they passed beneath this festal porch, and, clasping the girls in the darkness, were enchanted to wander in American hotels and boudoirs. And next morning woke again to ploughing. It was a fantastic transition. After dining with Miss Dolores del Rio, what did Giles think of his Madge, I wondered? But Madge had watched too, and assimilated technique. The shopkeepers of Stambury, intuitive, dangled garments which suggested the flat rather than the cottage. She waited at the cross-roads in silk-stockings and a flaunting frock. Giles tried to respond to the new suggestion also. A purple double-breasted suit was served to him by the Jew who shouted in the market-place, and this was his Sunday garment. The very next day I passed a sniggering and uneasy group at the cross-roads, dressed in a parody of metropolitan style which looked odd in the English landscape. It was expensive for these poor folk, of course: the material was shoddy, of ephemeral wear. So different from their father's corduroy coats at £1.

As we drove home that afternoon, we passed the local bus (another sign of the times) trundling its load back to Benfield. It was said to have diminished Mr Jolman's trade considerably, for the village wives liked to go to the town to shop for the sake of the outing, though the fares added to the housekeeping expenses.

As we passed through Benfield, the last rays were flashing on the windows of the empty Manor, as though all were bright within in preparation for a country ball. But the rooks settling into the elms were the only things stirring there. The village was without its gentleman, and lacked a figure-head. Old Mr Colville deputised, but he most of all regretted the days of Squire Lindley. The village, I judged, had been proud of that elegant flourish, of hounds and horses in its midst, and smooth lawns. It wanted an employer of gardeners and grooms and maids; and one to be preached at on Sundays in the name of them all.

4

On Sunday we breakfasted at nine. Dawn stole in silently, and I missed the hoarse voices and scraping hoofs that usually attended it. But at eight-thirty the separator was humming as usual as I came down, and there was the boy Jack clattering his pails from pig-yard to swill-house, and the horsekeeper was busy feeding his horses and pumping water for them.

Jack came towards the house with four dead hens in his hands. These he laid upon a tank near the window-sill of the breakfast-room.

'The fox had 'em last night,' he said. 'I reckon they'd been roosting up a tree.'

'But how could he get them if they were in a tree?' I asked.

'He's only to stand under a tree and look up at 'em and they fall down right into his mouth. Seems as though he sort of dazes 'em.' He added, 'You might tell the master when he comes down.' I said I would.

Now, the poultry on the farm was Mrs Colville's per-quisite; so also was the milk. It is usual in Suffolk for the farmer's wife to take the money for chickens, butter, and eggs. She has to keep the house on this, for she receives no housekeeping money, and if she has anything over it is hers to bank or spend.

When Mr Colville came down and saw the remains of the hens, and learned the cause of their death, he said, 'Take them away quick before the missis sees them.' But Mrs

Colville came down at that moment and caught sight of them.

'What a shame!' she cried. 'They are some of the best hens, in full lay. It has quite spoilt my breakfast.' She said some bitter things about the fox.

Afterwards Mr Colville said to me, 'That damned young fool Jack, to go and lay them right against the window there.' He added, 'I don't grudge the fox a hen or two; he gave us a good run the other day. If the missis hadn't seen them she might never have known.' When he came upon Jack, he rated him for his want of tact.

Our Sunday dress in winter was breeches of a smarter cut than those of every day, and clean leggings and boots. My original brown boots had been polished up, and seemed now the thing for Sunday wear. Mr Colville had a pair like them. They felt light as dancing-shoes after the working-boots.

Mr Colville rode across the fields to church. I lay in a horsehair arm-chair in the breakfast-room with pipe and book, and for once the bustling Millicent failed to stir me. One of the first questions put to me on my arrival at Farley Hall had been (*in camera*), 'Are you Church of England?' The object of it had been merely to inform me of the nearest place of worship of those of my creed. It was a question that had caused me some confusion in the past. Religion, in fact, had been full of perplexities, beginning with my first encounter – a painful scene with my nurse, who refused to allow me to rise from table before I had said, 'Thank God for a good dinner.' I had not the vaguest idea who or what God was, nor, since the dinner had included rice pudding, was I feeling particularly thankful for it. Then there had been my first day at a kindergarten school, which had begun with us all kneeling down (a new game, I thought) and muttering. 'Harold be Thy name,' I thought they said, and wondered. In any case, what could the word 'hallowed' mean to a child of six? My parents had been reticent about established religion – wisely so, I think; for how can the idea of God be conveyed to a child's mind in words, a Being about whom the adult world differs so furiously? How, without at the same time creating unnameable fears which cause children much private suffering?

Then there had been an interview with the head master of my public school on the first day of term. 'Are you Church of England?' 'Yes,' I faltered. But that was not enough. 'What church do you attend at home?' I sought wildly for a name. The memory of a visitor's conversation saved me. 'St Leonard's,' I answered.

But at school there was a short period of religious fervour, owing really to the persecution of larger boys, from whom one was safe only in chapel. Then becoming a larger boy oneself and insufferably knowing, atheism was the only possible attitude to the unknown. My housemaster – blessings on his memory! – hearing of this, laughed at me. Just when I was prepared, martyr-like, to suffer expulsion for my non-belief, he said in passing, 'So you are the young man who believes we go out like a candle?' 'Yes, sir,' I said. His answer was, 'Ha, ha, ha!'

From this I had drifted to the modern attitude of open-minded doubt which awaits, as it were, the next mystico-scientific discovery for light. So again the question, 'Are you Church of England?' was a poser. I made an inadequate reply, indicating that I was not a regular church-goer. This left an unsatisfied silence, and a few days later Mrs Colville returned to the attack.

'If you don't go to church, what makes you do good?'

My behaviour was instinctive and hereditary, not the result of reason.

'I suppose because it is usually less dangerous than doing ill,' I answered.

'But if you are not afraid of going to hell?'

I mumbled my way unsatisfactorily through these inquisitions. But to Mrs Colville and the ladies of the family I became 'a case'; they looked upon me curiously. The young man who behaved in an ordinary way, yet did not believe in heaven or hell! They saw nothing to restrain me from diabolical crimes, and for a while they regarded me much as a tiger cub, gentle and playful until one day it should taste blood. I mention this to show that here a pre-Darwinism faith still held good. It was the simple affair of the days of Tusser:

> Tithe duly and well, with hearty goodwill,
> That God and His blessing may dwell with thee still.
> Though parson neglecteth his duty for this,
> Thank thou thy Lord God, and give every man his.

Mr Colville, believing that every man knew his own business, kept religion a personal matter. But once, when his brother Arnold was going to sell me a gun, and I, meeting him on a Sunday, enquired of him his price, Mr Colville changed the subject, and, taking me aside, said, 'I shouldn't do a deal on a Sunday, if I were you. It may be my fancy, but it don't ever seem to turn out right. Once when I was a boy I bought some ferrets on a Sunday, and dash me if they didn't all die.'

The infallibility of parsons was no more an illusion here and now than in the time of Tusser. In fact, the inhabitants of Benfield liked a parson for his humanity rather than his godliness. The present one's predecessor had been a keen sportsman, who had boxed the local publican for a wager and beaten him, spending the stake money on drinks all round. He used to ride to hounds twice a week, and legend has it that seeing a fox cross the churchyard, he paused in his sermon to shout 'Tally-ho!'

On Mr Colville's return from church, we motored down to Benfield to his father's for lunch. This, I learned, was a weekly function, a gathering of the clan. Several cars were in the yard before us, and quite a crowd of people sat in the house. Brother Arnold was there, with his wife and two children. He had a general shop in a town some miles distant, and was a keen man of business. There was another brother, Dick, also in trade, with his wife and pretty daughter, who was charming, but the only one to feel a little bored. There were the farmer brothers and their wives, and a married sister with her husband (a farmer). I never came to the end of the Colville family during the years I knew them. Just when I thought I had met them all, another cousin, uncle, or sister-in-law would be introduced to me at a gathering.

Mrs Colville's father was there, Depden by name. He wore a lavender waistcoat with lapels, which compelled my admiration. He spoke in rhythmic periods, as though delivering a speech, but was a restive listener, always trying to cut a person short with, 'Just so, just so.' His three daughters had married three of the Colville brothers – that had been the outcome of dances in 'the good old days'. One of them was Arnold's wife.

Lunch was substantial and the party vivacious. We sat round a large table which almost filled the low-ceilinged room. Through the window I saw the mounting cornfields over the road, with a cottage in the distance, and on the left the trees of the Manor Park.

Having been caught many times in strange houses starting prematurely, I waited; but no grace was said. This, I learned, was the custom only when the parson was present. Then the company would wait for him to pronounce a blessing.

The antique servant, whose cap slightly suggested a Roman Catholic vestment, trotted round with slices of pudding and gravy. This traditional Suffolk dish (boiled, not baked, pudding) I was growing fond of, though it was not much to the taste of brother Dick's pretty and flighty daughter; she made a private face at me. I learned that her father's business was in a gay seaside town. She spoke of dancing and theatres, and I answered with shreds of pre-agricultural life. Then came a round of beef like a pillar, and after that trifles and plum pudding. Saturday in the old homestead had been a day of great preparation. Mrs Colville, the mother, and the servant did it all between them. They enjoyed the weekly reunion, and, old as they were, would admit of no help from the daughters-in-law who lived near. Besides the luncheon preparation, I learned that seventy buns had been baked the day before. Some of the brothers were staying over Monday for rabbiting.

After lunch, old Mrs Colville led the ladies into the drawing-room, and later upstairs to lie down. That siesta was an almost religious observance among them.

The men sat gazing at the fire, hands in breeches' pockets. A drowsiness overcame them, and conversation flagged. Old Mr Colville had his particular chair against the fire, an antique one with flaps.

Arnold said to me, 'So you think you'd like to go in for farming? There isn't a better life, but there's not enough hangs to it for me. The turnover is too slow.' Then he turned to his father. 'I see you've threshed those barley stacks at the side of the road. How did they turn out?'

Mr Colville produced a palm full of the grains from his waistcoat pocket and showed them to Arnold, who pronounced it 'rare good-quality barley.'

Old Mr Colville said to me, 'My pockets get right full of corn. I am always putting a sample in my pocket as I go about at threshing or harvest-time.' Then he turned to his son. 'But the price ain't nothing. They bid me for it, but I said, "I won't sell at that for nobody. I'll eat it first."'

I found in Arnold another exile from farming by his interest in events on his father's acres and his familiarity with them. A money-maker by instinct, he confided to me that his earliest recollections were of his elders grumbling about agriculture, the state of the weather, the poorness of prices. These complaints had sunk in and had determined him never to be a farmer. But blood will out, and he was at the moment proposing to his brother John to take a half-share with him in a farm which was being offered at a low price.

His first eager question upon meeting would be, 'What do you think of Courtauld's?' And I would have to admit lamely that I had not noticed what Courtauld's shares stood at that morning (as though by the merest oversight).

Arnold was a stickler for the last farthing in business but generous within the family. He was the bank. He was often impatient with his father over what he considered unbusinesslike procedure.

'It's my way,' was his father's invariable answer.

'The men,' Arnold grumbled, 'they don't help you get a living nowadays. When they had half the wages they were twice as content.'

Here brother Dick added an instance, and the company woke from its drowse. Dick, while shaving one morning, had noticed some men arrive opposite his house to repair the road. It was seven-thirty, he said, when they drove slowly up and began to unload poles and warning notices of 'Road Up'. Having made an enclosure for themselves they placed their braziers therein. It was then eight o'clock. Next they began polishing their shovels. This took a long time.

'Now what,' said Dick to himself, 'are they polishing their shovels for?' When they had done that they took them up, and, instead of setting to work, put bacon in them and used them as frying-pans.

I suggested to Dick Colville that of course he would speak of it to the surveyor or a friend on the town council, but he shook his head. 'That's the devil of it. You see, there are several Labour members on the council, and it would get round to the working people that I had complained, and I rely on their custom in my shop.'

About three o'clock, John Colville, who had been slipping gradually further down in his chair, roused himself and said, 'Let's go and have a look at those bullocks of yours, father.' Thereupon we all went out for the afternoon walk round, that great Sunday function of farmers. The dogs, waiting expectant at the door, bounded up in delight.

'Have you got a stick?' Mr Colville asked me. I hadn't, but it didn't matter, I said. 'You must have a stick,' he said, and fetched me a rugged one from the hall. A farmer would as soon go out without his hat as his stick, for it is a valued implement of his profession, as I found out.

We had not gone far before old Mr Colville paused, and with his stick filled in a rabbit-hole on the field, saying, 'That might cause a horse at plough to break his leg.' Arnold, meanwhile, was endeavouring to find which way the burrow went, by poking his stick into the earth here and there. When it went in without much pressure he knew he was over the burrow.

Coming to a plough, Mr Colville scraped away the earth from it to see that the man had not been ploughing with a worn breast or share.

We passed through a field which old Mr Colville said was sown with wheat, adding that he was going to have it harrowed in on the morrow.

'I reckon it's too wet after that rain yesterday,' said Arnold, and to settle the matter they ran the points of their sticks along the earth as though they were the teeth of harrows. As the earth did not clog on them, the old man was proved right.

While I was observing the horizon in the afternoon light, or glancing back at the village roofs and the church tower enthroned in trees, the eyes of the others were busy noticing things nearer their feet.

'I reckon a fox lies up in this tree,' said Dick, pointing to the bark, scarred in places.

Arnold thought he discovered the mark of a fox's pad in the mud.

'I'll ask Horace; he'll know,' John said.

Arnold had a terrier which glued its nose to a small hole in the ditch. As Arnold's dog was in his opinion the best ratter that had ever been known, the party had to pause for an exhibition of its prowess. But the rat was safely far in and had to be abandoned.

We passed through one of the farms, and, seeing the foreman at his door, old Mr Colville asked him for the key of the barn, as some newly threshed barley lay there which he wanted the others to see. The man was wearing a dickey; I noticed the word 'Reversible' stamped on it. The dickey was still in favour among the older folks of Benfield. As a swift smartener it appeared unbeatable. A tie was not considered necessary with it, as though it were a pity to hide the white starched front. Old Mr Colville wore a cravat built upon a framework of cardboard, which (in his everyday one) showed through in a frayed spot. It was too exact and flat to make any pretence of having been tied before a mirror each morning, but perfectly convenient.

Arnold thrust his stick deep into the heap of barley, and after a minute withdrew it and felt the end.

'It's beginning to get warm, father; you'll have to move it,' he said.

Mr Depden did not come into the barn with us. He was discovered bending over a heap of old iron in a corner.

'That's a handy piece of iron,' he said, lifting out an L-shaped strip; 'a bit like that will be wanted to hold something together one day.' He laid it carefully upon a ledge.

For a while we leaned over a paling in appraisement of a yard of pigs that were then being fed. The pigs lived in a kind of primitive bush dwelling with one side open. Rough posts supported the thatched roof. In respect of this John Colville said to me, 'Pigs always do well in rough old places like this, made of faggots and poles, much better than in modern brick and concrete sites. I don't know why it is.'

The horsekeeper had arrived to give his horses their evening feed. He was leading them to the pond to drink when one escaped and wandered off to a haystack and began pulling out mouthfuls. 'Never seen such a mare,' said he as he brought her back. 'She's allus arter her gut.'

On the way home, old Mr Colville began poking at the side of a ditch with his stick. 'There should be a drain hereabout,' he said, pointing to a track of glistening saturation down it. He unearthed broken pieces of pipe until a small hole was apparent from which the water spouted.

Arnold, not to be outdone in quickness of observation, claimed another blocked drain a few yards from it, on which he set to work. The others discovered one too, and began poking and scraping. I attempted one, interpreting, as I thought, the sign; but it turned out to be a rat-hole. In a little while there was a whole row brightly and briskly flowing, and the party stood back and observed them, pleasantly conscious of having earned its tea.

Old Mr Colville laid his hand on my shoulder. 'You see you can do a lot of good even just walking about your farm. Remember that if you come to have a place of your own.'

The windows of the Home Farm gleamed, welcoming us to tea. Old Mrs Colville presided over the tea-tray. The teapot was a silver monument.

'How do you like your tea?' she asked me.

'Weak, please,' I answered, observing my neighbour's dark cupful.

Arnold burst out, 'Mother, the fox has killed six of your best pullets.'

She had a pen of ten pedigree birds which she held in great affection, and kept for eggs for the house.

'You don't say that!' She looked round apprehensively, but John set her mind at rest. 'He's having you on.'

'Don't talk so foolish, Arnold,' she said. 'I know you like to tease me.'

'It wholly made you look;' and Arnold roared with laughter, pleased with his joke as a boy on April Fools' Day.

After tea, some went to church, others chatted by the fire. Horace Colville looked in for a while and confirmed the theory of the fox lying in the tree. George Crawley, the phlegmatic, also arrived. It was a Sunday observance with him to spend the evening there. He sat down in a chair, lit his pipe and, leaning one elbow on the table, listened to the conversation, pausing in his puffs to say, 'Ay,' every now and then.

I found the atmosphere of the gathering comfortable. One could speak or smoke in silence, as one pleased; there was no obligation to 'make conversation'. For the most part

I listened – to talk adorned with the picturesque names of fields, and similes new to me: 'A landlord without money is worse off than a toad under a harrow.' A tut-tutting over young so-and-so: 'A rare boozer – pity, too; he's got a good farm if it was seen after.'

It was an evening, I gathered, for general survey of crops and prices, people and their doings. 'Anyone come to Nordley Moat yet?' 'So-and-so had a rare bust up with some gypsies Thursday.'

Mr Depden was treating John Colville to a long account of negotiations with some men for the sale of oak-trees, which seemed to be sending him to sleep. Now and again he would murmur, 'No doubt'.

Driving home, he said to me, 'That old man would talk the hind leg off a donkey; he ought to have been a chapel preacher.' Further, he added, 'Sundays don't suit me; too much eating and sitting.'

The next day we were up with the lark again. Mr Colville stood in the yard of Farley Hall at the grey hour impatiently fingering his watch.

'They are always late on Monday morning,' he said. 'They get worse until I have a row with them; then they come at the right time for a week or two.'

When the men arrived and saw him standing there, they looked sheepish. Mr Colville gave an example of the emphatic use of the negative. 'You can all go home,' he said, 'and don't none of you never come back no more.'

The prospect seemed bleak, but Mr Colville had the knack of breathing thunder one moment and being in perfectly good humour with everybody the next. A few minutes after the threat, work was proceeding smoothly.

Breakfast was over early, and the brothers arrived with their guns for the rabbiting. Mr Colville bustled out, collecting boys as he went. There were always rosy young-sters loitering about, who followed him forth into the fields if he had a gun on his shoulder. When he shot anything, it was, 'Boy, pick up that rabbit,' which the boy did, and proudly carried.

This morning we were accompanied also by one Sim-mons, a spidery little man with a face of woe, who carried the impedimenta of our sport – a box of ferrets on his back, a rabbiting spade, slasher, nets, lines, etc. His coat was reinforced with leather at cuffs and elbows; pieces of bag were tied as pads on his knees.

Simmons knew the signs of the holes, whether there was any 'work' at the entrances which signified that they were used, whether this or that tempting-looking hole were a drain. If a loose ferret were allowed to follow a rabbit up a land-drain he was as good as lost. When a ferret disappeared into a hole and did not reappear, a line-ferret was sent in to locate him, with a collar round his neck and a cord attached, one end of which Simmons held. Then he laid his ear to the ground and listened. Sometimes one could hear the rabbits quite plainly thumping and scuttling about. The rabbits were not bolting well this morning. The ditch we had started upon was full of intricate burrows. Two ferrets had gone in and stayed; the line-ferret went in two-thirds of the length of the line. One of the little boys cried in a hoarse whisper, 'Look there!' A rabbit's head appeared at the mouth of a hole, with bright, apprehensive eyes. 'Keep still,' Mr Colville commanded, and was a statue: the dogs stood tense. The rabbit shot out along the ditch. Mr Colville fired, and the creature slithered back from the mouth of a hole he had just gained on, dead and kicking. The dogs brought it between them, and Mr Colville handed it to the biggest boy, who slit a hind leg with his knife, between the sinew and the bone, put the other through it, and hung the rabbit, thus cross-legged, upon the hedge.

But none of the ferrets had reappeared, so more rabbits must be in the burrow. The subterranean scuffling had ceased.

'I reckon they're laid up,' said Simmons. There was nothing for it but to dig for them. With his slasher he cut back the bushes. There was discussion among the brothers as to where to dig, each swearing he had heard them under his very feet. Simmons meantime dug where he thought and found the line, which meant he was in the right direction. Several holes were dug; sometimes the line was found, sometimes not. At length, getting as he thought near, Simmons broke a long piece of bramble from the hedge and thrust it as far as it would go along the hole. He twisted it round several times and withdrew it. Rabbit fleck was caught upon the thorns at the end. The ferrets were found where the ground was next opened, and taken out. Then Simmons put his arm deep in and drew the rabbits out one by one. The first two were in a sad state, for such is the animal's nature that it will often sit and allow itself to be eaten alive in its burrow rather than bolt out from the ferret, which it could easily escape.

At first these spectacles of suffering filled me with disquiet, but towards the end of the winter I had become used to them (the mind adjusting itself, as it must), and would pull the rabbits out with bloody hands and knock them on the head without concern.

The young boys picked up the rabbits, as Simmons flung them down and dived for more. They handled them without a tremor. I wondered what would have been the effect of the sight upon any half-dozen children then at play in Kensington Gardens.

Six rabbits were taken from that hole, the last four uninjured, having been protected by the first two. Of those mangled ones, Simmons murmured a perfunctory, 'Poor beggars!' as he ended their pain.

Mr Colville himself was a humane man, and liked rabbits to bolt and be shot clean. But ferreting, he pointed out, was the only way of keeping down the rabbits, who would ruin the corn crop of the whole farm if left to breed unhindered for two years.

The day had its comedies. I provided some amusement by my first attempt to handle a ferret. The creature came out of a hole near me, sniffing the air and flashing its pink eyes at me suspiciously. It snapped round at me like lightning every time I attempted to seize it by the shoulders, which is the only safe place. Simmons captured the more vicious by trailing a dead rabbit before them and making a chirping noise with his mouth which distracted their attention while his hand stole behind them.

At one hole he was listening intently when the ferret reappeared unexpectedly and fastened on his ear. This caused much merriment, especially among the little boys, but Simmons saw no joke, and used his favourite expletive loudly. Dick Colville's daughter was at that moment with the party, and, instead of sympathy, poor Simmons received a reprimand for swearing in the presence of a lady. Simmons, being slight and agile, was a born ferreter, as the job included much digging in crouching attitudes among entanglements of thorn. When an awkward dig was encountered, Mr Colville would leave him at it, and, taking a ferret, proceed, saying, 'We mustn't all stop about here or we shan't get anything done today.'

Sometimes after half an hour's patient digging Simmons would rejoin us, full of angry woe that he had found the ferret on the skin of a long-dead rabbit as the result of all.

After lunch (a bread and cheese picnic) we tackled the deep ditch that ran between the two slopes down to Benfield. Mr Phipps, the vicar, joined us there. Mr Colville hinted to me that he was a man to beware of when he had a gun in his hands. He would blaze off both barrels at a rabbit before anyone else had seen it. The spot was a thicket and full of bolt-holes; rabbits ran out and in continually. This, combined with the presence of Mr Phipps, in tweeds the colour of the surroundings, prowling among the hazels, bang-banging every minute, caused a state of nervous tension. The Colvilles frequently called, 'Don't shoot in this direction; I am standing here' to each other, but really for Mr Phipps' hearing.

Later in the day, in a clear spot, I had my first shot at a rabbit. Arnold Colville put his gun in my hands as we were waiting by a likely hole. The rabbit ran clearly across my view at about twenty yards. I pulled the trigger, received a violent blow on the shoulder, and saw the rabbit do a perfect cartwheel somersault.

'You'll never shoot a rabbit cleaner than that if you live to be a hundred,' was Arnold's opinion. I was pleased with my success. 'It's a good gun,' Arnold said.

The half-brother, Horace Colville, joined us, wearing an old tent-shaped hat with a jay's feather in it. He had an expert look of leisure and unconcern even in waiting for a snap shot between two close holes. He would raise his gun, kill a rabbit clean, and be returned to his dreaming attitude all in a moment, so that one almost wondered whether somebody else had not shot the rabbit. He puffed at his ruined crater of a pipe with its string-bound stem continually, stock-still: but his small blue eyes were alert to the quiver of a leaf.

I have seen the town brothers, Arnold and Dick, spend both their barrels on an escaping rabbit, Horace waiting (it being their outing), and then, taking quiet aim, kill it at long range.

Towards dusk we lost the line-ferret (he slipped his collar). Three of us returned after tea, Simmons and I and Horace meeting at the spot with lanterns. We looked a nefarious party, digging in the yellow gleam. We killed fifty rabbits that day.

I spent many days rabbiting with Horace during the winter. Mr Colville lent me a gun of his, but I did not live up to the reputation of my first shot. The rabbits usually ran out and along the hedge, popping in again where there was another hole. I shot behind or above them, and often had to cry shamefacedly, 'I'm sorry; I missed him,' over the hedge. But Horace was never put out; he merely remarked, 'Never mind; we shall come to him again.' We did, but it meant a digging job, for a rabbit will not bolt twice. In mud and in snow we crouched, poked, and peered. Often I froze, waiting for the rabbits to bolt, and when the moment came my numbed finger could not feel the trigger. Yet I enjoyed it, and tea-time firelight came to have a more than common glory.

We continued right into March, our last day being mild with the birth of spring, when we sat on a green-sprigged bank and basked in the sun as we ate our bread and cheese, our feet in young corn. But that was not yet.

5

November. Chilling mists, trees dripping half the day, and dampness underfoot. The out-of-doors had become distinctly inimical to life. The horsekeeper said the air was 'faint' and made the horses sweat. It was the worst time of the year, he said, for horses; they all caught cold. He had secret potions made from herbs gathered in summer, which he gave them. Tea, he called it; it smelt poisonous. He spoke enigmatically on this subject, with a smile that told of information withheld.

'If you give it them once,' he said, 'it do them harm. You must give it again a week after, and then it do them good.'

What this mysterious medicine was I have never discovered, nor could Mr Colville tell me much more.

'It's something he gives them,' said Mr Colville, 'that makes their coats shine. I don't know what it is. All horsekeepers do it. They are as artful as the devil.'

Mr Colville's horsekeeper could neither read nor write, but that had not prevented his faculties from being bright. He had an old book, he told me, about horses, which an old man had given him when he was young. 'My son Joe would give the world to see that book,' said the horsekeeper, 'but I keep it hid.' He seemed to believe that priceless secrets were contained in it, and if his son gained access to it he would come to know more about horses than he did himself, which would never do. So he kept it concealed, unread. Nor would anything persuade him to let me see it even. So there may be a first edition at the bottom of his chest to-day.

Now there was talk of 'the hounds' among farmers and men alike. 'Where do they meet to-day?' 'Will they run this way?' Several times I had heard the horn, and once I saw the hunt distantly, horses and hounds in full cry across a stubble like a handful of blown leaves.

Mr Colville asked, did I ride? I answered that I could, but had not ridden lately. I did not say how long ago it had been – to wit, at my preparatory school at the age of twelve.

At Farley Hall horses were always coming and going. At the present he had two hunters – a chestnut called Jock, a heavyweight retainer, and a roan mare, Cantilever, who was aged but a flyer, being half a thoroughbred. Mr Colville asked me to take Jock to be shod, as his hind shoes were loose and his front feet needed trimming. Now, though I had ridden I had never learned to put a saddle and bridle on, as the horses had always arrived at the door ready for mounting. Accordingly I asked the boy Jack to saddle the chestnut for me. He gaped and grinned.

'You ain't going to ride him, are you? He'll have you off.'

'Ride him? Of course I am,' I said.

'But you don't know how.'

'You'll see.'

Jack marvelled at my foolhardiness, for he was quite certain to himself that I had not ridden before; I was such a stranger to country ways in his eyes. However, he saddled the horse and I swung myself on to its back. I was not quite so confident perched up there; it was much farther from the ground than a motor-cycle. For a moment I almost doubted whether I had learned to ride or dreamed it.

'I reckon we shan't see you no more at all,' said Jack, waiting for the fun.

I touched the horse's flank with my heel and we moved off leisurely. Then, just to show that young man that I really could ride, I put him to the trot. I bumped several times, and began to fear I had forgotten how to rise to the trot. Then suddenly my seat felt soft as a cushion, and I knew I had fallen into the rhythm. I turned round to Jack, who stood gazing after me, and waved my hand, laughing. My sudden gesture caused the horse to start, and I lost a stirrup. I returned immediately to the business in hand, wondering whether I had shown any daylight.

I found the blacksmith lying flat on his back in the forge, and asked him if he were ill.

'Ill? No.' He laughed. 'I were just resting after my breakfast.'

I learned later that it is the custom of the Suffolk peasant to take a short siesta after his meals, wherever he may be. The usual interval is an hour for breakfast and an hour for lunch. He eats for half an hour, and for half an hour lies down.

That night Mr Colville said, 'The hounds meet at Borley Rose and Crown to-morrow. Would you like to come?'

I said I should like to very much, but – I was torn between a desire to taste the joys of hunting and a natural trepidation. My riding of many years ago had been no more than to trot sedately along quiet roads, one of a riding-class, and occasionally, as a treat, to canter on a piece of heathland. The admonitions of the riding-master still ring in my ears. 'Toes in, knees tight. Keep your 'orses well in 'and goin' down 'ill.' But I had never jumped or galloped over hunting country.

'At any rate you could come as far as the meet. You would like to see the meet,' Mr Colville said.

Next morning, after breakfast, the household was all of a bustle. The two women gyrated round Mr Colville as though it was some desperate cavalier venture he was embarking on. His hunting-coat hung on a chair before the fire, his tall boots stood beside it. His bowler hat was toasting on a rack over the kitchen stove. Damp was a grim ghost to Mrs Colville, and this was the first time her husband had hunted that season. She filled the whisky flask while Millicent cut sandwiches for us both, and Mr Colville, in check waistcoat and immaculate breeches, lathered his face vigorously before the kitchen mirror.

Midden, about again but hobbling, was supervising the preparation of the horses. They were led out, with leather shining and steel glittering, brightly groomed.

We mounted and were off. Mr Colville looked a typical hunting farmer with his round face under his bowler hat. He had lent me a bowler, that I might look the part, as I had not brought one, hardly considering it applicable to country life, the possibility of hunting being a fantastic vision in Chelsea.

He rode Jock, the heavyweight, while I perched on the nimble Cantilever.

'Rare good jumper, that mare is,' said Mr Colville. But the news at that time did not thrill me, only suggested a disturbing possibility of the mare springing suddenly from under me. 'She's safe, too.' That was better. 'But don't let other horses get too near her; she might kick. Only in play, of course; but people wouldn't like it.'

Apprehension again! Where did I go when she kicked?

A light wind was blowing. The mist had risen early, and the day was cold and clear. Conversation was cut short for the moment because a piece of paper in the road woke up and flapped, and the next I knew was that horse and I were on the top of a steep bank and then on the road again twenty yards ahead. I found I was still on the horse's back.

'I shouldn't let her do that,' said Mr Colville blandly. 'It's just that she's a bit bird-eyed, being fresh out.' He added 'But I like to see a horse show a bit of spirit.'

I noticed, however, that his was a model of decorum, with complacent ears (Cantilever's were a-twitch with nervous enquiry). Occasionally Mr Colville would make believe Jock had stumbled, and growl at him. I began to envy him his mount, though certainly Jock had not seemed as docile under me. Mr Colville's extra weight, no doubt. Jock moved with the magisterial surety of an elephant beneath his rider's fourteen stone.

Mr Colville exclaimed, 'I wish I were light enough to ride your mare. I'd show some of them how to go. Now, you're a nice weight; you could ride anything.' He sighed. 'Ah, well, you are only young once. I never cared what I rode one time of day, but I have to be careful now. I'm no light weight to fall.'

As we progressed, he pointed out places where he had made daring jumps or sustained skull-cracking falls. He had been a devil of a fellow, I gathered, when he was young. He harked back to the famous runs of his youth, telling me where they had found, where killed, and the hazards in between. Though the names meant nothing to me, I gathered something of the spirit of the thing by the enthusiasm of his telling, tinged with a melancholy that such irresponsible days were done. How he had ended up miles from home at dark (so few of them in at the kill), and had given his horse a drink of beer at an inn. The long hack home in moonlight with a friend – 'Poor Tom Barclay; he was killed in the war.' He went over his horses, dwelling on each by name, and after an account of every one it was, 'I shall never have another horse like that.' I think the sight of me perched on the flyer Cantilever made him begin to feel old.

As we passed a double hedge with a considerable ditch

between, he told me how he had seen his father (on a black mare of glorious memory) take it flying, and then another out of the field again. I found it hard to see the breathless old man so vigorous. The obstacle looked to me highly dangerous. Was that what we were in for?

As we proceeded, we were joined by others going to the meet. Mr Colville seemed to be equally at home with everybody, farmers, second horsemen, and pink coats. A small-faced man with glittering blue eyes and grizzled white hair (altogether like a bright frosty morning), dressed in immaculate pink, cried, 'Well, Colville, where shall we find to-day?' At his appearance the second horseman dropped back behind the farmers; the farmers themselves retired a little, and our group became a procession headed by Mr Colville and the gentleman in pink (Brigadier-General Sir Somebody or other, Mr Colville had muttered at his appearance). I stuck to my place on Mr Colville's other hand – largely because Cantilever seemed to desire it.

The hounds were gathered in front of the Rose and Crown, with the huntsmen and whips near by. The small space was packed with cars, horses, and people. There were horses sleepily still, horses restive, horses rugged and being led to and fro by grooms. Smart young men, mounted, ambled from one group of ladies to another, paying their respects. Hats were doffed right and left. There is something about being on horseback which gives a touch of old-world courtesy to a man's gestures.

Just before the hour the MFH drove up in a Bentley car. He doffed a white apron, which had protected his breeches from the slightest mark *en route*. His dappled horse was led to him, the rug swept from it, and the bridle held while he mounted. It was a ceremony to which the eyes of all were turned. The master was young, and would have graced the occasion perfectly, I felt, but for pince-nez with a chain to the ear, which gave him a somewhat studious look. The roots of his affluence, I learned, were in the grocery trade, and among some (non-hunters) there was always a snigger at the apron as having a double significance. But he used his riches to the noblest purpose. Here he was MFH, a title above pedigree.

The hunt prided itself on being a democratic hunt, and the bulk of the field consisted of farmers. A number of labourers stood viewing the scene, and one burly farmer, as near an embodiment of John Bull as I have ever seen, rode up to the inn porch, and handing silver to the landlady, said, 'Give all these chaps something to drink.' Thereupon there was a touching of hats and a growl of thanks.

The ladies were nearly all in side-saddle costume. They looked ungainly on the ground, but suddenly graceful mounted.

The whole scene was animated by the men's greetings to one another and the ladies. Nor were the ladies lacking in condescension, but chatted to their husbands' tenants on the day's prospects. Everybody knew Mr Colville, and I kept alongside him. Cantilever was a-quiver with anticipation, and I had some apprehension in guiding her between shining limousines and the haunches of other horses, especially those with red tape on their tails – a danger sign of which Mr Colville had informed me.

The hounds alone were unaffected by the subdued excitement. They lay about with lolling tongues and sleepy red eyes, and occasionally yawned.

Consultations were in progress between the Master and the huntsman, a shrewd old leatherface. There came a short toot of the horn and they were moving off.

Mr Colville turned to me. 'What do you think about it? Coming on or not?'

Before I could decide, I found myself swept onward in a crowd of horses. Cantilever was in no mood to retire. I went with the tide and hoped for the best.

'The only thing is,' I said, 'I have never done any jumping.'

'The mare is as safe as a church,' answered Mr Colville. 'All you have to do is to sit back and hold tight. Hug her well with your legs.'

I hoped my legs would be equal to the occasion. I was balanced, I felt, rather than seated. But to me, a stranger, there was something stirring about this laughing, chattering throng, the bright coats, the gleaming leather and steel – a flavour of old chivalry. I determined to let events take their course.

The horses were afire with impatience. They jogged their riders up and down and would not walk. We entered a field and spread. As soon as their feet touched soft earth, many of the horses tried to canter, and one or two bucked sensationally. I held Cantilever close, for she seemed disposed to give an exhibition of high spirits herself. Mr Colville's mount was magisterial as ever, his only sign of enthusiasm being to lift his legs higher and jog occasionally.

'We shall find here,' said Mr Colville, indicating a wood ahead. 'We always do.'

We stood under the shadow of the trees. The whole hunt seemed to have vanished, and silence reigned. A crowd of pigeons flew out of the wood. Rabbits lolloped silently towards us, paused, and scuttled away. A hare dashed past with a swishing noise through the stubble.

''Ark!' whispered Mr Colville, 'is that a 'oller?' – his aitches forsaking him at the moment of excitement.

I listened obediently, for what kind of noise I knew not; but Cantilever continued to champ her bit restlessly. Mr Colville raised his fist at her threateningly, but I saw no means of causing her to desist.

Suddenly a yelping and roaring filled the air, which immediately flashed upon me a childhood memory of the lions waiting to be fed at the Zoo.

'Ah!' said Mr Colville, 'that's the music at last.'

The horses were all of a twitter at the noise, and mad to be off. The horn sounded a rapid note. There was a thunder of hoofs behind, and half a dozen horses went flying past.

'Gone out towards Sedley Willows,' shouted somebody. Earth spattered on me. Next moment we were flying in their wake.

We turned the bend of the wood, to see the hunt streaming down a long slope. I had a glimpse of blue distances before I turned my attention to the curbing of my mare. I had made up my mind to follow Mr Colville as best I could, but it was with difficulty I could keep Cantilever from getting ahead. My arms ached; my fingers were numb. The mare made that noise that the Bible translates as 'Ha, ha!' and bounded on. It was downhill, and all were converging towards a single gateway. I could no longer hold Cantilever. I saw disaster ahead, and resigned myself. I understood then the intoxication of the Gadarene swine in rushing down a steep place into the sea. I did not care what happened.

The gateway was a stampede of horses. Somebody in a pink coat went crashing through the hedge to the right with a catastrophic din. Horses squeezed me on either side. Stirrups clanked against mine. Hosts were behind, indicated by fierce panting breath and squelching mud. Cantilever's nose was against the warning red ribbon on another's tail; but that was nothing to me now. Somebody said, 'Big dog fox, going like smoke.' Suddenly the pressure on cither side of me relaxed. We were through the gateway. Cantilever started into a gallop again. Where now! I looked round, but saw no sign of Mr Colville. I was careering along a tarred road. I had been taught that one should never canter on a hard road, and tried to pull Cantilever to a trot. In vain. At least half the hunt was galloping ahead; others were mounting a slope to the right. A man in front of me swerved his horse to the hedge and jumped it cleanly. I wondered, should I do that? I thought, not yet. So many were keeping to the road that there could be no dishonour in it.

We dashed through a village street with a terrific clatter. Women stood in doorways, children clung to mothers' skirts; at the inns, mugs paused half-way to mouths. The good news from Ghent to Aix; yes, that was it. Cantilever's hoofs between the houses begot echoes of a more heroic purpose than the chasing of a fox.

Ahead, a gate was being held open by a yokel, and the hunt was streaming through. A man in a pink coat paused to press money into his hand. Sign of hounds and huntsmen there was none, but I was surprised to see Mr Colville standing just inside the gateway watching the others go through, as though they were so many sheep he was counting. I thought he was far behind. His face lit up on sight of me, and he cantered alongside.

'I was wondering if you were all right,' he said.

I was so much out of breath by ten minutes' hard galloping, not having ridden for eight years, that I could only manage to blurt out, 'How did you get here first? I thought you were behind,' to which he answered, 'It don't do to follow the others always. You get a lot of galloping about for nothing. I knew they would come here, so I cut across.'

I began to realise that my hot-headed progress was not the true soul of hunting. I was glad I had found Mr Colville again. Cantilever, having exhausted her first wind, was now more manageable, and I was able to hold her in. There was a long stretch of meadow ahead. I discovered the hunting seat, standing up slightly in the stirrups and leaning forward. Immediately the bump went out of galloping, which had exhausted me, and I found myself rushing easily through the air balancing to the mare's motion.

Those ahead seemed to be vanishing one by one into the ground at a certain spot. When we came to it, I saw a steep bank to a depth of twenty feet. Surely, I thought, a horse can't get down that without falling head first? Or, horror, were we to jump it? But agile as a cat, Cantilever slithered down, and I blessed her. Mr Colville came thundering and bounding with a 'Hold up there! Steady!'

Next, a wide ditch was before us. I saw George Crawley on his horse's neck, its hindquarters being deep in the ditch, which was not encouraging. I had a further glimpse of him standing on the bank, hat askew and muddy, while his horse struggled agonisedly out.

'A bit of luck for George,' said Mr Colville. 'A wonder it didn't break the horse's back.'

But our turn was now come. Mr Colville went first.

'Let the mare have her head,' he cried back to me.

Jock leaped the ditch with a grunt. Cantilever paused on the edge and looked in. The ditch seemed then a precipice. The mare's front feet began to slither; she gathered herself in time and sprang. Her body seemed to leap from under me; but I found we were across and I was still mounted, but on a different place. I had been flung back in the saddle.

'You're all right,' said Mr Colville encouragingly, 'but you want to let yourself go with her. She jumps big.'

I was about to continue after the others, but Mr Colville put up his arm. 'Hold hard; let's see where they are going to.'

His eyes were upon a distant fallow, where I saw the hounds for the first time since the meet. They were casting about. The huntsmen turned and cantered towards some willows, and the hounds were whipped in that direction. On the edge of the plantation one began to give tongue, then another, and another, till the whole pack were again in full cry. They strung out, heads down, and were going to the left. Those of the field who had been to the fore were now no nearer to the hounds than we were. I was turning to follow the new line, but Mr Colville said: 'Wait a minute. I know where they are going. The fox is sure to run to Sarrow Park from here; always does when it's down wind. Come on, we'll be a bit artful.'

He led the way, and, ignoring the direction the hounds had taken, made obliquely away from them. In a minute we were alone, cantering gently over empty fields. In a little while we drew up at the entrance to a park, and stood looking along a private road.

'Listen,' he commanded; but there was no sound. Suddenly, 'Look there,' he whispered excitedly, and pointed. The fox, rich brown, with a brush as big as its body, slipped across the road twenty yards from us. 'That's the one, I'll bet you. A rare great fox, and brush up, fresh as a daisy. He'll give 'em a doing.'

In a minute or two the hounds came streaming prettily across the green sward among the oak-trees. 'Keep well back,' Mr Colville said, 'or they'll be saying we headed him.'

Next moment the flashes of scarlet were visible among the green trunks, and the huntsmen and whips dashed by, together with the Master on his big dappled horse. Behind came a few of the field.

'There,' cried Mr Colville triumphantly, 'you'll hunt for many a long day before you get another view like that.'

We cantered easily through the park, being well to the fore and not many others visible. We came to a hedge, and a gap with two rails across it. The brigadier-general came up with us; his topper had a concertina look, and its nap was ruffled like an angry cat's fur.

'Had a fall, sir?' asked Mr Colville.

'Some bloody ass,' spat the general, 'galloped right across my line just as I was about to jump; put the horse out completely.'

Spurning the gap, he rode full tilt at the straggling hedge, and, with a military-sounding command to his horse, shielded his eyes and crashed through. We made for the rails.

'Hug her well,' Mr Colville advised me.

Jock nipped neatly over, for all his master's weight. Cantilever was close behind. I gripped with all my might. But suddenly I found the saddle slipping away from me as though my legs had been two straws. For a moment I floated in air. I came down again with a bump, the empty stirrups clanging upon my boots. My head was upon the mare's neck. I struggled back and found my stirrups.

Mr Colville laughed. 'The mare caught you well.'

'A cup and ball existence,' I thought, remembering an old joke.

'The mare draws herself up so behind when she jumps a place standing like that,' said Mr Colville in extenuation.

We came out of the park and saw the hounds checked in an open field. We waited, and others joined us one by one, coming up with horses wet and panting.

'Can do with this check, by Jove,' said the image of John Bull, wiping the dews from his brow. 'You and your friend look as cool as can be, though.'

'Ah, we've been a bit artful. I guessed he'd run to the park.'

'He might have gone to Dudley Grove, then you'd have been done.'

'The wind lay wrong,' said Mr Colville sagely, and added to me as the man moved away, 'That's Will Westray; one of the best. His family have been farming in Suffolk for generations. I think I'm big; look at him. He has a rare job to find a horse to carry him now. We used to have some sport together when we were young.'

His waistcoat, I felt, should have been a Union Jack. He was a monument to England, the shrewd, merry eyes, the slightly aquiline nose, the lips firm yet ready for laughter, the strong chin. The man he was at the moment chatting with was his opposite, lean to emaciation, with a pointed beard and tightly buttoned coat, riding with long stirrups, that hardly bent his knees, on a bob-tailed hack as skinny as himself. He was like Don Quixote. 'A bad doer,' Mr Colville dubbed him.

Of those who had started from the meet, not more than half, I reckoned, were here. All groups were proportionately represented – immaculate youth, grizzled and dapper age, ladies, yeomen. The ladies now and again patted their buns of hair to make sure that they were still there. There were several crumpled hats and muddy backs. The general's wife, much younger than he, pale and proud and beautiful, sat with her nose in the air, as though disdaining the reek of the horses. There was a little monkey of a man, aged yet ageless, with a second horseman behind him; a young horse-dealer who kept leaning this way and that, admiring his latest mount; a youth on an unmanageable thoroughbred which he was riding to hounds in order to be able to race it in the point-to-points. He kept at a distance, luckily, as every now and then it bucked and reared. And then, of course, the man with the terrier, its head poking from the box on his back, indefatigable in the rear. These were some that Mr Colville pointed out to me.

The men had some of them dismounted and were tightening their ladies' girths and their own. Cantilever, who, I found, was always interested in the food-value of her surroundings, was plucking some coarse withered stalks, experimentally.

'Grimwood's casting forward,' said Mr Colville. The huntsman was leading the hounds to the hedge on the other side of the field after casting back without success.

'If we don't soon get on to his track we shall lose him,' said someone.

'That we shall,' Mr Colville agreed. 'Strongest fox I ever see in my life. Hullo! They are on him again.'

The hounds gave tongue, and, after a moment or two of uncertainty, turned back towards the far end of the park.

'Slipped along the ditch and doubled back, I'll bet you. That means he's off to Cropley. Sure to lose him if he gets in there.'

We followed cautiously. 'Hold hard, hold hard!' cried the Master; then, to one too ardent spirit, 'Hold hard, damn you!'

The unmanageable steeplechaser came swerving and plunging uncomfortably near, and caused Cantilever to leap aside.

'Sorry,' cried the harassed youth, as he was carried to a far corner of the field again by his hyperbolic steed. I did not envy him.

Back in the park, we became split up into little groups galloping here and there among the broad grass rides, with the horn sounding intermittently always just out of sight among the trees. Two groups would come galloping in opposite directions, pull up and ask each other questions; then become one group, going in one direction, till somebody, having an opinion of his own and influencing others as they ran, would detach himself and, followed by his converts, strike off in a new way. Then a group would pause and wait. Two or three horsemen would be waiting a little further off, a single one at a distance on the corner of the ride-way. Suddenly the single one would be seen to canter off. The group of three would be exchanging glances, and in a minute they too would be cantering away. The larger group would then become restless. The horn had not sounded for some time. A vague sense of being forsaken would steal upon them. Somebody would cry, 'I believe they've gone away.' Immediate panic. Next moment we were all helter-skelter towards where the others had vanished. Rounding the bend of the trees, we would find them, the single man, the group of three waiting patiently along the length of another grass ride, and the horn sounding it seemed from the very spot we had left. I began to think of Harris in the Hampton Court Maze. Then, when we were settling down, one of the whips would come flying past as though his life depended on it, and put us all in a flurry again.

I had temporarily lost Mr Colville, and found myself tacked on to one of these groups. Then I saw him standing in a gateway. Three times I passed that spot, flying to false alarms, and he stood calm, immovable. The third time he beckoned me.

'I should stay here if I were you. They don't do a bit of good galloping about like that; only tire their horses. Half the art of hunting is not to lose one's head.'

So we stood and admired the autumnal trees and the pigeons floating among them. A dozen mummified corpses of vermin dangled on a line stretched between two trees near by, and Mr Colville had begun telling me what they were when suddenly he broke off. The horn had been sounding at intervals, but now he recognised a different note.

'Come on,' he cried, digging in his heels, 'they're off again.'

Two or three were added to us as we went, then a whole group, then another. All were converging in one direction, like the dead at the sound of the last trump. Doubt was at an end.

We came out of the woodland and thundered past a fine old mansion, whose chatelaine waved to us from the terrace. A herd of deer came running inquisitively, stopped at a distance, gazed, and fled in panic. Watching them, I narrowly missed being beheaded by a low bough of an oak. Unable to contain their curiosity, the deer came upon us on another quarter, peeping fearfully, like naiads, and lithely fleeing our approach.

The fields again; hounds and horsemen streaming into a hollow and up the opposite slope; the whole hunt in a vista. 'The river,' shouts somebody, and we pass a bearded old yokel, lusty in excitement, hat held high, shouting, 'The river, gentlemen, that's where he's gone.'

Now we squelch through a miry farm gateway. I am close behind Mr Colville, and feel wet mud splash on my neck. Through the stack-yard we fly. A threshing-machine is at work there; it runs empty. All hands hang idle as we pass, all eyes gaze, mouths are agape. We pass a pen of bullocks. A sow scrambles up and leans its forefeet over the door of its sty; a horse in a stable tries to break out. Chickens fly right and left; a cow prepares to defend its calf.

'Damn good bullocks in that yard. Wonder whose they are,' Mr Colville cried back to me. Always the farmer.

Hounds invade the vicarage garden. The vicar runs out, his sermon forgotten, and watches us into the distance, shading his eyes. Ploughmen hold the heads of their teams, which stamp and whinny with excitement. Six Suffolk colts at grass gallop beside us, then pause, frustrated, as we leave their field behind. Cows gather in groups, angry and afraid. Women and children run from their houses to points of vantage. Cantilever is striding easily a neck behind Jock.

'The river.' I wonder about that.

'We are getting into some hairy country,' said Mr Colville. There were small fields with ragged hedges and ditches. We came to a hedge seven feet high. Half a dozen people were waiting at the only feasible opening. It was awkward; a tree with low boughs growing over a ditch of more than usual width left a kind of hole into which in turn the riders disappeared crouching. Mr Colville bade me go first. The man before me came off, his horse not getting across and falling sideways on the opposite bank. But he lugged him out and mounted again in a moment. Cantilever looked at it. I bowed myself to her neck and hoped for the best. Twigs thrashed me; we sank; we rose. I opened my eyes, and we were on the opposite side. Cantilever had not tried to jump it, but crept into the ditch and out again. I heard Mr Colville swear lustily somewhere in the hedge as I cantered on between two spinneys. In a minute he came flying past, fuming at Jock, his bowler hat awry and a big dent in it.

'The damned old fool tried to jump it,' he said as I came up with him, 'and hit my head the hell of a crack against the bough.' He looked so like the comic man on the stage, with his hat askew and indignation in his face, that I could not help laughing. I dropped back so that he should not see my mirth, and the more I looked at him the more I laughed. It seemed no end of a joke, especially as I had had a tot from his whisky flask a little before; I could hardly keep on my horse.

However, another unkempt place ahead toned down my amusement. Mr Colville made for a likely spot, but Jock, still smarting from his master's wrath, examined it well and took his time. I was waiting when a pink coat came up, chose a place, and scrambled through. I put Cantilever to it, and we got across. I did not wait for Mr Colville, as the queue at the last hedge had put us behind, and we seemed likely to lose the hounds, as they were going well. The pink coat, on a bay, was flying along, and I followed him. The young horse-dealer came past me. Next was a ditch but no hedge. The pink coat was over. The dealer was next, but his horse refused, frightened, it seemed, by some running water there. He kept him at it, delaying me. I sought another spot, but the opposite bank was covered with stubs and I would not risk it. At last the dealer's horse swerved away. Cantilever, who seemed as anxious as I to get on, immediately dashed across, gathered herself with a snort, and raced ahead. The pink coat was a good field in front of me. I saw Mr Colville some way behind, and the dealer looking for a new place to get over. There was nobody else in sight. I urged Cantilever, though she needed no urging. The speed and the mare's eagerness beneath me were exhilarating. Gone were all qualms of my security of seat. I was confident. I felt that I could never fall off, that the mare would never stumble. It was as though I had known her for years. We took place after place without a thought, Cantilever jumping, creeping, and scrambling, I toppling and recovering. I was close behind the pink coat. Where he went I went also. I found that flying an obstacle was not nearly so unseating as jumping it standing. I was congratulating myself, saying, 'You've been a first-rate horseman all these years and not known it.' I began to enjoy the hazards. A hedge ahead. Pink coat was over. Cantilever sprang at it.

Next moment her head seemed miles below me and I was flying through the air. I found myself turning a somersault, and as I did so I remember thinking, 'You are coming the deuce of a cropper.' I hit the ground with my shoulder, then stood on my head. I seemed poised thus for ages. It felt undignified; I kept wishing my legs would come down.

As soon as my legs reached earth I made the mistake of jumping up. Many thoughts had been crammed into the space of a second, and Cantilever was only just galloping towards me from the hedge. Had I lain still she would have sprung over me, but I was on my knees and her hoof hit my side and winded me. I rolled over.

Mr Colville, the horse-dealer, and the man in the pink coat were gazing down at me, and I, flat on my back, was gazing up at them, unable to speak or breathe. They were wondering how much I was damaged, but I knew (remembering a football incident at school) that, though at the moment I was dying of suffocation, my breath would suddenly return. I felt an impostor, being so anxiously gazed upon, and longed to tell them to go on with their hunting and that I would be all right in a minute. Strangled words actually escaped me – 'Nothing . . . be all right . . . minute.' They gave advice to one another.

Suddenly my breath returned. Mr Colville was saying something about laying me on a hurdle and a farmhouse near. But I jumped up. I felt as right as rain. I found I was clasping the bridle in my hand all this time. Where was Cantilever! She stood near, plucking at the hedge and champing twigs. Mr Colville laid a hand on my shoulder.

'Wait a bit, young fellow; go steady.' He could not yet believe I was not seriously hurt.

I slipped on the bridle, undented my bowler and remounted.

'Lucky thing you pulled the bridle off, or she'd have stamped on the rein and broke it most likely,' said Mr Colville.

I apologised to the others for delaying them, and thanked them, and we rode on. I had less confidence than before. Mr Colville said, 'You should not have come off there, really. The mare only pecked.' I had thought at least that the mare had turned a somersault as well as I.

We came to the river, and found the hounds checked there. We had to dismount and lead the horses under a low railway bridge. One or two bold spirits waded the stream, their horses lurching in deep mud; but they did no good by it, save to show daring, for the hounds retired, having lost the fox, and they had to cross back again.

We mounted the railway embankment, and for a while the whole hunt ambled along between the rails of the single branch line. I had a feeling that had the train come along the Master would have held up his hand imperiously and the train would have stopped and shut off steam while we went by. For I had seen that the hunt was king of the road, and that the more plutocratic the car, the more respectfully it edged by. I gathered that our presence caused trade delays, too, for delivery vans would stop and watch the sport. It was an accepted fact among farmers that, if the hounds were about, little work was to be expected from the men, and short measure of hedging or ploughing for that day was generally excused. If a yokel saw a fox and hallooed the hounds to it, he was rewarded with a ten-shilling note by the Master.

It was now late afternoon. The smoke of hedge-row fires hung in the air; distances grew hazy. The sun burned behind a ruined rampart of cloud. We ate our sandwiches, and had another tot from the flask. George Crawley rode with us, his conversation consisting chiefly of responses. 'Ay – ay,' he would reiterate to everything that was said, till one waited for the monosyllable, like the regular drip of water on one's head in the Chinese torture.

We found another fox, but I was feeling very stiff and had really had enough. Since my fall, jumps had again become crises. Not that the majority of the hunt jumped anything big; only about half a dozen really dashed at things as people did in old pictures, from which my apprehensions had been drawn. The rest kept together, and seemed to have an instinct for the easy place in any obstacle ahead, through which they filed like a giant centipede. Exhilaration had overcome my prudence in leading me, a novice, to follow the pink coat, who was an old hand.

Mr Colville said in reference to that, 'It don't do to go following chaps like him. It pleases them to lead you over big places. And all right too if you've got two or three more horses in the stable, but if you've only one horse you want to save him to hunt another day.'

As we went away after the second fox, John Bull shouted, 'It's Cropley this time,' as he galloped by. I noticed several people on the horizon, who had abandoned the hunt and started for home, looking back uncertainly when they saw us in full cry once more.

'Don't mind if he runs for an hour like this,' said Mr Colville; 'it's homeward for us.'

John Bull was right – Cropley it was. Cropley was a wood of vast extent, a virtual sanctuary for the fox. Once he gained it, it was almost impossible to get him out again. It was getting dusk, and there was much galloping along shadowy wood rides, halloos and yoicks and toot-tooting of the horn. Eventually I stood apart and listened to the sounds about me – the crackling of twigs, sough of hoofs, voices grumbling or laughing. It must have been like this, I thought, to be a Cavalier or Roundhead at the end of a dubious skirmish. No wonder life was then full of alarms and adventure, when the next valley might shelter an army and news came by horsemen only.

At length the horn sounded a long waning note, as though proclaiming truce with the evening, and there was an end.

We jogged homeward under the rising moon.

Mr Colville said, 'You kept up well, considering you hadn't ridden for so long.'

Several people asked him, 'What's my best way home from here, Colville?' He was consulted on all questions of topography. As he said to me, 'I think I know every field in this part of the country, and the best way out of it.' Many a time since I have been with him when he would take a line of his own, saying, as others dashed away, 'They can't get over there; there's a ditch ten yards wide.' And, sure enough, in a minute or two they would have turned and be following us.

On our way home this evening a group of labourers leaving their work asked us as to the day's sport. Mr Colville recounted the happenings, while they stood round in a half-circle attentive as to news of the rout of a foe.

Old battle-zest is surely half the huntsman's joy. There are memories of it in his bright clothes, his spotless setting forth, his mingled courtesy and fury, his 'neck or nothing' creed. To me the day seemed like one long cavalry charge.

All who passed us on the road asked if we had killed a fox, even the children. At an inn at which we stayed for a drink the bar buzzed with tales. The yokel boasts exclusive knowledge of the fox, for it passes him as he works in the fields. The hounds may lose it, but he sees it slink, draggle-tailed, from hiding when all have gone. We suffered ourselves to be told all about it, and how we could have killed it if only we had followed old Ben's halloo. We were admonished by old Ben.

Mrs Colville honoured us with a hot dinner when we reached home, which was welcome. Afterwards we drank port, and Mr Colville said to his wife, 'I reckon he'll be so stiff he won't know how to move in the morning.' And I reckoned I should.

I was asleep as soon as I was in bed, and never ceased galloping all night. It ended, I think, by Cantilever leaping the railings of the square in which my home stood. As I remember, we found in Battersea Park.

6

I was not only stiff the next morning, but slightly lame, having bruised my leg in falling, a fact which I had not noticed at the time. I was an onlooker for the present, and did not go beyond the yards before breakfast. Pigs were being loaded into a tumbril there, for this was Friday. It was the day of a local market, and from the farms around floated the panic protestations of pigs being lifted into carts. Farley Hall contributed its share to the music of the morning.

It is a curious fact that the pig, though naturally a timorous animal, is yet moved to pugnacity if his brother is attacked. Half a dozen in a pen next to the ones that were being loaded into the tumbril became transfigured by their neighbours' distress. Instead of cowering away, they came to the edge of the dividing hurdles, barking and foaming at the mouth. Yet it seemed to me, observing them closely, that their barking (quite unlike the usual voice of a pig) was not a conscious menace, but a nervous reaction that was as involuntary as the others' shrieks of terror – an extremity of fear. Sometimes when a piglet has trapped its head between two palings, and is shrieking as no other creature of its size can, the whole yard of swine has become an inferno of this panic-fury. The shrieks of one of their kind seem intolerable to them. It is bad enough certainly to the human ear, vibrating the eardrum and boring into the brain.

On the present occasion the stud boar, a tusked monster, who was safely pent, as we thought, in a brick enclosure, became so maddened that he put his snout under the heavy five-barred gate, lifted it, and carried it, like Samson, on his back for several yards. Midden turned to deal with him with a 'There, what d'ye think of that, now?' and smote him across the snout. This begot a terrific trumpeting, and Midden roared in answer and smote again. 'Ye damned old devil, ye would, would ye?'

The boar, champing, and frothing and glinting enmity from his little red eyes, kept his face to the foe, but Midden was not intimidated. The pigs had been troublesome to load, and this intrusion was the last straw. The boar was beaten back snarling into his yard, and the gate re-hung with the help of the men who were loading the pigs. Midden fetched five-inch wire nails and hammered them in over the hinges. The boar tried the gate again, but the nails held. Throughout the rest of the pig-loading the gate rattled and shook. Every now and again Midden topped the din with a thunder of abuse to the creature.

Midden was noted for his voice. Early and late from the yard it was heard, even within doors. Mr Colville would exclaim, 'There's Midden's fog-horn again.' Yet when he chose he could 'roar gently as any sucking dove.' In the cowshed his voice would keep up a vibrant undertone of, 'Stand still, old cow; come over then,' no louder than the rustling of the straw. I have heard him calling the cows in when I was dressing. In winter they would come readily, as hay would be awaiting them in the shed; but in summer they were loath to leave the meadow, as nothing was provided for them in the crib.

Midden would go to the gateway and call, 'Come on then, old dears; come up, come up,' in a soft, persuasive tone. The cows would lie still and look at him. Then he would try again, and, bored by his chanting, they would cease even to regard him. Then, being compelled to stride through deep wet grass to the far corner where they lay, and rouse and drive them, he would burst out in a voice that made the leaves tremble, 'Goo on then, you awkward old devils!' The cows were used to him, and, as they gazed at him with the dreamy puzzlement of their eyes, seemed to regard him as a slightly irritating but provident deity. They let him handle their calves without fear, whereas the figure of a stranger in the doorway would make them lower their heads.

In memory I can see Midden now (for he is dead), trailing through the yards, knee-deep in straw, driving a bullock or pursuing a horse, always with a rumble of complaint. He was a pessimist, foreseeing mishap in little things. He used to irritate Mr Colville sometimes to such an extent that he said to me, 'I had to walk away or I should have sworn at him straight.' Occasionally he would say, 'Damn it, Midden, you're always complaining; if you can't do the work, I'll find somebody else who can.' Then for a week Midden would jump about with an alacrity that was foreign to his clod-shaped figure and never murmur. He had been with Mr Colville ever since he had started farming. He was implicitly trustworthy (keys were always left in his charge when Mr Colville went away); he kept to no rigid hours, but was about in the yard with a lantern sometimes towards midnight.

'He's an old fool,' Mr Colville would say, 'but he's good with animals, and the place wouldn't seem the same without his fog-horn.'

One of his functions was to throw a piece of gravel at Mr Colville's bedroom window at six every morning. Sometimes Mr Colville would be up before that, but if not he would lean forth and give his orders from the window in his nightshirt.

This morning Mr Colville rode in from the fields just as the pigs were loaded into the tumbril and the net fastened over them. With his nimble eye he immediately noticed a fault in the bridle.

'The mare will be having that off when she chucks her head; then she'll see the wheels and run away.' He called to the horsekeeper, who was at that moment bringing a plough-team in to breakfast, to get another bridle.

Later in the day we motored to the market to see the pigs sold. It was situated conveniently behind the chief inn of a small town – not a very salubrious spot, the haunt of the higgler and the Jew poultry-buyer. A number of people stood about listlessly waiting for the selling to begin. Faded gigs drove up with crates of hens tied on the back. As each was unloaded the Jews (there were about six of them, voluble, of unpleasing countenances) seized the hens one by one and squeezed them, turned them upside down; and each Jew, having examined one, flung it to his neighbour – the hens, with wild bright eyes, enduring all this silently, without struggling. They were put into pens which lined the market. Sometimes a Jew lifted the door of a pen, stirred up the inmates with his hand, drew out one, felt it, and shoved it back again by the legs. All the time they chattered to one another and gesticulated, while the simple rustic, for want of a better entertainment, watched them, and occasionally remarked to his neighbour, 'They are a nice lot, they are'; and his neighbour in time would reply, 'Yes, they are a nice lot, if you like. God nor Devil can understand what they say.'

There were, besides livestock, several old tanks to be sold, a perambulator, a red-horned gramophone, an oil stove, three bicycles, and six sacks of potatoes.

The auctioneer now arrived via the back door of the inn.

He was a jovial man, wearing a magnificent buttonhole (November notwithstanding), and was heralded by a man ringing a bell and esquired by his clerk on the one hand and a bright-nosed drover on the other, and attended by a retinue of pig-buyers still laughing at his final story over the final drink.

They all gathered round him at the first pig-pen as closely as swarming bees round their queen. I was squeezed nearly to death, breathed on, smoked at. I could not see the pigs, so I watched the Hogarth faces opposite me. Every shape and manner of whisker was there. A London crowd would have been as like as sheep compared with them. There was one old man Mr Colville pointed out to me, standing next to the auctioneer, amplifying his ear with his hand. He wore a beard in a fringe round his face, which was fine and kindly and was the exception to my theory that those who dealt with pigs grow to resemble them; for he was a noted pig-buyer who could guess the weight of any pig to within a pound at sight. For this reason he was disqualified from the guessing the weight of a pig competitions at Vicarage fêtes.

After each lot had been sold, the whole gathering lurched compressedly two yards farther to the next pen. The unfortunate ones were those who came up against the posts. The human body is at least soft, a humane crusher.

'Six-ten,' cried the auctioneer, 'six-fifteen – six-seventeen-six – who says seven? Seven? Half-a-crown anywhere? Going for the last time at six-seventeen-six.' He tapped his book, then turned and said, 'Name, please?' No answer. He asked again, 'Who was it? Somebody behind who nudged me.' Thereupon the pig-buyers burst out laughing, for they knew that there had not been a bid of six pounds seventeen and six at all, but that the auctioneer had been running the pigs up and had been left with them on his hands. This was his usual way of coping with an awkward situation. The auctioneer grew red, and cried, 'I tell you somebody nudged me. Well, don't press on me at the back there. I don't know who is bidding and who isn't.' Then the lot was sold again, this time for six-ten apiece.

Meanwhile a lesser auctioneer was selling the poultry. This went on in lightning fashion, bids being mixed up with chatter bewilderingly. Even as they were being sold the hens were hauled out from the pens again and passed from hand to hand. The Jews were in a ring buying mutually, but every now and again they started to squabble. On the outskirts stood the owners, bidding up their poultry, as they knew there was no real competition. One dame was so anxious that hers should make a good price that she topped her own bid, and the auctioneer remarked as a favour, 'No, lady, I won't take your bid against yourself.'

There were some tame rabbits also. Six pens contained white Angoras, marked impressively 'Pedigree.' But it did not avail them. They made two shillings each. That seemed to me to be the short last chapter of an enterprise started with gusto and dreams culled from text-books: 'Pedigree White Angora, 2s.'

The Jews wore East End suits and patent leather shoes ornamentally inlaid. They were a contrast to the breeches and buskins and clod-scarred boots of the rest. One of the Jews discovered an egg in a pen of hens he had bought. He cracked it open and swallowed it. They carried their hens in bunches of four in a hand (holding each by a leg) and put them in their crates. Then they sat on the crates and quarrelled about them among themselves. The sight of them jabbering and gesticulating collected a pleased crowd. 'As good as a Punch and Judy show,' said one.

Lastly the dead-stock was sold. Each object was many times examined in an honest endeavour to discover merit in it. The magical phrase 'Might come in handy' was heard. The man who bought the gramophone bought also the perambulator, in which he put it. He was the object of much banter. 'Hello, Tim. I didn't know you were in the family way.' 'Ask me to the christening, Tim,' and 'You won't want that there gramyphone – you'll have plenty of music without that.'

I recognised one or two in the market who had been out hunting the previous day. John Bull, *alias* Will Westray, was there, and called out across the market, 'Hullo, Colville, how's your old bottom after that great run yesterday?'

The pigs were sold. The day was raw and the spot cheerless. I was glad to go. Mr Colville said to me, 'This ain't nothing – not what you'd call a market. You must come to Stambury on Christmas sale day. There's something to see there. Best market in the eastern counties. This is nothing but a higgler's show.'

The higgler was a common phenomenon in the district, and in time I came to know him well. With a blistered spring-cart and a hoppety old pony, he jogged along staring at the country. He would have a load of anything, from chicken-crates to worn motor-tyres. Seeing a farmer, he would draw up and comment on the nearest crop, and then ask, 'Anything to sell?' Much of his trade was probably due to the farmer's love of 'a deal.' He cannot resist being drawn into a verbal fencing over prices. The prices creep closer, and suddenly the farmer finds he has sold some cockerels over which he started to haggle just for the fun of the game.

When the higgler has done a deal with a farmer he regards a bag of chaff as his perquisite. He also asks the farmer to sell him a truss of clover hay (stover) or some mangolds.

In this way he keeps his horse. Usually he has an acre or two of land (who hasn't in Suffolk?), and he begs some seed at a nominal price. He is often irritating, but just as often amusing. He retails gossip as he trundles about. The market is his club, lots marked 'Sundries' his rallying-points. There is more joy in the higgler's heart over sixpence made by buying a thing and selling it again than over one-and-sixpence earned at a straightforward job. He scrapes a living snatching at minute profits. The word DEAL is written on his heart. He often wears a stiff coat of antique fashion, with many flapped pockets and tight trousers giving him a Dickensian appearance. He carries one-pound notes crushed like waste paper in his trousers pocket, and silver rolled up in them. They are unravelled one by one on completion of a deal. Whatever the faults of the higgler, he is a cash customer, and usually pays on the nail. The compensations of his hacking life are an illusion of independence and the spice of possibility. Those cockerels he bought for four shillings apiece may make five-and-six in the market. Or they may make three-and-nine. The successful among them is the judicious risker. He buys boldly, prepared to chance a loss. The farmer likes him for it; he admires a sport and wishes him a good profit. If a farmer sells something to a 'little man', he wants him to get something out of it. It is almost a matter of honour. He hates to profit at the expense of a poorer man; at least, Mr Colville did.

The smallholder is another matter. He is the importunate widow of the agricultural world. He is a slow payer. He buys some seed corn and will pay after harvest. Harvest usually goes by without the appearance of the money, and the debt drags on for years. He has two bony nags to plough with, fat-bellied through eating bulky food of poor nourishment. Mr Colville used to rail against such persons.

'They don't do a ha'porth of good. They always work like the devil and they've never a shilling to bless themselves with. They'd be better off by half if they went to work for somebody.' He warned me, if ever I started farming on my own, not to sell them things, as I should never get the money. He stoutly maintained they were the curse of agriculture, and that he would never listen to their fiddling requests. I thought he was a hard man till I discovered that in practice he did sell his smaller neighbours seed corn at long credit, and lent them his implements. He has even advanced them money to tide them over lean months till harvest, stipulating, for the favour, that he might drive over their land on the occasion of a shooting-party. But it would never have done to get a reputation for philanthropy.

On Friday evening the wages were paid. Mr Colville employed upwards of twenty men. They came to the window of the breakfast-room for their money, and the window-sill became a counter. Mr Colville paid the money, while I stood by and noted down the sums opposite each man's name in the labour book.

'Irishman's rise this week,' said Mr Colville. The group at the window murmured, 'Oh!' not very cheerfully. Men were receiving forty-five shillings a week in those days, and wages had just been reduced to forty-two and six. That is what was meant by an Irishman's rise. These things were all settled by the Agricultural Wages Board, as to-day. Mr Colville added to me, 'If it's the other way about, they soon let me hear of it.'

Besides the paying of wages, there were small requests of different kinds, and enquiries. One man asked, 'Would you do a little something to my cottage, sir? The thatch has blown off in one place and the water comes through.' Another said, 'Will you give me that hedge on Dead Hill?'

I wondered what the man wanted a hedge for, and learnt that it was to cut it down for faggots for his winter firing. Another asked, 'Will you sell me a couple of pigs?' and the proceedings paused while master and man came to terms over the pigs.

Sometimes, when Mr Colville came upon the 'cad' pig (or weakling) of a litter moping about the farm buildings, he would say to the nearest man he saw, 'I'll give you that pig if you care to take it home, but I reckon it'll die.' Many a one like that I have seen a few months later fat and flourishing in the corner of a man's garden.

While these discussions were in progress I turned the pages of the account-book. It was a skilful compilation, with numerous classifications, cash accounts, and summaries. A few of the headings were:

Inventory and Valuation of Produce.
Hiring of Servants; Wages, etc.
Dairy Produce – Yield of Cows.
General View of Cultivation.
Summary of the Labour and Cash Account.
General Statement of Crops.
Consumed in Household.
Statement of Profit or Loss for the Year.

Never had I imagined anything so intricate as the keeping of farm accounts. This book was priced ten shillings and sixpence. It was both diary and ledger. There was an introductory preface by one Clare Sewell Read, Esq., which in rounded and fluent periods urged upon the British farmer the necessity for keeping strict accounts. Not only did the book teach him to keep accounts, but even how to farm. There was an Agricultural Calendar after the preface, divided into months. Under October (the first month in the farm year) I read that Old Michaelmas is a good time to begin to drill wheat. Also that fences, ditches, water-courses, and the mouths of all under-drains should be looked to. In November, 'Thresh and convey grain to market as may be convenient.'

Under December I learned that the 'Swedish turnip, which is the foundation for fattening cattle, should be cut into convenient slices, strips, or pulped. The turnips during the frosty weather will freeze in the bins, therefore during the day give them as much only as they will eat by a little at a time, throwing the frozen pieces to the pigs.' (Poor pigs!)

Under the heading June I found a proverb contradicted. 'The old saying is, "Make hay while the sun shines". Our advice is, keep the sun off as much as possible, and dry it on cocks, or with as little sun as may be necessary to wither it. Hay made this way retains the saccharine matter.'

But, coming to the month of August, the calendar writer cannot restrain a solemn fervour. The feeling hidden under his meticulous instructions breaks forth.

'The farmer's brightest prospects are now bursting upon him, and the fields are all ripening to harvest, while the wavy corn recalls many bygone years of "peace with plenty crowned", and the happy harvest homes. This is indeed to the farmer the happiest and the busiest of all the months; and heaven's rich reward of industry and patience; now are the almost deserted barns opening wide their doors, awaiting the treasures of the field. But,' he ends up, 'should the weather prove showery, muck may be carted and spread on the fields intended for wheat,' and 'Pigs, when turned into the new leys, should be well rung or they will injure the grass.'

The advertisements contained in the book were also of interest to me, and there was a fascination in their strange terms. Cupiss's Constitution Balls, for instance, were for horses, cattle, and sheep in cases of Swelled Legs, Grease, Cracked Heels, Broken Wind, Staring Coat, Hidebound, Epidemic, Scouring, Surfeit, etc. It was adorned with two dim but dramatic vignettes, the first of a horse in a stable hanging its head without interest while a groom showered a tempting sieveful of oats into the manger. This was entitled 'Out of Sorts' (without specifying to which of the diabolic diseases mentioned the horse was a victim). The second picture showed the horse prancing excitedly towards the manger, so much so that the groom was obliged to hold up one hand in mild reproof while he emptied the sieve with the other. The title of this picture was 'All Right.'

Then there were Willson's Canadian Pig Powders. They published a photograph, remarking, 'This group, taken at the Royal Show, Darlington, represents the absolute Cream of British Experts in Pig Raising. They were most enthusiastic users,' etc. Well, there they were, some smiling, others looking stern and responsible, armed with flat sticks wherewith to guide and goad the pigs.

Cannell & Sons gave a picture of their New Century Mangel, adding that 'the skin is a bright orange colour and the flesh is golden.' There was a letter from a user. 'Dear Sirs, I have grown your seeds for the last Forty years and have always found them most reliable,' of which Cannell & Sons remarked modestly, 'Forty years is a fairly good test.'

There were also Denniss's Lincolnshire Pig Powders. They were represented by a silhouette of a pig like a zeppelin, with comically inadequate legs and a small white suspicious eye.

There were pictures of complex ploughs, of stack-cloths on half-finished stacks, with workmen standing proudly by; of tents in parks, of wagons of corn setting off well protected with the advertised wagon-cloth. In most of them there was a vista of pleasant country for background, and many had an outmoded grace of lettering.

Seeing that I was interested in the account-book, Mr Colville explained some of the terms and headings to me when the wages were paid. Then he took me into the attic and showed me his old account-books, of which he kept every one from the first on his entry into farming. This he treasured most. The pages became pictures when filled with his meticulous writing, every letter sloping exactly as its fellow, and the neat double lines drawn beneath grand totals. During the war period the labour list became meagre, and the names were continually changing. He even had some land-girls for a short time. I asked him how they did, and he said, 'They'd smoke everywhere, among the stacks and buildings; you couldn't stop them. It was a wonder the whole place wasn't burnt up. But they worked well.'

He spoke of a strike once, before the war, and how the farmers banded together, and went from one holding to another getting in each other's harvest, and how the men stood and barracked them, crying, 'How do you like the taste of work, masters? It's something new to you,' and how they drank so much beer it had to be carted to them in a water-cart.

An attic is always interesting for the view from its window, and its contents representing the dead wood of a person's life. A group of framed photographs arranged in a heart-shaped pattern on an end wall attracted my attention. Each of them was of a lady, and in the middle of them was one of Mr Colville himself when young, handsome in a high collar.

These, I learned, represented his early amours, and the group was the work of his wife in teasing mood. 'Mary likes to act foolish sometimes,' he explained. The work must have been something of a triumph also, I considered, for it seemed he had been an attractive young man, and it was she whom he had married after all. 'Not you,' she might have mused as she hauled them out of limbo and hung them one by one, 'nor you, nor you.'

Mr Colville went over his affairs, dwelling on each portrait in turn. 'She was a pretty girl,' and 'This one, Betty Corbett, she was a damn good sort. I wonder what's happened to her,' and 'She was a smart girl, she was.' They seemed women to me, with their pancakes of hair, tight waists, and high-collared blouses, but girls he called them, and I took his word for it.

He used to think nothing, he said, of driving twenty miles to a dance in a gig in the winter and returning home in the dawn in the snow. He would arrive just as the men were coming to work, and give his orders in evening dress. He did not think much of modern dancing.

'They look so serious about it, and dance with the same girl all the time. In my days, if you danced with a girl three times you were engaged. We used to do the two-step and the Boston, and in the Lancers we fairly used to twirl 'em round.'

The grooms used to sit in a room in the inn, and every now and then one of the men would go in and treat them to drinks all round. He gave me a picture of their country dances in the days before the fox-trot, held in a large upper room of an old inn. A committee of men used to invite the ladies, and then a committee of ladies used to give a return dance and invite the men. And after the dance the merry young bachelors used to jump on their horses' backs and ride races down the street, much to the annoyance of a severely teetotal gentleman attempting to sleep near by. He complained to the police inspector, who then laid a ban upon their dances there.

'But we got over him,' said Mr Colville.

'How?' I enquired.

'Well, the inspector had two pretty daughters. We sent out invitations for another dance, and we invited them. We held the dance.'

Dancing, hockey-playing on Saturdays, shooting, and hunting – these were the pastimes of a young farmer of substance in the winter. In the summer, Mr Colville used to go to the seaside every week-end after working hard all the week. Altogether it had been a great life in his agile days, the fearless days before the war, he told me.

The night after the County Ball at Stambury there was held a Yeomen's Ball in the same ballroom, the decorations of the first remaining for the second. The yeomen, as I was learning, were a corporate society like the county gentry, having similar pastimes. There was no doubtful border-line, but a clear space between the classes. The yeomen esteemed the gentlemen; the gentlemen comraded it with the yeomen on the hunting-field, and entertained them on the days of tenants' shoots, etc. When a leading gentleman of the district was summoned once for driving his car recklessly on a country road, it was generally deplored, much as though a prefect at a public school were found smoking and thrashed for it. As Mr Colville said, 'He's supposed to set an example to those round. The police, I believe, were most uncomfortable about it.'

To the yeomen, the gentry still dwelt in an ambrosial upper air; their parks were aloof, Elysian, for lingering and strolling. Mr Colville said once ingenuously, indicating a neighbouring mansion, 'Rare good family they are; why, nobody less than a lord ever dines there, I believe.' Old Mrs Colville, his mother, used to supply cream to a certain country house. The family had gone to town without countermanding the order till the last moment. 'But there,' remarked the old lady, 'that's the worst of gentry, you can't expect them to think of these things' – attributing the failing, not to the individual, but to the class.

But anyone in Suffolk who is not engaged in farming, and appears to exist on private means, is designed 'gentleman'. If a farmer retires, his friends say, half ironically, 'So and so's giving up this Michaelmas; he's going to be a gentleman.' There is only one work – that of the fields; and anyone not actively engaged in this, if he lives in the country, is considered independent, and therefore rich. If the stranger knew what romances are woven round him in the inn, what power and authority imputed to him! A person in any way connected with London is darkly important. The city paved with gold reigns still a ghost in the rustic brain. At the same time, imagination will not conjure anything much greater than the market town, of which people say to one another, 'Oh, I'll see you there,' without being more specific, and do. Thus it was that the local rate-collector, an altogether delightful man, who used to like to talk politics with me, asked, 'Does your father have much business with Lloyd George?' The news that my father was in the newspaper world had got round to him, and the question seemed natural.

'Pleasure garden' is another magic phrase, part of the gentlemanly spell. It is made much of in placards of the sales of little houses as indicating the respectability of the dwelling, and calculated to draw the man of independence, who will pay a larger price. For in Suffolk there are two

values, actual and possible. It is known what a perso
gets his living from the land can afford to pay for a dw
that is a matter of necessity. But with a 'gentleman' i
affair of fancy. (In Suffolk they are just beginning
aware that a stranger 'sees something' in an old cot
They do not know what.) Therefore the price is fanci
At the time of writing, which is 1930, the discrepancy
this extent. Land values have fallen so that some farms w
sold the other day for £3 10s. per acre, including house a
buildings. A friend of mine, 'a stranger', thinking of settli
in the district, was asked £850 for a barn converted into
bungalow. The ordinary price of a labourer's cottage is £
to £100. Thus two hundred acres, plus the buildings, are t
be bought for the same price as a bungalow. There i
all the difference there between the idea of farmer and
gentleman. The farmer's concern is with the land entirely;
his wife views the house. One farmer I knew, having looked
over a farm, hired it. His wife asked, 'But don't you want
to see in the house before you decide?' He answered, 'No,
I get the living from the land, not the house.'

But to return to the days of my apprenticeship.

Mr Colville's horsekeeper, who read the sky instead of
books, learning that I came from London, said, 'I have a
brother lives in London.' We were riding out to the fields,
each on a plough horse; I was going to have a lesson in
ploughing.

I asked, 'What does your brother do?'

The man replied, 'Bless you, he don't do no work;
just sits a-writing all day!'

I discovered that he was in a responsible position in
office of a suburban Water Board.

'He comes down here for his holiday sometimes at
vest-time. I tell him he ought to pitch some sheaves.

got a belly on him like an old mare in foal. So should I if I didn't do anything.'

In this district they used old-fashioned wooden ploughs without wheels. These required more skill in handling than the wheeled ploughs, as the large wheel, running just inside the furrow, kept the plough straight and the work even. I knew a small farmer, in fact, a man of energy, who sent his plough off alone across the field, hedging meantime, and his boy, also hedging at the other side, turned it when it reached him and sent it back. They were quiet horses.

But there is all the difference between this and the use of a wooden plough as between playing the piano and hearing it on the gramophone, or so they think in parts of Suffolk. The wheel-less plough is suited to heavy lands, as wheels would clog with mud in the winter.

I laid my hands on the plough handles. The cord reins lay across the handles before me, hooked round an old cotton-reel.

'Hold the handles tight,' was all the man said, knowing that experience only could teach this thing.

'But the reins?' I asked.

'The horses know the way,' he replied, and called one of them by name, and they started off. Next moment he cried 'Woa!' The plough was digging deep into the earth and scouring up yellow clay. 'We're set. We shall soon break something like that. You must bear on the plough so that it rides level in the ground.' He extricated it for me, and we started again. I bore on it, and it skimmed along just scraping the bottom.

The plough seemed to come alive in my hands. Every variation in the solidity of the ground was translated into a quivering of the handles. The plough attempted to jerk aside or up or down, and a kind of prescience was necessary

in hands and arms to check these tendencies. My eyes were on the furrow that the share lifted and the breast bore over wave-like. My concentration was on keeping it eight inches wide. I received an impression of speed as is gained from watching the prow of a ship where it cuts the water. When I glanced up I was surprised to see the horses treading so slowly. This too, I thought, must appear a sleepy occupation to the passing poet. One hears talk of the monotony of ploughing, but I found it a keen exercise of hand and eye.

When we reached the end of the stetch the horses stayed, then slowly began to turn. The man murmured to them a long-drawn chant of admonition, 'Worree-eee.' Then, 'Bear against the plough,' he said, but before I knew what was happening the plough was flung upon its side, and I almost with it. Turning upset the equilibrium and I had to lean the plough almost over upon the outside of the turn to counteract this. I was surprised that such a slow motion of the horses should have such a lightning effect on the implement. It was full of tricks and moods, in fact, according to the natural conditions, which I learnt in course of time. Dead-heavy and stubborn at rest, in motion it became nimble as its arrowy shape suggested, and answered to a touch. The secret was balance, and in turning it and setting it for the next furrow one worked upon the principle of the lever, with the earth for fulcrum. Every plough had its own character, and ploughmen knew their own ploughs and disliked using another's.

The horses, too, needed guiding at the turn, since if the traces (the chains by which they pulled) were not kept at tension they stepped across them and got them between their legs. I should have been an excellent ploughman, I felt, had I had four hands. Luckily, the old man was beside me to unravel my entanglements. When I had got the plough into the wrong place for starting, and it seemed fixed, immovable, with a thrust of the wrists he would displace it and set it right.

When we had been once up and down the field we paused and surveyed the result. 'That ain't half bad,' he said, 'for one who ain't never touched a plough afore.' I, too, was secretly pleased, for the furrows seemed straight and good. But of course I had had his faultless furrows for a guide, and as the morning went on I seemed to get worse, being unable to correct my own errors. There would be a kink about the middle of the field, an outward bend some-what farther on. As I stood preparing to voyage across the field once more I made my plans. In the middle I must shave a narrower furrow to straighten the kink, and farther on a wider one to rectify the bulge. But it was impossible to see when one was at the right spot for the variation, and on reaching the end of the stetch I found sometimes that I had made another kink and another bulge. Then, at the end of the day, the man took the plough into his own hands and made all right in a single bout up and down. What instinct told him when to narrow and when to widen his furrow I know not.

The sky looking dull, I apprehended rain, but the man, after a moment's survey, said, 'No, we shan't get no rain, not while the wind follows the sun. But when the wind go against the sun, then we may expect it.' I learned that he meant that when the wind shifted in the direction of the sun's motion there was no fear of rain, only when it went contrary to it, i.e. anti-clockwise. Ploughmen, I found, were always conscious of the direction of the wind, and could give an account of its veerings throughout the day.

Once, in summer, an inky cloud threatened from over Benfield, and I expected a shower, but the horsekeeper said he doubted it. 'We don't get rain from Benfield hardly ever.' The cloud passed over us, turning noon to twilight without a drop falling. Rain always arrived to us from Jim Crawley's direction. Storms from the other direction for some reason split and went harmlessly round us on each side. Time and again I noticed it. The horsekeeper prophesied by rings round the sun, the shape of clouds, the quality of light, the feel of the air. A man highly attuned to natural variations, sensitive and swift to interpret, subtle in humour too, of a riddling mind, he could neither read nor write. He had worked on Farley Hall all his life, and his father before him. He rose at four every morning to attend to his horses before it was time for them to go to plough. He went to bed at eight. He lived in a white cottage with a thatched roof. It had once been a farmhouse, they said. Its chimney was a noted one, being so wide that the folks around used to hang their bacon and hams in it to be smoked. His recreation was to sit before the fire (one of the old open kind) for an hour and smoke before bed, and to sit in his garden for an hour in the twilight in the summer. His summer bedtime was about ten o'clock.

He hated disturbance. There was a small cottage in the lane opposite his, and for a while a woman with children lived there. 'Them children,' said the old man, 'shriek fit to craze the Devil, and then the old woman hollers at them and she's worse than the lot.' Luckily for him, the woman got bitten with the desire for a 'front room', and nothing would content her till she had persuaded her husband to take one of the new Council houses perched austerely on a hill, at double the rent they were paying for the cottage. This house had a parlour as well as a kitchen; this she furnished on the hire-purchase system, and felt much elevated in the social scale.

The local baker knocked one of the children down with his van and bruised it. It was proved to be the child's fault, but he generously paid the doctor's bill of thirty shillings. 'More than the kid's worth,' said the harassed horsekeeper. He rejoiced at the family's departure, and to ensure peace for himself in future, paid the rent of the cottage, which amounted to half-a-crown a week, to prevent anybody else coming to it.

He was a noted ploughman, and had received offers from farmers at different times, but he would not move from his ancestral home. 'As long as I'm treated civil I shall stay where I am,' he said.

And Mr Colville said to me, 'I don't reckon anybody would ever shift Bob out of his house, not unless they burned it over his head.'

Although the younger folk preferred modern box-shaped houses of brick and slate, and despised antiquity, the older people had often an extreme affection for the plaster cottage in which they had lived for many years, especially those who lived alone. Often I have seen a single curtained window in a cottage half in ruins. An old woman would be hanging on there in the last habitable room of her crumbling home, her husband dead and her children scattered in the world. There she would sit, defying the inspectors and authorities till forcibly removed to a safer abode.

By the latter half of November all the wheat had been drilled, and the days had settled into a routine of ploughing, ploughing. Rains soaked the ground, and the ploughshares pared glistening furrows that lay overlapping one another, exact and unbroken. The horses came home muddy, and the men's boots were hidden in dumplings of mire until they wiped them in the straw. It was then that Mr Colville demonstrated to me the suitability of the Suffolk horse to local conditions. He has little hair (or 'feather') about the hoofs, whereas the Shire horse has a great deal, which gathers mud so that a Shire horse would come home, as Mr Colville said, bringing half the field with him. This begets cracked heels and grease, that infector of stables.

The Suffolk is fine-legged, of classical build, compact, and spirited. Mr Colville was proud of his Suffolks. Just before I came to Farley Hall, he told me, he was offered £1000 for five mares and their foals. It was a tempting price, and he went indoors and thought about it. Then he saw them through the window feeding in the meadow, a view that always pleased him, and he said he would not sell.

'I shall never be bid that price again,' he told me, 'but, you know, I like to see them about.'

The men that were not ploughing were hedging and ditching. At breakfast-time they made bonfires of the black-thorn they had cut (it being useless for faggots), and gathered round it. They flung their coats cloak-fashion over their shoulders, and sometimes, if it were cold, wore hoods of sacks, which gave them a mediaeval look. Their breakfast was a dexterous meal. In the left hand was firstly a half-loaf, and on top of it a hunk of cheese. The left hand also managed to encompass an onion. The right hand held a clasp-knife, which cut off a piece of bread, cheese, and onion in turn in due proportion and conveyed them to the mouth. Rarely was a fragment dropped. When they had done, they took out short clay pipes and smoked. They were not, of course, allowed to smoke near the yards; that was a strict rule. Yet such was their avidity for an occasional puff that often, when their work lay among the buildings, at chance intervals they would steal round corners and light up. The very prohibition seemed to increase their craving.

Their pipes were so short that Mr Colville used to say of

one man, who had a bushy moustache, that he could not see if he were smoking or not.

'Joe, there, he has such a tiny mite o' pipe he hides it in his whiskers; I reckon plenty of times I've been by him and he's been smoking and I never noticed it. One day he'll catch his moustache on fire, then he'll be done.'

As for our own breakfast, the Suffolk ham was done and in its place we had a piece of cold boiled bacon. There was actually no lean upon it at all; it merely flushed a little towards the centre. Yet I ate it eagerly along with peeled boiled eggs. It seemed just the thing for the weather and the life. I wondered what I should have said to it a month or two before.

7

Now, though there were days when I enjoyed my new life, at other times I disliked it.

What I gained in health was reflected in my outlook, certainly: I had come to admit that imaginative moods might not be the most important things in life: had glimpses even of the fact that the mind, to be any good, must build itself on foundations which did not exclude the dunghill; but there were occasions when the handling of cold muddy iron at 6 a.m. was too much for my faith.

Yes, I have groaned at Mr Colville's tap on my door, and lain pleading with myself for a minute more of bed. And I have stood with the wind driving through my clothes, holding a post steady for Simmons's mallet repairing a fence, when the thin grasp of my hand round it seemed to tell me I was a fish out of water here. I have looked to the south-west on desolate afternoons and thought of London there, and the warm, bright rooms I had left; heard in memory the laughter of friends, and asked myself why on earth I was standing here miles away, alone in fields.

I was far from fitting into the country scene yet. For the first months, when not with Mr Colville I was at a loose end. I wandered from one lot of men to another attempting to lend aid which was a hindrance rather than help. Then I would give up, and moon away by myself into a wood, and try to compose a nature poem. But the impetus of a sonnet printed by the *Westminster Gazette* just before my country venture was spent. If I had any poetic faculty, it was in abeyance; my mind might march in blank verse metre: language would not, and pigeons scared to sudden flight from the boughs above would startle me from my abstraction.

In December and January, the first strangeness of the life being over, my agricultural enthusiasm burned low. I had to endure the ardours of physical work of which I could not yet catch the labour-saving rhythm, and at the same time answer with a smile the laughter of yokels at my awkwardness. I had little conversation. If I opened my mouth about farming, I made a fool of myself. The men's dialect baffled me: everything had to be said to me twice, as though I were deaf. Even then I often missed the meaning, but tried to pretend I hadn't, being ashamed to ask again.

There were bodily compensations. I enjoyed my food enormously, and my pipe (it never made me dizzy, as in Chelsea), and I had come to know fatigue. These were good things, but not enough to outbalance the obvious amenities I had abandoned. Besides, I asked myself, was there any future for me in farming? At every meeting of farmers I heard talk of falling prices, grumbles that soon there wouldn't be anything in it. (Had they but known how far it was to fall in ten years, and that most of them standing there talking half seriously of 'no profit' would then be bankrupt and facing a portionless old age!) In any case it was certainly no fortune-getter.

I used to motor-cycle home for occasional week-ends. I had spoken so brightly of my life at the first that I did not care to admit that I began to doubt the excellence of it. So I still assumed the robust faith among my friends. But that word 'assumed' is not quite true. For, curiously enough, finding myself in a studio party again, and remembering suddenly that I had been hedging only that morning, my country life really did seem good to me. Watching the throng, listening to them, 'I am the only one in touch with reality,' I told myself. While the gramophone played, and a glass was broken occasionally, and the air grew denser, and more people came crowding in, there would flash into my mind scenes of the farm, the lantern-lit stables, Midden, wood-firelight, rabbiting . . .

I discovered I was two persons: one slipped back easily into studio life; the other was glad to be returning to the fields. That was the strange thing. However depressed I might have felt about the business, I could not be away for more than a day or two before I felt the place pulling at me again. I did not reason these likes and dislikes; but there grew in me half-consciously a premonition that, though I should experience further reactions against farm life, ultimately that was to be the life for me. I cannot say how it was; only that, looking back, I now realise that I was dimly aware of it all the time.

My mother was pleased with my looks. I was a different person already, she said. My former 'artiness' (and general weediness) had worried her in Chelsea, and she had been prime mover, really, in getting me out of it. She, before marriage, had been an artist, and 'an artist's is a dog's life,' she told me, including in that all the arts. I might not make much money at farming; at least I should be sane.

An uncle raised a doubt. I overheard him by chance, in conversation with my mother. 'It will be all right till he wants to get married; then there'll be nothing for it but a farmer's daughter, as far as I can see.'

But I did not speculate on that at present.

The first week, in December, was spent threshing. This was hard work. The tackle (engine, threshing-drum, and elevator) had arrived overnight and been set in position beside a stack. The man in charge of it used a spirit level, so exactly true was it necessary for the unwieldly drum to stand in order to work properly. Its angle could be altered by a fraction by a blow on one of the wooden wedges driven under the wheels.

The next morning Mr Colville tapped on my door earlier than usual. Dressing quickly, I was down before he had made the tea. He always boiled the kettle in a large scullery in which was an old open fireplace. The kettle hung upon a hook, and underneath was a great heap of sticks. Almost as soon as the sticks were lighted the kettle was lost in a sheet of flame. It boiled in a minute. I have no hesitation in affirming that this ancient method is quicker than coal, gas, or electricity. That was why Mr Colville used it in preference to the kitchen grate or oil or Primus stove. 'There's nothing like a faggot,' he said.

Time was of consequence this morning, for he wanted to get the stack stripped of its thatch before the men arrived, so that there need be no loss of time in starting. A little before six-thirty we ascended to the roof of the stack in the hardly abated starlight, cut the strings, pulled out the pegs (or springels), and flung the thatcher's neat work in confusion to the ground. It was a matter of some hazard creeping about the steep roof, the smooth thatch of which offered little hold. But when the men arrived we had most of the stack laid bare.

All the organisation had been done overnight, and the men had only to take their tools and each go to his post. Mr Colville hurried about, seeking by example and brisk commands to check any tendency to dawdle at the start.

The engine-driver, ruddy in the glow of his fire, waited with his hand on the lever till all were ready. He had been there early, getting up steam. The engine started, the long belt to the drum-pulley clapped, grew taut, and the drum revolved with a deep murmur. It was so dark that a man could hardly see his neighbour as the first sheaves were scattered into the drum. I was posted on the stack with two others. The work was easy at first, as one had only to dislodge the sheaves with one's fork and they rolled down upon the platform of the drum. As the two men already there could not keep themselves wholly occupied with this, and the space was small, I stood at the edge of it and watched the dawn.

Light came gradually. First, slender clouds of fire floated in a desert sky. Then came piled clouds, ash-grey, which suddenly flushed and became a rosy palace of morning. The whole sky glowed and put a splendour upon common things – the wind-ruffled water in the tub; the engine-smoke, the horse and cart waiting to carry the grain, the muddy ground. The straw fell in a golden shower from the elevator upon those who stood below building it out into a stack. Their faces had a bacchic fervour of hue. Even the dust that floated from the machine was impregnated, and the half-daft youth who laboured among it, clearing the cavings, moved in a mist of light. The tines of my pitchfork were bright as with monarchist blood, and seemed eager for fresh affrays. I stabbed a sheaf and tugged, but could not pull it up. I tried another and another. One of the men had been called from the stack, the other could not now pitch the sheaves fast enough to keep the drum fed by himself. I heaved desperately, and at last pulled one out, nearly falling over backwards. Yet the men seemed to lift them easily enough.

Mr Colville, seeing my labour, came upon the stack, and, taking the absent man's fork demonstrated to me how the sheaves were laid in layers, and how one unbuilt the stack by exactly reversing the building process.

'If you always take the top sheaf it will be quite easy,' he said.

I found this was so, and that if one tried to raise any other than the top one the labour became herculean.

Mr Colville worked with gusto, so that I had to shift here and there, as the sheaf I was standing on always seemed to be the one he wanted.

In a little time the platform of the drum was piled with sheaves. Then Mr Colville mopped his brow and departed.

Said the man with me, 'That's just like the master – he come and work like hell-o for five minutes, then he go off and we don't see him no more. He couldn't stick that pace all day.'

Of course, Mr Colville had other business to attend to, but the men seemed to leave his function of organising out of account and thought his demonstration was made for effect.

The pile of sheaves on the platform was melting rapidly. A man stationed there took them one by one, cut the bands with a knife, and, as they were about to dissolve, passed them into the arms of one beside him, who let them fall a little at a time into the mouth of the drum. The men on the stack with me appeared to work in a very leisurely fashion. I acted most of the time as intermediary for one or the other of them, as the stack was now far across, and for all their sluggard look I found it difficult to fling the sheaves to the band-cutter as fast as they came to me.

The engine-driver stood at the back of his engine taking a comprehensive view of the proceedings. Occasionally he walked to the straw-stack and examined the heads to see that no grain had been left in them; then he walked round the drum, inspecting the corn that came out of the various spouts.

Mr Colville had asked me to bring in a sample of the wheat at breakfast-time, having given me a little bag for the purpose. I went down to the drum and found wheat streaming out of two spouts. I filled the bag from one, and was walking off with it, when the engine-driver came after me to tell me I had taken the 'tail', or second-quality wheat. There was a broad grin all round at my sample. I was mortified secretly to think that I had not taken the trouble to ascertain the difference between good corn and bad. But I laughed with the others, for I found that the best attitude to adopt at first was to pretend to be even a greater fool than I was. To be afraid of being laughed at was to court annoyance.

I was glad enough when at a thrust of the engine-driver's arm the machinery came to rest with the waking of stars in that part of the sky whence the dawn had sprung. Hour after hour we had ministered to the threshing-drum as to some insatiable pre-Christian deity. It gobbled the sheaves as fast as we could feed it; it poured out chaff as fast as the youth could bag it and carry it into the barn, and straw as fast as the men could stack it. The absence of any one of the dozen people grouped round it would have thrown the whole proceeding out of gear. As it was, owing to Mr Colville's organisation, the business went with a rhythm; we, the humans, were vital parts of the machinery. The operation, in fact, was an example of the rigid limitations of machinery. It can thresh and winnow corn, divide the good from the bad, yet it cannot lift the sheaves from the stack, it cannot stack the straw or deal with the products of threshing.

In the sanctuary of a workshop machinery may be supreme, but outside it, nature imposes her limits. The tractor wheels skid helplessly upon the softened earth, a shower slips the belt from the pulley. Variability only can cope with variability. Agriculture needs legs and arms.

By the end of the week the corn-barn looked like a treasure-house, with the rich heaps glorifying its gloomy corners.

The drum was heaved out of the rubbish which had collected under it, the elevator from the straw in which it had become embedded. The engine-driver manoeuvred his engine to the head of the procession, and it moved away down the road. Mr Colville sighed with relief.

'I am always glad to see the back of them,' he said. 'The farm work is all upset while we are threshing, and things get into a muddle. As for the mess they make, look there!'

The usually tidy stack-yard was a litter of straw and heaped dust.

'It will take days to clear up.'

Already the men were shovelling and forking into carts. The boy Jack was retrieving tub and pails which had been commandeered from his pig-feeding paraphernalia. 'I've bin in a rare muddle without them,' he said. The horsekeeper was reclaiming valued cords, bags, and tarpaulin; Midden bearing back hurdles filched from the cowshed, for the penning of his calves. Simmons, who did the thatching, was collecting thatching-stakes, that he should not have to cut more for next harvest.

The next day we were sacking and weighing some of the corn that was already sold when I noticed a rough-looking implement standing in a corner of the barn. It consisted of two poles, one long and one short, hinged together with a leather thong – a flail (called 'frail' in Suffolk, where they boggle at difficult consonants), precursor of that murmurous giant we had been lately attending. There was something almost comic in its rough simplicity after that.

'My father made that one,' said Bob, the horsekeeper. 'I should like to have as many shillings as that has threshed coombs of corn.'

It was not a derelict, but still used for threshing beans and peas for seed, as the modern drum cracked them. In the old days the taskers, as the threshers were called, used to work the whole winter in the barn with their flails. They were not allowed to wear nailed boots, as they crushed the grains. Bob showed me the action of the flail, and I attempted it, and cracked myself on the skull, as he said I would. The swingel, or swinging end, performs antics of its own in the hands of a beginner, bounding back at him and behaving more like an enemy than an ally. It would have made an excellent weapon, and I wondered if the rabble used it in the French Revolution along with the other implements of agriculture.

Cottagers in Suffolk use flails to this day. If his garden is big enough, the cottager likes to grow a corn crop on part of it for his hens or pigs. This he reaps, shocks, and stacks just as though he were the lord of acres, and afterwards threshes with a flail. They always speak of 'farming' a garden in Suffolk.

Now the flail is being collected as an antique. Other ancient tools still lurk in forgotten corners. Probably one could gather together Tusser's whole list of husbandry furniture.

That evening two road-wagons were loaded with sacks of wheat and covered with cloths. At three the next morning Bob and another ploughman set off for Stambury, where the wheat was to be delivered, with lanterns hung on the wagons. They returned with loads of coal at five in the evening.

Bob said, 'You want an easy pair of boots for roadwork.

The boots I get nowadays wholly perish my feet. There was an old chap used to live up the lane what was a shimmiker.'

'A what?'

'He made boots.'

'Oh, a shoemaker.'

'Yes, a shimmiker. He made boots for fifteen shillings each that'd last a year, clod and road-walking, and never let the wet in as long as you kept 'em greased. But he's dead, and now I can't get boots that don't perish me to walk, and let the wet in pouring.'

The next Wednesday was Christmas sale day at Stambury and Mr Colville took me with him to see it. The town was full of cars and farmers. Inn yards were crowded with gigs. The market-place was at one end of the town, a vast space divided up into pens and selling-rings under cover.

Dealers hailed Mr Colville near the entrance with, 'I've got a pretty bunch of heifers this morning that would just suit you, sir,' and 'Do you want to see some real fine beasts, now?'

'They're Irishmen,' he said. 'They bring Irish cattle over, and rough ones too, sometimes. The trouble is, the Irish won't pay enough attention to quality – they use any old bull. But the cattle are hardy. There was an old chap used to farm in a big way near here; as mean as could be, he was. He'd buy fifty Irish cattle, and all he'd give them to eat through the winter was barley straw. They used to come out of the yards in the spring looking like scarecrows. He was the luckiest old man on God's earth – if they belonged to anyone else half of them would have died. It was wonderful how they pulled together, though, on the grass when they were turned out.'

There was a great bustle of unloading, penning, and

marking the creatures. A variety of gross persons with sticks were driving cattle about the alleyways between the pens, shouting, 'Mind your back – hup-ho! hup-ho!' Whichever way I turned I seemed to find a herd of bullocks charging down upon me.

The pens near the rings contained the fat beasts, and were garnished with holly and laurel. A piece of mistletoe (somebody's joke) dangled over the auctioneer's head. The prize cattle wore rosettes, and cards were tied to their pens with 'First Prize', 'Second Prize', 'Highly Commended', printed on them. The first-prize winner, a red shorthorn steer, was a breath-taking spectacle as he strode round the ring, supreme in width and depth. He was like a creature of legend sublimated in the telling.

So was the second, snow-white and classical – Europa's own. A man with gold rings in his ears and a woman of lascivious curves tattooed upon his arm urged him round.

'There,' said Mr Colville, 'how would you like a joint off him for your Christmas dinner?'

The auctioneer, searching the throng with swift eyes, enumerated the bids. Old men fingered their beards, pronouncing judgment on this year's quality. The bidders, simulating unconcern, nodding imperceptibly, shot occasional flashing glances to spot their rivals. It was a battle royal of butchers for the prestige of having a carcass with a red rosette hanging in their shops, a carcass split, showing inner qualities of meat and fat corresponding to those outward proportions for which he had been famous. Butchers who cater for farmers have a clientèle of connoisseurs, and at Christmas-time something extra special is expected.

'Turkeys be damned,' said Mr Colville before this brave show of creatures, 'give me beef and plum pudding.'

What, indeed, was turkey to him, who had pheasants or

partridges for the pointing of his gun? Not cooked *in camera* in an oven, either, but turning upon a spit close above brilliant wood embers on the old hearth in the scullery, well basted, hissing and browning, their flavours sealed within them. His wife kept turkeys for the Christmas trade; all day at Farley Hall their melancholy calling filled the air.

'Their row gets on my nerves,' said Mr Colville more than once. 'Thank God when they're sold and gone. I don't want to see one again for a long while, least of all on Christmas Day.'

The first-prize steer made £85, the second £80. 'A tidy price, but they won't forget to charge us when we want a joint,' said Mr Colville.

'Ha! You're right there, that they won't,' laughed a man beside him.

We strolled past the pens of store cattle, where the Irish dealers were stationed with eagle eyes for any that so much as paused before their beasts.

Mr Colville pointed out to me the points of good bullocks – 'Tails well set up, and good wide backsides on 'em. Now, these are a nice lot, a choice little bunch, all roan. They'll sell; roan is always a favourite colour, and a matching lot is always worth more than a lot all colours.' We passed to some others. 'These are a rough lot, narrow and bony. Rotten doers; I wouldn't have them at a gift.'

I was all eyes and ears, and tried hard to differentiate in this matter of backsides and tails, but for lack of practice could not. Whenever I expressed an opinion I found I had been led away by some irrelevance of smooth or rough coat.

The dealers came about Mr Colville. 'Now, sir, I can see you are in the mood to have a deal to-day. Why, sir, what with Christmas at hand, I expect I shall be fool enough to half give you a lot if you just try me. I must get rid of them; can't have them hanging on over Christmas. Sure and you shall have them at your own price; grand beasts, man, grand beasts.'

Mr Colville smiled and shook his head. 'Not to-day. I haven't got any money.'

'Money,' they laughed. 'Why, you're poisoned with money.'

'Bad time of the year for farmers,' said Mr Colville. 'All the bills soon coming in.'

'Come, sir, I am prepared to be very reasonable to day. I'll have a deal if you'll give me half a chance.'

Mr Colville allowed his glance to rest on the pen of roan bullocks he had commended.

'Yes, sir, grand lot, they are. I'll have 'em out so you can see 'em.'

'No, don't trouble to do that. I shan't buy them.'

But in a twinkling the dealers had them out into a clear space. For a time they haggled over them; then Mr Colville strolled away. But the men came running after with a half-crown concession.

'That's the worst of them chaps,' he said. 'If you so much as look at their bullocks they follow you about all day.'

Then he told me a story of the etiquette of dealing. The dealer always asks an exaggerated price at the beginning, and treats any offer, however near it be to his real selling price, as absurd. Then the bargaining begins. Now, there was a farmer who had been run up by a dealer at a sale and determined to have a revenge. He went into the market and bid the dealer for some bullocks more than they were worth. The dealer was prepared to take much less for them, but, as a matter of custom, treated the farmer's price as inadequate.

'Couldn't take that, sir; it would be giving them away.'

'Very well,' said the farmer, and walked away.

'Hi! Wait a minute!' cried the dealer, but the farmer went on, chuckling to himself, while the dealer, seeing the trick, indulged in vile epithets. Nor would he deal with him or even speak to him again. There had been a breach of etiquette.

In another part of the market we came to some cows.

'That's a good cow,' I ventured, selecting what I considered a likely beauty.

'Horny old devil,' said Mr Colville. 'I shouldn't like her in my yard. If she was to turn round on you she could wholly give you a jab. They're funny things with calves. Never buy bullocks either with much horn; they're sure to damage one another.'

The cows had calves by them. Their anxiety for their offspring in this crowded place, with likely buyers invading the pen, was a sad sight. In addition, although their udders were distended and milk dribbled from their teats, their calves were muzzled and were exhausting themselves trying to suck, hungry as they were. It was a sight that angered Mr Colville. 'They don't milk them the night before the sale so as to make their bags look bigger. It's cruelty.'

As we walked on we heard that turkeys were making a good price – two shillings a pound. We came to that part of the market where they were, in netted pens, through which they poked their heads, expressive, as ever, of faint disgust, like old maiden ladies imprisoned by Hottentots. Here, too, there were rosettes and cards. There were several first-prize winners, according to classes, with a bronze glitter upon their feathers.

'Good lord, it will take them all night to sell these! I never see so many in my life,' said Mr Colville. 'That's it, you see; you never know what turkeys will make at the last minute before Christmas. Sometimes they go to silly prices; sometimes you can hardly give them away.'

We inspected the Christmas show of pigs. As I cast my eye across the market, congested with fat beasts, it seemed almost incredible that in a few days' time the human mouth would have devoured the lot, and all these prize bullocks, pigs, turkeys, become assimilated into humanity.

'Just a minute,' said Mr Colville. 'There's a man over there I want to have a word with.' I leaned upon the rails of a pig-pen and waited for him. An old man with a beard was surveying the beast within.

'A rare sow,' he remarked to me.

It lay diagonally across the space, huge, lethargic, and pink.

'A rare sow,' I agreed.

'A rare show of stuff here to-day,' continued he.

'A fine show,' said I.

He laid a hand upon my shoulder. 'My eighty-ninth Christmas,' he said. 'I have seen many changes in my time, young man. Good times and bad. You take my word, people are better off to-day than ever they were before. Everybody has a Christmas dinner now. Why, I have seen twenty men walking to the workhouse about this time, and their wives and children following in a wagon. My father was only a horsekeeper, but he had a good master. I remember the master passing the blacksmith's one day about this time, and he saw some men standing round the fire, and he said to them, "Why are you chaps standing idle there?" And they said, "Because we haven't any work, master, nor anything to eat neither, nor a bit of firing in our houses." So he said to them, "Go to the mill," he said, "and say that I sent you and you are to be given three loaves of bread apiece, and then come to my kitchen door and you shall have some pork, and when you have eaten I will give you some work to do. Everybody in this parish must have a Christmas dinner."

'Ah, those were cruel times, young man. And we used to work in those days from four in the morning till dark. I hadn't anything when I started. I come from the Fen country. I used to earn twelve shillings a week, but I managed to save something somehow, so that I hired a bit of land. Part of it I got a man to plough for me and set with barley, and the other was grass. Well, it got on towards harvest, and I had a tidy little haystack off the meadow. But the man that had done the ploughing and drilling for me wanted his money, because he was only a poor man too. I hadn't got any, so I could only see that I should have to sell my haystack, which was a rare disappointment, because I'd looked forward to keeping a cow with it through the winter. Then I went to my old master and said, "Will you help me, sir?" And he said, "What do you want?" I said, "A hundred pounds." He thought, and looked at me very searching, and said, "I'll lend you fifty pounds, and if you use that well I'll see about the other." So I paid what I owed, and with the rest and my harvest I bought a cow and two horses and a plough. But then I hadn't enough for my rent, so I went to my old master again and said, "Will you let me have the other fifty pounds, master?" He replied, "Let's come and see your land." So he came and saw how I was doing it, and, after he had looked round, said, "I see you mean to get on. Yes, you shall have the rest of the money."

'In two years I'd paid him back, and interest too. That's how I started. Then I married, and my wife helped me a lot. A good wife is a great thing, young man, you take my word. She died a year ago, and I don't seem to have the same interest in things since.'

I saw Mr Colville parting from the man he had been talking to, so I bade the old man good-day and left him leaning against the rails, a wizened and grizzled figure gazing into the distances of his life.

'Have you been talking to old Jim Bradley? A real old Fen-man he is. It's wonderful how he keeps about. Why, I remember him as an old man when I was a boy. Yes, he's got pots of money; he's one of the biggest sheepmen in the district.'

Every few yards Mr Colville was accosted by somebody he knew, who had some confidential remark to make. Our progress was therefore slow, and I had plenty of time to gaze about me. The ground was cobbled in the wide ways between the rows of pens, and trees grew there. These and the roofs over the pens gave the market the appearance of something between a boulevard and a railway station.

Everywhere men sat perched in rows of three or four upon the rails like roosting fowls, and seemed to have nothing to do but gaze in front of them and smoke. When a cartload of pigs drew up, the loiterers gathered round and watched them being unloaded by one leg and an arm under the belly. Two old deaf men stood in an alleyway bawling at each other, their beards almost intermingling.

All the while the air was filled with the lowing of cattle, the slithering of hoofs, pigs quarrelling, and bells ringing.

The large pigs seemed indifferent to their surroundings, sleeping until the auctioneer came to them and the crowd poked them to sudden panic. Each, as sold, received an indigo blue hieroglyphic upon its back, and was soon once more in deep slumber. Death, I felt, could make little difference to them, except that they would not eat.

The little pigs, though, crowded together in fright, and tried to hide among one another.

Everywhere sticks waved: one of the undertones of the place was the continual tattoo of them pattering upon hides.

Men stood conferring solemnly with their hands upon a bullock's back, as though it were a sacred relic they were swearing by, or raised themselves and stood on the rails to get a comprehensive view of a particular penful.

As we were passing an auctioneer's office, Mr Colville pointed out to me a man who looked like a beggar or mendicant.

'He's as rich as he can be.' We paused as the man entered the office. 'I bet he's bought two or three hundred pounds' worth of cattle.' Through the open door I saw him taking wad after wad of notes from an inner pocket. 'He never writes a cheque; he can't sign his name,' said Mr Colville.

It was half-past one, and smells of cooking wafted across the market-place.

'I don't know how you are, but I begin to feel a bit peckish,' Mr Colville remarked.

I agreed that lunch would be welcome; I began to feel chilly with long loitering and looking. At the entrance we were again besieged by the Irish dealers, but Mr Colville had a way, by a smile and a jest, of brushing past them without seeming brusque. We passed down a street where I saw lofts full of trussed hay, where granary doors stood open, revealing sacks and hanging chains. We entered a dim hall of beer-barrels, and so came by a back way, familiar to farmers, to the Three Tuns Inn, and mounted wooden steps from the courtyard to a lofty chamber where the Market Ordinary Luncheon was to be had.

The floor was of scrubbed boards, the walls whitewashed. A long table went down the centre of the room, and at one end was a serving-table on which stood various joints with spirit-flames beneath them keeping them hot. Behind this the landlord and his wife were stationed, wielding carving-knives worn thin as rapiers, while aproned wenches went to and fro with plates and dishes.

We had roast beef and brown beer. Beside us sat a butcher in his dark-blue coat. Mr Colville was greeted all round. It was a variegated throng; corn merchants in smart suits, with buttonholes, sitting next to tradesmen snatching half an hour in the market-day rush. The merchants were leisurely, oracular; the tradesmen swift of speech; the farmers wryly humorous, but interested mostly in their luncheon.

Mr Colville and the butcher were discussing the quality of the beef, which the butcher had purveyed to the inn.

'It comes from Manton Hall. I bought one of Sam Sneep's fat beasts. He took third prize here to-day, so you know he keeps some good stuff. It was a picture. There he is, sitting over yonder.'

I saw Sam Sneep, a bearded farmer, eating of his own bullock.

After the beef we had bread and cheese and celery. The farmer never eats biscuits with cheese. The actual menu of the market luncheon was soup, joint, sweet, and cheese, two and threepence. The price was based, I think, on the fact that the farmer does not take a sweet. I noticed small bowls of stewed apples and custard, but they were untouched. They seemed to be included merely to swell the menu, for every farmer shook his head and reached for the cheese at the servant's mentioning the effeminate word 'sweet'.

Mr Colville's father came in towards the end of our meal, a bit short of breath and glad to sit down. He said, 'I've been coming to Stambury market for fifty years, and I've only missed twice in all that time.'

Another, even older, told me he had been an attendant there for fifty-five years, and in his early days they used to

143

take their places at the table according to the number of bottles of port they drank at a sitting – the three-bottle men at the top, the one-bottle men at the foot. 'In those days we used to do all our business in the morning, and sat a-drinking and card-playing the rest of the time, till very near the next morning.'

After lunch we went to the Corn Exchange. It was one of the chief buildings of the town, of exuberant late Georgian architecture, with pillars and stone flourishes, surmounted by a benevolent Ceres presiding over symbolical figures in bas-relief – the reaper and his sickle, the ploughman and his team.

Within was a vast chamber, the roof chiefly of glass. A deep hum of many persons talking filled the air. 'Always puts me in mind of a hive of bees,' said Mr Colville.

Row upon row of desks stood each a few yards from another, with a merchant's name and trade inscribed on the front. Behind stood the merchant himself. Each was surrounded by a shifting group of people, who in turn offered him samples of corn in small black bags (black makes the corn look brighter by contrast – farmers neglected no details). The merchant poured some of the corn into his hand, kept shifting it with his finger as he examined it (sometimes with a magnifying glass), while the farmer stood before him and the others craned their necks, awaiting his pronouncement.

The form of the group (the merchant at his desk stood a foot higher than the farmers) suggested irrelevantly a master and his pupils to me. The merchant wore a professional nonchalance, convincing in its air of 'I don't care whether I buy or not,' whereas the farmer's growl of independence – 'I won't sell at that price for nobody' – by its assertiveness hinted at bluff.

When the merchant's opinion was unfavourable (and he had a way of wordlessly handing a farmer back his bag after a mere glance), it was almost as though he were reproving a boy for bad work. I remembered a sarcastic master who had been my terror at school.

Mr Colville had a sample of barley with him, which he offered to a merchant.

'I don't know whether it's quite good enough for him,' he had said to me beforehand. 'He's a good buyer, but he only wants the best.'

The man opened the bag, and, having gazed upon the barley, plunged his nose into it, to which, when he lifted his face, several grains adhered. He poured it in and out of his hand, cracked some grains with his teeth, then asked the price.

'Seventy shillings,' said Mr Colville, in an uncompromising tone.

'Heavens, man, what are you thinking of – not this sample?' returned the merchant. He held up the bag. 'I'll bid you once, and more than it's worth – sixty shillings.'

Mr Colville shook his head, and, taking the sample, walked away. He showed it to another merchant, who offered him fifty-seven shillings, and a third, who offered him fifty-five, and who, when Mr Colville said he had already been bid sixty shillings, said, 'Take it, man; you'll never get more.'

Thereupon Mr Colville returned to the first merchant, remarking on the way, 'I don't reckon he'll stand word.' He didn't. His bid was now a shilling less per coomb, but agreement was at length reached by the mutual concession of sixpence.

While these negotiations were going on, a confidential fat man tried to sell me some patent pig-meal, taking me for a farmer. He conjured rosy visions, but as soon as I could get a word in, and told him I was not in farming, he ceased abruptly and went elsewhere.

Wheat and barley lay spilt about the floor and on the desks, but Mr Colville said, 'There's not much business being done here to-day. It's too near Christmas.'

As we left the building, Mr Colville said, 'I think I'll treat myself to a new hat for Christmas. The missis is always on to me about this one,' and walked into a shop and bid the proprietor for a hat as though it were a pig or a bullock. Nor did this seem entirely out of order, for the latter (who seemed on terms of long-standing friendship with his customer) laughed and said, 'Aren't you going to allow me a little profit?'

Mr Colville turned his attention to some gloves, and, having heard the price, said, 'I can see I took up the wrong trade. I ought to have been a shopkeeper, not a farmer. You all retire about forty; no wonder. You can charge just what you like; we have to take what we can get. Farmers never retire; they can't afford to.'

'I don't reckon you've much to grumble at, though,' answered the hatter. 'You haven't wasted all away yet' – indicating his increasing portliness.

After five minutes' chaffing each other, they returned to the hat and gloves. To Mr Colville, haggling was an amusing exercise. He offered to take the gloves at the man's price if he would sell him the hat at his own. The bargain was clinched, but, as the hatter was making out the bill, Mr Colville said, 'Five per cent discount for cash, remember. That's worth a bob or two.'

'Ha, you're a terror, you are, Mr Colville,' murmured the man with relish. He deducted the five per cent.

As we stood outside the shop, 'It don't do to give these

chaps just all they ask,' he confided to me. 'I saved a bit there, you see. It all mounts up.'

In later days I came to know that hatter quite well, and remarked upon the farmer's shopping methods.

'Yes,' he said, 'but, you see, when a farmer comes into the shop we put a few shillings on to the price of things, just to give him the pleasure of knocking it off and feeling he's saved some money.'

Mr Colville now said, consulting his watch, 'I have a business appointment in five minutes. Perhaps you would like to look round the town. I'll meet you in the Old Butter Market at four o'clock.'

The Old Butter Market was one of the many open spaces of Stambury, surrounded by shops – no longer a market in any sense of the word except that on market days it was thronged with stalls, much to the annoyance of the shop-keepers.

Stambury was a fine and ancient town, containing squares of Georgian houses, and churches in the noble Suffolk style. It had its polite street, where on days other than market-days the county gentry shopped, and large cars rested, and car-riages, too, of unusual shapes with technical names, while grooms stood at the heads of horses. Although the motor-car was universal, there was a certain pride, among those that had the money and ability, in driving a prancing grey in a yellow gig through the streets, with floating whiplash and all.

To be a master of the horse, round Stambury, was like being a master of life. The children of the great drove in their own miniature tub-carts with shaggy ponies, and the grocer came out of his three-gabled shop in Churchgate Street and waited on them when they stopped outside.

There were agricultural streets, too, converging on the

cattle-market, where bright-blue horse-rakes and harrows stood upon the pavement before a shop, and grinding-mills and oil-engines within. One shop window was full of blades, saws, sickles, slashers, bill-hooks, scythes. There were gun-shops, with some antique pistols for show, and decoy pigeons and cartridge belts – all that the sporting yeoman should require. Within, there was much trying of the weight of new guns, aiming of them, and discussions as to whether five or six shot was best in a particular case.

'These,' a shopman was saying of a small cartridge for a rat-gun as I passed, 'will kill a rat easily but won't hurt your barn.' It was taken for granted that every customer had a barn.

There was also an agricultural tailor in this vicinity who cut breeches just suitable for a farmer's better occasions – not exaggeratedly Newmarket, nor yet unassumingly narrow, but with a hint of style about them.

I met George Crawley hereabout. His only vanity was his legs, which he encased in such close and elegant leggings I wondered how they could move. I endeavoured to talk to him, but he stood saying, 'Ay, ay,' and waiting for me to be done, as he was busy. He carried (like all farmers) a leather bag under his arm containing samples, chequebook, wages from the bank, and all to do with his business.

The chief shopping-place of the day was the Old Butter Market. Here beef and pork and poultry were turned by the alchemy of the coin to feminine adornments, tobacco, silks, and scents. Here wives and daughters strolled.

Where this joined the agricultural neighbourhood stood a shop devoted to clothing of a rural kind. A line of dickeys hung down the window. Some were blue, with a pattern; some striped. There were both soft and stiff ones, the former with a system of tags at the corners for fixing. The most interesting kind were those which were compounded with a collar. This was in two halves. You put it round your neck; the two parts of the dickey met upon your chest; you buttoned them together, and in a trice were both collared and shirted. Then, putting on your better coat to hide the make-believe, you were ready for market. On your return, you had merely to unbutton and whip it from your neck, and you were in working trim to milk the waiting cows. They were only a shilling each; without collars, eightpence halfpenny.

There were corduroy coats with black velvet collars, stiff blue trousers, scarves and ties for 'courting' in, of sugary hues. There were underclothes also, but of a grim hairiness.

At the end of the town opposite to that at which the cattle-market was situated were the ruins of a great abbey, a memory of old ecclesiastical significance. Public gardens had been laid out within the walls. They were deserted to-day. I walked the lawns under bare boughs tranced to the stillness of stone in the frosty air. Shattered arches stood up lonely from the grass. A door stood open in an enclosure of ruined wall. I looked in, and found a gardener there sweeping up the last leaves. It had been a family burial-place, he said. 'The mossyleum, they call it.' He looked around. 'There ain't much moss there now but doubtless there was at one time.'

At the end of the gardens a river ran, and a monks' bridge spanned it. All this was in grave contrast to the bustle of market-days beyond the walls.

The tufted abbey walls flanked one side of a sloping space, called (on account of the inn that stood opposite) Angel Hill. As I passed out of the gardens a traction engine stood fuming before the gate-tower, with a timber-drag sent to deal with a fallen tree within. Here it was a dragon which the blunt-nosed saints in the niches confronted with holy calm.

Cars were parked all across Angel Hill – not the immaculate ones of townsmen's recreation, but old cars, with carriage lines about them and high seats. These had the advantage to farmers of the old school of allowing them to see over the hedges as they drove, and criticise their neighbour's crops. In the back of one lay a calf snuggled into a sack, his head peeping forth; in another, some hens were murmuring in undertones. And in all were mountains of parcels.

What a packing up was going on there before starting home – a fitting of one another in, wife and daughter, and the neighbour who was being given a lift. Fringes of rugs were tucked in, doors slammed.

The sun was setting; it seemed to have dissolved and dyed the air. The sky had a bronze glow, purple-hazed where a plume of smoke expanded. The air was nipping.

On the third side of the hill stood Georgian houses, and on the fourth an eighteenth-century Assembly Rooms. It was here that the County balls were held. Clear the space of cars, and one hundred years had altered nothing. Standing there, it was easy to picture a Georgian occasion – carriages depositing ladies and their squires at the steps of the inn, where they always stayed the night, or what was left of it when the ball was over. I imagined the moving lanterns, the cries, stamping of horses, visions of elegance flitting from gleam to fitful gleam . . .

But it was now four o'clock, and I returned to the Old Butter Market.

8

One day just before Christmas was spent in killing and plucking the hundred or so of Mrs Colville's turkeys. She had sold them to a London buyer, as she always did, preferring an agreed price of so much per pound to taking the chances of the market.

The turkeys were hung by the legs from a beam in the coach-house, and one of the labourers with a swift, strong twist broke their necks. I and the boy Jack each held a wing while this was being done; the automatic muscular reaction was so strong that I could hardly keep hold of mine as the creature kicked and flapped, dead.

'They take some killing, they do,' panted the man, perspiring, though the day was bitter.

And yet, as I was to know, when they are young turkeys will die almost of a lack of the will to live. They are nothing but an anxiety from the moment they are born. They have to be coaxed to eat. Wet is fatal to them when small. They must be collected and put under shelter if it rains or they will just stand and die. Their depressing squawk continues all day without intermission. Vermin seem to consider them the tastiest morsels possible. Their foes come from the air and the earth and under the earth. Hawks and crows swoop upon them; cats and foxes ambush them; rats, stoats, weasels, burrow to them under the coops. In addition, they become enemies to one another. For they never grow evenly, though hatched at the same time. Some grow quickly; others remain puny and weak. Then the strong attack the weak, killing them unmercifully.

When they become adult they make up for strengthened constitutions by becoming more troublesome. They take to roosting in trees. As the fox has only to look at them for them to fall into his jaws, it is necessary during the later months of their lives to clamber about precariously every evening, poking them down with a pole and herding them to safety. It was thus that Midden came to grief.

The half-dozen biggest turkeys of a flock band themselves together into a bullying gang and institute a reign of terror in the farmyard. Their pleasure is to prowl round in a crafty way, slowly, with head stuck forward, as though looking for stray grains of corn on the ground, but in reality seeking whom they may destroy. Woe betide any hen that is not feeling as agile as usual that day, should she come within their view. One turkey will approach, eyeing intently the fictitious grain of corn, and suddenly, with a vicious peck, seize the unhappy creature's head with its beak and hold it to the ground, while the others stand round and peck at it in turn with the rhythm of wedge drivers. They do it slowly, deliberately, and in silence, as though performing a solemn rite. That particular atrocity may last them an hour. When the hen is beyond all doubt dead, they lose interest in it and seek another victim.

But now their hour was come, though a more merciful end meted to them than they had meted to others, and by evening they were all naked corpses A motor-van came for them, and Mr Colville sighed with relief really to see the last of them. There was a respite of three months. In March it would begin all over again.

In the old days, turkeys used to be driven to London alive. From Norfolk, flocks of thousands started upon the pilgrimage in October, feeding upon stubbles as they went and arriving in London at Christmas.

I went home for Christmas, of course, while the Colville family gathered at Benfield for theirs. I have spent many Christmases there since, but, as every reader has a country Christmas of memory, there is no purpose in my re-enumerating the signs, from the early bells to the mistletoe on the yokels' caps (a fancy that even cinema tuition in what's what cannot eradicate).

The morning has even been one of virgin snow, on occasion, when cottage and tower stood forth with a sim plicity incommunicable in our now sophisticated language. I remembered at such time approaching the village over untrodden whiteness (save for birds' faint mazy patterns), and hearing the bells start suddenly to ring with chimes that seemed not to break, but only stir, the wintry spell (as the wind a dew-hung cobweb), the tranced cold echoing to them like a fine glass tapped with the fingernail.

But such a moment of vista and old summons is as fragile as the snow it is engraved on, and melts and cannot be told of.

More homely and nearer the heart of every day was the bustle and congestion in the post-office the two days before. The office was a cottage room converted – if frowning signs and notices, or all the insignia of officialdom for that, could ever make a thatch and plaster cottage anything but a happy, homely place. It became a gathering-place hardly second to the Cock Inn – a rustling, breathing, expectant crowd waiting while the postman performed his mysteries of sorting and franking under a hanging oil lamp, and music from his son's gramophone ('When Father Papered the Parlour') sounded from within – a noise which one felt the Postmaster-General would have considered out of order here.

Gifts flowed in from the outer world, and Benfield gave in return. Rabbits and game lay on the counter, tied and labelled.

On Boxing Day the bell-ringers went round and serenaded the chief houses with chimes on the handbells, and wished the people good cheer, for which they were invited to drink with them to the coming year, and favourable sun and shower upon the fields to harvest.

Of these and of the Colville gatherings the reader has probably an instinctive idea, and of such homely rites as were the soul of the occasion to those beyond the bafflement of boredom. That modern snake, the question 'Are we enjoying ourselves?' did not raise its head here. Unimagined, it was not.

The little daily contest of men's minds which is every-where and eternal was stilled by the tradition of the occasion, the 'Play thou the good fellow' (again to quote Tusser), and

> *Good husband and huswife now chiefly be glad,*
> *Things handsome to have, as they ought to be had.*

It was just and only that. (To the cottager his firelit, 'mantling' beer; to the Colville grandchildren, their paper crackers.)

I returned home to London, to a world of narrow sky and no darkness, to find the old life half strange already. My brown Sunday boots, in which I motor-cycled home, once again seemed uncouth there, and I was asked to change them, as they would ruin the carpets. These 'gentleman's' boots!

I re-entered a world of nervous significance, where the very furniture was a complex language, and a piece placed *so* had, to some perception as acute as Bob's for weather signs, the subtle rightness of a *mot juste*. This world fearful of mud-splashes, that yet breathed grimy air (I remembered the threshing-men grappling muddy iron while they breathed air like well-water); a world of hurtful probing into personality.

I noticed most keenly the brilliance of electric light after oil lamps, and the absence of anything worn, or uneven, or overgrown. Interiors had the illusory quality of flashed scenes of midnight storm. In fact, the whole Christmas sojourn had a flashed effect, flat and unrooted, with people gesturing and smiling as in a charade. I was called 'Giles' or 'Hodge', and treated to enquiries of "Ow be thoi mangel-worzels?' Either that or I was a courageous self-emancipator, the wind whistling through my hair.

Said one, 'How splendid to be free of dress formalities; hats for instance.'

'But I always wear a hat,' I replied.

Another asked, 'What are the names of the pigs? And the cows?' I told her that they had no names; only pedigree stock and horses had them, and that was a matter of convenience; to which she replied, 'How heartless,' and liked me less.

Somebody else spoke of a friend who had a farm. It turned out to be five acres in Surrey, which he visited at week-ends.

Another week-ender with a cottage had noticed that pigs use only one corner of a sty as a lavatory, which was considered commendable.

The value of my agricultural smattering to them was that it gave me a character part. I was set to preach robustness among cushions. 'Have you met our farmer?'

I reclined on a divan (there was that or the floor or a gilt chair like a shell). Before me a cocktail, and salted almonds

in a red saucer with white spots ('like a workman's handkerchief – such fun!') on a baroque table whose legs were
entangled dolphins diving to their reflections in the polished
floor. On the black wall a design of fountains and flamingoes
done with pasted scraps of coloured paper ('a revival of old
patchwork pictures – quite the newest thing'). Electric bulbs
were hidden behind lotus-shaped shades. On the mantelshelf
was an orange-tree of spun glass and black candles that had
not been lit – never would be . . .

'Why are we all so complex nowadays?' was the self-
congratulatory sigh after my account of the country.

Whatever I said, the week-end attitude was unalterable;
the yokel was a museum piece, and the whole subject an
excursion in the grotesque or the picturesque.

Here, when the waiter, with the flourish of a conjurer,
produced the omelette at its moment of perfection, I thought
of how Mr Colville had cried, 'Boy, there's an old hen lays
up in that stack. Go and hunt the eggs up,' and how they
had jogged many a mile in the higgler's cart.

And the elegant shoes of the gentlemen dancing there,
how they had been tapped round the cattle-market by the
man in the gold earrings, and bid for and bought and led
into the slaughter-house; and how his faultless dress suit
had been penned once with other sheep and felt by many
a farmer's hand; and the lady, his partner, so complexioned
by skin-foods, creams, elaborately potted and made mysterious by advertisements repetitive of the words 'exquisite'
and 'fragrance', yet sprung from the turned furrow just the
same. Then it seemed to me that this world had forgotten
that it sat on a tree and ate of the fields and the creatures,
but made of the word 'exquisite' a talisman, if not a fount
of life; and it appeared to me then that the cattle-market,
gross and tumultuous, and the Corn Exchange, were the

twin lungs not only of the agriculture of the district, of the little town, but of all civilisation.

Two days later I was back at Farley Hall, having changed my brown boots for not lighter but heavier ones, and was painting agricultural implements in the barn.

This was bold, impressionistic work. There was a pot of blue paint and one of red. Mr Colville painted the woodwork red while I painted the ironwork blue. We made the thing look gay and at the same time preserved it: blest marriage of use and beauty.

'A coat of paint saves pounds,' Mr Colville exclaimed at intervals when he had finished a wheel or a beam. We were painting a horse-hoe in the middle-tree of the barn. Outside, it rained intermittently. Four men were dressing barley on a raised wooden floor at one end of the barn. As three of them bent over the dressing-machine, roughly cradle-shaped, and the fourth knelt making some adjustment to it, at a glimpse it might have been some old mystery play they were engaged in, I thought, with beams arching into a Gothic vista above them.

Hens came to the doorway and paused, leg in air, and watched, faintly querulous, with head on one side, as much as to say, 'Oh, so you are there, are you?' Small pigs, too, came gaily trotting, with an 'Ah, the barndoor left open; now for a feed,' but halted precipitately at sight of us, grunted imprecations, and fled.

We chatted as we worked, when the machine was not actually turning, and Mr Colville entertained the men with an account of how on Christmas night the lights of his car so dazzled Simmons, making unsteady progress from the inn, that he had fallen into the ditch.

We were a happy party, for it was homely in the barn out of the cold and damp. Two of the men had their coats off, and I noticed how their shirts were striped with the same contrasting red and blue with which we were painting the horse-hoe.

During a period of persistent rain I came to realise the extent of the farm-worker's wardrobe. Since his clothes are never thrown away until actually worn to shreds, and since the clothes of his forefathers were made to last, many a cottage has an interesting store laid away, usually in an old chest. When the need arises they are brought forth. His ordinary clothes being soaked, one meets him wearing forgotten fashions – that which was once a gentleman's driving-coat, maybe, well waisted, and a large hat.

The colours of his clothes and of the things he handles echo one another; his corduroy and the Suffolk horse he drives, his handkerchief and his plough-beam. With red-blue shirt and necktie he rides out to the harvest-field in a wagon the colour of the sky. His face, too, contributes a tone, and his copper-coloured arms. In dawn-flush or sunset-glow I have seen him, an illumined figure. These same colours laugh together in the pictures on his cottage walls.

He only wears an overcoat if it is raining or he is driving or is ill. He wears it over his shoulders like a cloak, the sleeves hanging empty, if he is working, as he is freer so.

Only on Sunday does he elect to quench himself in black, or, worse still, the pseudo West-End suits I have spoken of. Corduroy takes on an easy grace in wear, but Sunday clothes imprison him.

So I painted in a barn that was a cathedral nave, and wondered what earthly use my liberal education was to be to me here save as a pleasure-garden for the mind to wander in. I had only this more conscious pleasure in things than these men – of catching in the cloistral gloom of cowshed or stable those gleam-lit attitudes of strength and patience which the old painters turned into religious masterpieces.

January drew to an end with a spell of severe frost, which the Colville farmers welcomed, saying, 'This will make the land work well for barley seeding.' Ploughs were frozen into the earth, and farm traffic rattled briskly over the iron ground that all winter it had soughed and slushed through. Horses and cattle were littered knee-deep (never could they be too well littered for Mr Colville). ('Deep-plunging cows their rustling feast enjoy.')* Pigs burrowed into the straw tipped into their pens and lay invisible but sonorous. Fires where the hedgers had been at work beaconed the darkness. Mr Colville went the rounds with dog and gun (hedging was the only work possible), and was himself loath to leave the charmed circle of fire, and, making work an excuse, seized a fork and fed the flames.

On the first of February our last shoot took place. It was a family affair, like the others. The Colvilles, with an uncle or two and the neighbours, easily mustered a dozen guns.

We had at this time a new clergyman at Benfield, Mr Phipps having returned to the Colonies. Mr Maglin, his successor, was a man of means, and had lived hitherto in a westerly London suburb. He was anxious to be on the best of terms with everybody, but, as their language and outlook were entirely different, he was finding it a little difficult to get to the hearts of his people. His 'Yes, rather, by Jove,' struck a stranger note than Mr Phipps's 'I reckon so'.

Although his gun was from Pall Mall, it was not yet the comfortable companion that Horace's was to him. As we were moving round a wood for the first drive, a hen pheasant got up under his feet, which so startled him that he shot it point blank to annihilation.

* Bloomfield: 'The Farmer's Boy'

'Here's your bird, Mr Maglin,' said Dick amusedly, picking up half a wing, the only visible remains.

'Ha, should have given him more rope, what?' laughed Mr Maglin, himself appreciating the joke. It was the only bird he killed that day.

We were not shooting hen pheasants on that occasion, either, only cocks, the season being almost done.

But who am I to talk, myself then an erratic novice? However, I enjoyed those days – the tap-tapping of the beaters among the trees, the expectancy at their cries of 'Over – mark over!' and the cock pheasant, whirring like machinery with bright plumage and tail streaming and quivering as he broke from the thicket. The barrel of my gun searching for him, an instinct within crying 'Now,' and the bird suddenly becoming a ball of feathers and crashing down into a hedge. I was a savage then (and still am when standing outside a wood with a gun). I did not want to see him escape, that beautiful bird. Then the lunch in a barn – pork pies, bread and cheese, and beer – which the ladies brought to us, themselves riding over the fields with it in a new-painted tumbril. John Colville afterwards (he always had charge of the proceedings) being the first to jump up, impatient to be getting on with the sport, standing among the beaters like a Napoleon, giving his brisk commands, pointing this way, that way, encompassing the horizon with his gesture. Then, as we, the guns, moved to our positions, Arnold and Dick, loitering, conferring, and Mr Colville's cry, 'Come on, pray do, don't keep talk, talk, talk.' And then mumbling to me, 'They will wholly keep jabbering worse than a couple of old women. The birds'll be by them before they know anything about it.' When Arnold fired, he would cry, 'That bird's hard hit. Watch it, watch it,' and obediently we watched it floating away unscathed and alighting where it chose. After the drive Arnold would be searching for it with the dogs, but John Colville, knowing it useless, would push on to the next stand, Arnold murmuring.

It was generally arranged that Horace Colville stood next to Mr Maglin, and when a bird flew by between them, and Mr Maglin fired and Horace also and the bird fell, Mr Maglin cried, 'Did you shoot that or did I?' And Horace would generously make answer, 'That was your bird, sir.'

But partridge-shooting, that was a very different thing from downing slow pheasants. We crouched beneath a bank, waiting as though that ploughed field were no-man's-land and we were to repulse the approaching line of beaters. This was the last drive. A cold mist came over. The others were invisible suddenly. I heard Mr Colville's voice, 'Why couldn't it have waited?'

Whistles and cries out of the mist ahead. 'Look out – coming over!' My fingers tense, my eyes straining; a rush of wings passed my head. Bang – bang – and, farther down the line, bang-bang – bang – bang. A voice to a dog, 'Here, Gyp, here in the hedge.' A fluttering and scurrying, then silence again save for the voice of a wounded hare, some-where behind us, crying like a child . . .

In a few days the frost gave, and, though the sky still lowered, the rain held off. Nature was no longer silent, but birds added song to the workaday stirrings of the early mornings. Then, at the end of the month, there came a day of full sun, and timorous airs played warmly on hand and face. Young foliage peeped; water was bright as a blade, and, ruffled by flashing-white ducks, seemed cool, not cold. This was spring's ambassador.

The day showed in all our faces. The men sat under a wall to breakfast and basked. Mr Colville ordered the har-rows into the wheat.

'It's too early really,' he confided to me, 'but I don't like to lose such weather.'

To my view it seemed destruction to the young growth of winter wheat hardly yet greening the earth to put tearing harrows over it. The earth, crusted already to a light dry colour, was darkened again as the harrows broke it and made the wheat even less evident. But Mr Colville said, 'It doesn't matter how much you pull wheat about; it does it good. But oats, that's a different thing. You mustn't cover oats up.'

We viewed dubiously the winter oats, looking very grey after the frosts, especially on this day of green. But the young beans began to show the rows. By midday coats were being doffed. Other harrows were crumbling ploughed land.

'We'll put some peas in to-morrow,' Mr Colville said, and that evening the drill was brought out, cleaned, and prepared.

This was the beginning of spring seeding. Though the weather turned cold again, and for one temperate day of sun we had a week of shivering dullness, the hedges were breathing green and the ground dried after rain.

Three men went with the drill. Bob, the old horse-keeper, was in command; he steered, one of his sons drove the horses, and Simmons walked behind watching the corn scooped up in the revolving cups and showered down the funnels that led into the earth, seeing that none got blocked and that weeds did not clog the points that furrowed the earth.

Bob's hand is on the steering-lever; his eyes are fixed on a faint mark in the earth made by the off-side wheel in their last bout. Now he must keep the nearside wheel upon that mark so that no land is missed. He has a reputation for straight drilling to hold against younger men. He is, as it were, writing in invisible ink upon the earth. When the sun warms it, the corn will spring up and every thin green line will be almost as straight as though drawn with a ruler.

His son holds the reins and watches the horses, to see that they keep straight and each pulls his share. As they approach the edge of the field, he warns them for the turn. They pause at the headland, and, in response to a tightening of the reins, their feet move sideways clumsily. Their legs overlap and they jostle, tossing their manes and shaking froth upon one another.

Simmons, at the back, winds a handle which lifts the points out of the earth which has polished them bright as spearheads. Bob, gripping the lever hard, pulls the front wheels straight with an effort, the moment the machine has turned enough, shouting 'Whoa!' A lid is lifted, and hands buried to the wrists level the grain in the hopper. Sacks line the headland at intervals; more barley is poured from one of these into a bushel measure, and the hopper is filled. The men take up their positions, and at a word all start across the field again.

March was a cold, dry month, and by the end of it much of the barley had been drilled and covered well with harrows. I spent considerable time and ingenuity in ambushing rooks. They haunted the newly sown fields, and rose in clouds at the scarer's shout, but were extremely difficult to shoot. They always left a sentry posted on a tree, who saw one from afar and began uttering his dismal note of warning. 'They can smell a gun,' is the popular saying. Certainly they would walk fearlessly behind a plough or harrows, and, if one was unarmed, would only stir if shouted at, nor fly far then. If, however, I was walking with a gun, they rose before I was within a field of them.

I lay for hours in a ditch waiting for them to come over. They would fly in twos and threes across the ditch about fifty yards away. I changed my place and sat there. They then seemed to pass over the spot where I had been sitting before. But one windy day they came over against the wind slowly and very low, and I shot several and mounted them on stakes in the barley-fields, scattering their feathers about; for rooks will never alight where there are evidences of a dead one of their kind. In one place the remains of a black hen (a victim of the fox) was put up, but it had no effect.

Now rabbiting was at an end (already there were nests of young ones), the point-to-point races had been held, and there was an end to hunting. The barleys were sprouting up, vivid green. Winter was really over.

9

There came a day in April that was like a summer breath, not the timorous, tender wish of late February. It was a Wednesday, and I attended market with Mr Colville. Mrs Colville came too, tempted out by the day.

When farmers take their wives with them to town on market-day they part from them on getting out of their cars, and do not meet them again till it is time to go home. No Market Ordinary for madam; she lunches delicately in a restaurant with small tables.

Mrs Colville asked her husband for some money.

'Ah, no!' He wagged his head, wisely jocular. 'What you buy you pay for.'

But she, with a smile to me, filched his note-case from his breast pocket and helped herself to a pound.

'There now,' he said, 'that's what it is to have a wife.'

Stambury is aware that summer is imminent. The stalls are crowded close. Some are golden with fruit – pyramids of oranges and tumbled heaps of bananas. Some are spread with sweets – glistening slabs of hardbake, batons of rock thick as barbers' poles, white squares and oblongs of nougat shining in the sun like flat-roofed villas of Babylon, and others with almonds embedded like fossils in strata of pink and yellow. There are stalls that bear silver-shining mounds of fish; others are hung with gay flapping garments and festooned with lace; others overflow to the ground with ornaments, accessories, polished pans. Some beneath canopies are dim and lustrous with blossoming plants.

Nor are the vendors shy. They shout and hullabaloo with one another; they wield codfish and gesture magnificently with frying-pans. They strain at indestructible cycle-tyres, and wind garlands of unbaked toffee upon hooks. They fling new farthings into bags of their wares, pretending that they are giving away half-sovereigns. They hold mock auctions. They squabble eloquently with one another to collect a crowd in their mutual interest.

It is, perhaps, this confused effect of colour and vivacity set about with steep old houses that breathes a suggestion of the exotic; perhaps it is the thin music of a street piper somewhere in the midst; perhaps just the beautiful day. The people are out with new hearts; there is an air of unrestraint. For now the corn will grow, the earth crumble, and the grass make rich milk. This might be the festival of spring, they laugh so together. They all seem to know one another; they meet acquaintances at every step, and long-lost friends at every corner. The stalls hum with trade, for to-day they buy a little more than they can afford. The women flaunt airy clothes, and one catches at moments some bewildering bright expression, some breathless look or daring turn of the head.

But at dusk, perhaps, the vigour of the scene is most apparent, when the flares are lit along the stalls and the flames leap fanatically and search the darkness, making the shadows of people dance upon the canvas backgrounds. They add a touch of the barbaric, for their light is the light of torches flowing with the wind. The stalls become islands of light into which the people are born out of the night; in the glow their faces have the over-expressiveness of masks. Everywhere trembles the fingering of fire. The face of a church clock stands like a yellow stage moon on high. A cracked bell sounds the hour slowly.

But there are two things here that are portents, that sound, amid this flourish of life, a note of self-consciousness. One is an antique stall set a little apart from the others, hung about with engravings, passionate and dim. It has old silvers, brasses, coppers, and veined and pictured china, and wineglasses with spirals in their stems. There are books, too; tattered volumes of religious treatises by eighteenth-century clergymen, tucked in among Victorian school prizes and mirrors of the times. Sometimes there are choice flat volumes from ancestral libraries – classics usually, their leather bindings laced with gilt patterns, looking like inscribed golden bricks dug from ancient tombs. Here people linger. Often it is just a person in search of an Ethel Dell or a book on horses, but sometimes it is a more insidious type that looks at the undersides of china and brings out a magnifying-glass to the engravings.

The other portent is an 'olde' tea-shop. It succeeds, one hopes, in spite of the 'olde'. It has black oak beams awry, cream-washed walls hung with little windy autumnal impressions of Versailles. Blue and yellow check curtains hang half-way up the window. Between curtains and window are glass shelves with iced cakes on them, so dainty and pure, one feels. The girls who serve wear no uniforms; one suspects they are 'superior'.

Now, these things are contrary to the settled dispositions of the countryman. He likes wallpaper on the wall; he likes irregular beams well wrapped up out of sight; he likes a carpet on the floor, not oilcloth imitating wood; he likes large pictures that you do not have to peer at, and for frames he is not afraid of plush; he likes lace curtains that begin at the top and go the whole way; and he likes currant cakes with nuts on. And he likes a serving-woman to look like a serving-woman. Yet this place succeeds. As a symptom it is dangerous, for it is patronised by the younger folk. The older men, what have they to do with four o'clock tea?

I met Jim Crawley, who asked me how I was getting on, how I liked farming. He scanned me with his bright eyes.

'We need new methods. I keep on thinking something ought to be done.' He became suddenly diffident. 'You may think it silly of me, eh? I've not your education, but I'm interested in – ideas, if you see what I mean.' He became still more hesitant. 'There's a Debating Society here; I am going to-night. I don't know if it would interest you at all?'

It ended by my staying with him to attend the debate, Mr and Mrs Colville going home alone. The debate was not till eight o'clock, so we went to the cinema first. There was a war film showing, an affair of restaurants and champagne in contrast with grim hours at the front. But we had to leave in the middle, which was a wrench, as it had become of deep importance that I should know what happened next, the villain having just escaped in an aeroplane enemywards with secret documents, and such a man surely could not be allowed to prevail.

But the strains of martial music died, and we were walking down the dark street to the sound of our own footsteps. In a large room a few people were huddled together. The subject was whether men of science or of imagination had contributed most to the cause of progress. A lady with a metallic voice seized upon the great thinkers in turn, held them up like laboratory specimens for disdainful examination, and cast them squirming, as it were, upon the table before her. I was dazed by such slaughter of great minds. A clergyman attempted to reply. In vain; the lady's tin voice echoed and echoed long after she had finished speaking. The very electric lights, cold-shaded, were against the man of God. Imagination, forsooth! Poetising! Progress!

Jim Crawley leaned forward, brilliant-eyed, in an agony of comprehension.

As we walked away to his car he said, 'If I had had more education . . .'

A week later, at his invitation, I went to tea with him, and he showed me round his farm. In lanes and odd corners stood rusty monuments to his ideas, his 'new methods' – machines for simplified cable ploughing, for stacking sheaves, for drilling root-seeds. Each of these, sinking slant-wise into the earth, had once been an enthusiasm, a fever in the brain. But his mind was not limited to these tangibles, but voyaged into agricultural polity, economics, social reform even. His farm overlooked an immense vista of country; to stand on his lawn was to seem to be on the top of the world. There he walked to and fro and looked down and thought and puzzled; while his wife bit the cotton with which she had been sewing as she wrestled with the more immediate problem of household expenditure, and called him in to tea for the third time.

Mr Colville said, 'If Jim would content himself with seeing after his farm, that's plenty for him to do, without meddling among things that don't concern him.' His brother George sat in his valley farm where he could see no more than a field ahead, and said nothing. Perhaps, had they changed farms . . . Did not Jim, I wondered, with his disposition, suffer from too wide a view?

In May, trefoil and clover seed was drilled in the corn on those fields where Mr Colville had elected to set it. In this matter Bob the horsekeeper's memory was consulted. For, by a law of nature, clover will grow on the same field only after an interval of eight years. So Mr Colville said to Bob, 'I thought of setting Shinns Field with clover. Has there been any on there lately?' And Bob, after a minute's cogitation, answered, 'The last time Shinns Field was clover was the year them three stacks of Mr Crawley's up Red Dock Lane was burnt down; that's ten years ago.' And it was so, as an old account-book showed.

So the young corn in these fields, just recovering from the first harrowing, was again harassed by the drill tearing through it, depositing the minute clover seed in the earth, and by the harrows covering it in, and trampled by horses and men. But no harm was done to it. The horse-hoe was put through the corn where no clover seed was set. This was a machine with a number of pointed shares on it, set a drill-row apart. A man led the horse, another held the steerage handles behind. If the hoes were not held exactly between the drill-rows the machine cut nine rows of corn at the same moment. It required concentration.

The wheat was harrowed and rolled and harrowed again, which made it sturdier, so that the plant, instead of shooting upwards, branched and spread about the ground. As I watched these operations the wheat-plants seemed agriculture's counterpart, in the line of the modern poem, to 'the sturdy, unkillable children of the very poor.'

Now swishing tails and shirt-sleeves were a sign of summer in the fields. Teams of men, eight abreast, hoed rhythmically through the corn with hand-hoes. I admired their strong and easy motion, and took a hoe and placed myself by their side. Again I found that their leisured look masked speed, and was soon perspiring, close-bowed to the ground, to keep up with them. They were as trained oarsmen to one who, vexed into twice the exertion, yet loses the race.

The fields were busy as never since autumn. Over all the valley the hoe was urgent. It was repulsing an attack that never wearied. Hardly had the hoers, one regiment of thistles being cut down, turned their backs to defend another field, than a second regiment was standing there, thick as the first.

The horses no longer lay in the yards at night, but were turned into the meadows to graze after their work. As soon as their harness was off them they trotted one after the other towards the meadow gate, and, when inside, galloped round and kicked up their heels, so that the ground thundered, before settling down to feed. The bullocks, too, were turned out, and gazed about them strangely after their long confinement, and ran hither and thither; then, having explored the limits of their new domain, stooped their heads to the grass.

One day in June, Mr Maglin came to tea at Farley Hall, and afterwards, as we walked through the meadow where the Suffolk horses were, asked, 'And do you hunt on these?'

'No,' said Mr Colville, with a private smile, 'not on these.'

I was pleased to find that I now knew not the least, but the least but one, in Benfield about agriculture. I was able to smile with Mr Colville over a stranger's ignorance; it was a great moment. The question was just the kind that I had asked at first. I was at least beyond that, though still unable to be an intelligent companion to Mr Colville. But he had a kind manner of gently setting right my little slips, and conversed with me as with one who knew a great deal more than I did.

Bob, I learned, had received a visit from Mr Maglin, too. In the old horsekeeper's words, 'I was a-sittin' havin' my tea within doors when my son Alf comes runnin' in from the garden. "Here comes the bloody parson," he says, and pops off through the back door. So in comes the parson, and he says, "Good evening," and I says, "Good evening, sir," and just sit where I was a-lookin' at him. I wasn't goin' to be disturbed from my tea for he. I shouldn't mind his job. He don't do only one day's work a week, and the rest of the time watches other people workin'.'

That, I am afraid, was the general rustic opinion of the clergyman's function.

Mr Maglin himself told me that, at one cottage where he called, the woman half-opened the door and said, 'Not to-day, thank you,' as though he were the grocer.

Now the whole valley became green, so that, had I passed here before I knew anything of agriculture, I might have imagined it all rich grassland; only an occasional fallow remained of its deep brown winter hue. But actually the corn was of a green much more vivid than grass, and trembled in the light winds, bearing alternate sun and shadow, so that the fields really did seem to 'laugh and sing'. When motoring, Mr Colville would exclaim, 'That looks a strong bit of wheat,' or 'That barley shows well.' At first it was a mystery to me how he could discriminate at a glance between one kind of corn and another at that stage of growth, but after a while subtle differences showed themselves to my eyes. Wheat had a deeper green; barley a twisting blade that gave it a hazy look; oats had a blue, broad blade.

Then the beans blossomed and made the air fragrant about them, and the clover-fields also. The valley now became clothed as with diverse carpets – red clover, white clover, the yellow of mustard (with a faint scent of its own) and trefoil, the silver blue of beans, and occasionally the wine-glow of a field of trefolium.

In June I went with Mr Colville to an agricultural show which took place in a park near a certain garrison town. A city of pavilions was pitched among the trees, and its flags and pennons were seen from afar.

The day promised to be hot. Although Mr Colville and

I arrived early, streams of cars and people were already converging at the gates. Strings of pennons had been stretched across the streets of tents, and we walked beneath their fluttering colours till we came to the grand ring, a space of wide circumference, the heart of the show. Beside it was the bandstand, where a military band was playing Gilbert and Sullivan music. The red coats of the bandsmen showed bravely against the prevailing green and white of the surroundings, and the sun turned the edges of their trumpets to flame.

The Gilbert and Sullivan operas are somehow just the music for such sunny festivities; garden-party music, jolly old gentleman music; music that carries on at a comfortable jog-trot and keeps pace with pleased idle meanderings; uninsistent, but there, should you care to listen to it. There were seats round the bandstand, many of them already occupied. Said Mr Colville, 'There are some people, first thing they do, get round the band at a show like this, and there they sit all day.' I noticed that it was indeed a relapsed, dreamy-eyed type of person that sat there in waxwork attitudes and looked like sitting there all day.

In a corner of the show, farm machinery reared itself like primitive artillery against a bastion of trees. We went to inspect this section, as it was not yet time for the horses to be paraded round the ring. Small oil-engines coughed and spluttered here, while the flywheels of large traction-engines revolved slowly with the faintest hissing from the engine, and their drivers clambered about them with oily rags. There were threshing-drums, binders, elevators, wagons, tumbrils, painted boldly red and blue. Mr Colville noted improvements here and there in details, was nearly persuaded into buying a tractor, but moved away without finally committing himself, even though he had knocked something off the list price, saying, 'I'll think it over and let you know.'

As we returned towards the ring we paused at the butter-making competition. Here, beneath an awning roof, spick and span maidens were turning the handles of churns or lifting off the lids and looking inside. A cool smell floated out to us from there. Though they worked hard, they contrived somehow to appear cool, and, despite exertion and the fashion of the day, they were rounded in face and figure. Their cheeks were rosy and their bare arms comely and vigorous.

Now we return to the ring. The music languishes and surges lazily. The flags set round the ring on crimson-bound staffs swoon and rally, unfolding continually like scrolls. The boughs of trees lift and fall, sending cataracts of shadows across the roofs of the pavilions. The heavy horses are being paraded. The Suffolks come first, plump and glossy. Sometimes they break into a tense, slow trot, as though to ease an overflow of strength. Then they hardly seem to touch the ground, like fabled creatures working an aerial treadmill for the gods.

After them come the Shire horses, ponderous living machinery, magnificent and ungainly. The hair spreading about their hoofs gives their legs a tree-trunk sturdiness. Their manes and tails are plaited and beribboned, and they wear halters of red or yellow leather studded with brass that flashes starrily when they toss their heads. A man leads each horse, twitching the rein occasionally. There are old men walking with rolling rustic unconcern and younger ones with traces of army bearing, whose unnatural sternness of expression marks the importance of the day for them.

Now a prize-winner passes, a rosette upon his temple, and a rumble of applause goes round the ring.

Now come mares with foals whinnying and prancing at their sides, now yearlings in the gawkiness of youth, but giving promise of future greatness.

Still they come, a lumbering armada of horses, approaching from beyond the dark masses of the people opposite, their heads nodding against a white background of tents as they walk. The band plays them all in, seems to play also those gay white clouds across the sky.

At length the whole ring is full. The horses are halted in a vast regiment facing the grand stand, some pawing the ground, others with feet well spread, immovable as rocks. With deeply arched necks and shining flanks and ebony hoofs, they are like some old peace-offering between kings; there is a munificence that is Arabian here in the heat and fierce light.

The next function was a public luncheon, which Mr Colville and I attended. It took place in a large pavilion, and was crowded. At the chief table sat the president of the show, a few lords and parliamentary notables, and others of importance. Waiters attended that table, waitresses the others. There hardly seemed enough waitresses. A plate of cold salmon – that fish indispensable to summer festivities – waited at every place, but after that an interval elapsed before the arrival of the cold beef. I was thirsty particularly, and the slightness of the possibility of obtaining a drink seemed to increase my thirst. Suddenly, as by divine ordinance, a tankard descended beside me and a voice asked, 'You said ale?' I hadn't, as I didn't think it would have been of the slightest use, but accepted the favour eagerly, while somebody farther down the table gesticulated furiously at the waitress. How long he had been waiting and imploring for that tankard I dared not guess. But I buried my face in it.

The formality of toasting all who should be toasted was gone through, but Mr Colville was impatient, desiring to hear Captain P—, our Member of Parliament.

'A rare good speaker he is; understands what he is talking about.'

He made his speech, very brisk and to the point after the careful eulogies of the others, and was applauded. I noticed Jim Crawley at another table, listening eagerly and looking as though he would have liked to say something too. After the speech, he turned and entered into ardent discussion with his neighbour, and I saw his hand steal to the pocket where he kept his pamphlets.

After lunch, we returned to the ring and took seats on the stand. The ladies' hunters were about to be judged. The ladies, in riding-costumes, were being mounted by their grooms. They then walked their horses to and fro till they might enter the ring, whence a caravan of veritable bulls of Bashan was winding slowly away. A big chestnut hunter reared suddenly among the crowd, startled by a *fortissimo* passage from the band. He presented a momentary spectacle, beautiful and awful. The rider was perched untroubled, as he plunged. The crowd turned a few heads, shifted uneasily. The music returned to its lazing tone, and the horse was calmed.

The hunters are admitted to the ring. They walk round, trot, canter, gallop. The chestnut hunter is getting out of hand. 'If she don't take care,' says Mr Colville, 'he'll slip down with her at the corners.' He leans dangerously as he goes round, his hoofs pouncing at the ground, which is hard and slippery. Winged and white, he would be Pegasus. His flowing mane is a vision of wild autumn.

The hunters are halted and lined up. The two judges, Lady This and the Honourable Mrs That, stroll up and down the line, pause, observe, deliberate, making little gestures with their riding-crops. They mount each horse in turn, ride round in leisurely fashion. They sit their horses well, with that nonchalant grace that is their heritage.

'That big chestnut is the winner,' says a knowing spectator. 'I can see that from here.'

Doubly beautiful as Lady This and the Honourable Mrs That appear on horseback, the crowd begins to feel that it is possible to have too much of them. Speculation as to the next event – something exciting by the military – is making it restless.

'This isn't a mannequin parade,' grumbles one.

The rosettes are affixed at last, half an hour overdue. The chestnut takes first prize.

'There, what did I tell you?' cries the knowing one. 'I picked him out from here. Talk about women knowing their own minds! If men had been judging, it would have been settled in half the time.'

'At least they were thorough,' replies his wife, defending her sex.

The military dash in with a fine ardour. There are a dozen of them, and their horses are exactly alike. They leap six hurdles in line, taking off their tunics as they do so. Then they leap them again, putting on their tunics. They remove their stirrups as they gallop round; they undo the girths and take their saddles from under them. Then they jump again, hurdle after hurdle, with saddles held high in one arm and stirrup-leathers in the other.

The crowd becomes vociferous.

'And yet,' says Mr Colville, 'it's a funny thing, if these chaps ride in a point-to-point, half of them fall at the first fence. I saw an NCOs' race at the garrison steeplechases. They all went like devils at the first jump, and those that didn't fall, why, dash me if they didn't go galloping clean off the course altogether. People hollered to them, but, bless you, they didn't hear. They enjoyed themselves, that was one thing.'

An old staid farmer near says, 'A little of this trick riding is all right; it draws the people. But an agricultural show is an agricultural show, and should be kept as such. That's my opinion.'

After we left the ring, we went the round of the tents and stands. Every man who supplied an agricultural need – seeds, implements, manures, sacks, physic – had pitched a tent in the showground. Here they treated their customers to drinks and gossip, and enquired, 'Anything you may be needing?' By many of them Mr Colville was well known, and time and again he would be detained by the arm. 'Now, come in and have a little something, Mr Colville; please do.' In the warm twilight within, men stood talking with red or amber-coloured drinks in their hands, and the agent and his lieutenant went round being pleasant to everybody. In one tent – that of a large firm of feeding stuff manufac- turers, Charlwood & Co – a waiter dispensed the drinks, looking like an old-fashioned butler.

'I knew old Charlwood – he's dead now – regular old toff. Always would have things done properly. Why, before the war he used to give his old customers a champagne lunch,' Mr Colville said.

We stood in the tent of a manufacturer of horse-cures (I was beginning to realise I had had enough drink), sipping sherry while a man with an order-book in one hand flourished a bottle at Mr Colville.

'The finest thing for cuts and bruises,' he said; 'used by all the leading hunts.' It contained a blue-green liquid. 'Or can I send you some gripe drinks?'

'I've still got some left of those you sent before,' said Mr Colville.

'Some blood salts, then? Indispensable this hot weather, you know.' He stands, pencil poised, grows confidential. 'Now, look here, sir, I'll put you down for just half a dozen bottles.'

'I'll see what I want and write to you.'

'No, you'll forget, sir. There's no time like the present.' He takes up another bottle containing a red liquid. 'Half a dozen of these, then.'

At that moment his partner enters, and, taking in all at a glance, cries, 'Yes, of course Mr Colville wants them.'

Mr Colville expostulates, laughing.

'Now, sir.'

'Put it down. Of course he wants them,' says his colleague.

'But I don't even know what those are for, anyway,' Mr Colville interposes. The man, his pencil now busy, soon banishes that objection. 'Full directions on the bottle.'

At this moment a man in the congenial stage of drunkenness enters. He is well dressed in a grey suit and bowler hat. He holds up further conversation, addressing the assembly with weak gestures.

'Now I'm goin' talk for a minute. Mus' jus' ask you this riddle: Why are Bass's breweries like the wells of Palestine? Now think it over.' Holding up his hand to the man with the order-book, 'I know you want to talk, but I'm goin' talk instead with your permission. Just think of this riddle: Why are Bass's breweries like the wells of Palestine? Of course, I should prefer to drink what comes from Bass's breweries – vastly – va-astly – but that's *en passant*.' Wagging his forefinger, 'Now, what I want to ask you is this little riddle . . .'

Everybody gives it up. He leans closer; his finger becomes

portentous. 'Because he brews drink in them. Simple, isn't it?' He turns and lounges away, but pauses at the entrance. 'Do you know, I have a dog. Yes, and I have a cook. The dog takes the seats out of the tramps' trousers and the cook sews them in again. Good-bye.'

In every tent a drink was put into my hands, usually different from the one before. I sipped, looked round me, listened. Into many pavilions we were persuaded: such friendly terms existed between Mr Colville and the merchants that they would none of them take a refusal.

Before long it dawned on me that the show was even better than I had realised: indeed, it was the pride of England. I lost all sense of strangeness in my surroundings. It seemed I had become a real agriculturist at last, for I felt pleased and familiar with everything about me. I admired the old County gentlemen with their neat check ties, their yellow gloves turned back at the wrists. I would grow old like that.

I found I was at heart a rigid Tory. Yes, the old things were best. When England ceased to have pleasure in them it would surely be the end of her. This show, for instance; why, it *was* England, her very soul. All that remained of tournaments and the country festivals of old was to be found there. It was the holiday of farmer and labourer alike: the country gentleman's gesture of self-justification, the landed proprietor's answer to Socialists and reformers. For how, I asked myself, should such creatures come to be bred as were to be seen here to-day but by men of wealth and tradition?

Said a man beside me in a certain tent, to all in general but to me in particular, a whisky and soda having brought his approval to the brink of exclamation, 'I don't care what anybody says, this is the best show in the eastern counties.'

He found no contradiction in my eye.

'Always has been, and always will be,' I said, echoing Mr Colville, and sipped my drink sententiously. 'Nobody seems able to run a show like this – everything to time.'

'You're right, no hanging about,' my neighbour agreed. 'A fine class of Suffolks, eh?'

'Even better than last year,' I said, again echoing Mr Colville.

'Did you see the prize-winner?' he asked.

'Ah, a fine stamp of horse, that.' I liked the *cliché*. I added to it. 'Never saw a Suffolk with such bone.'

I tasted for the first time in my agricultural experience a feeling of being master of my matter. Sherry had spirited away that old hampering suspicion that I still knew nothing.

'Are you showing anything here to-day?' my neighbour asked.

I confess that did take the wind out of my sails for a moment. True, I had dressed myself pretty smartly for this occasion, but never dreamed of being taken for an exhibitor.

'Er – no, not to-day – that is to say, this year,' I replied, and sought new sang-froid from my glass.

Emerging from that pavilion, and safe from exposure, I indulged in complacent reflection on the man's remark. No, I wasn't showing anything here to-day. True, I hadn't even a farm. But I should have. Forgotten then were the discon-solate, the rainy days; the days when I had made a fool of myself over some simple thing; forgotten the miry winter dawns. In this place of sunshine and groomed, beribboned cattle, I saw my future clear. It was a vision of natural prosperity that was like a biblical blessing. I saw my fields whitening to harvest: my horses ploughing. Heifers equal to any here stood in my yard, and pedigree sows lay prolific in the pens.

Mr Colville had remarked to me once, 'If you've got

anything extra good, it's bound to sell.' I should have everything good. I should show them, and they would take prizes. They would sell for large sums. My declining days should be spent in a Georgian manor set in a park. The welfare of the village should be my care. I should die honoured and mourned, leaving sons to take my place.

'That's a good patent.' Mr Colville's voice woke me from my dream. He had his eye on a portable fowl-house, with a single swivelling wheel in front. 'You can lock it round sharp as you like, you see.'

I examined it and found it excellent. 'Jolly good idea,' I was about to say, but seeing the salesman at hand, changed it to a critical 'H'm, not bad,' satisfying myself that I had acumen in not showing enthusiasm in his presence.

The salesman took me for a prospective buyer and began enumerating the advantages of the hut. I walked inside, hoping he would turn his attention to Mr Colville. But he followed me in. I was appreciative as grudgingly as I could be, for really I could find nothing to cavil at; it appeared an ideal villa residence for fowls, with every comfort. Panes of glass had been let in, allowing a view of the country from the perch; nest-boxes of decent privacy were provided, and ample scratching accommodation. In a minute or two I began to have an uneasy feeling that the man had already half sold the thing to me. I beat a retreat to Mr Colville, who was examining the roof. In the end the salesman (hardly a psychologist, I think) woke up to the fact that he was the likely buyer and not I. He did indeed buy the hut (but not at list price), for he had promised Mrs Colville one for a birthday present.

Now as we sauntered round the show I observed things with a more personal interest. I had definitely embraced agriculture: was determined to have a farm of my own; and everything I saw I considered in the light of my prospective farming stock. I wished my year's apprenticeship would hurry and be over. Not that I had the least idea whether my father was prepared to buy and stock me a farm. In Chelsea that would sound about as reasonable as a request to equip an expedition to the North Pole, I considered. But to-day was not a day of doubt. Somehow it would be done.

We passed an enclosure of wattle hurdles in which were summer-houses, rabbit-hutches, beehives, dovecotes. I was rather attracted by the dovecotes, and would have lingered, though I felt that as a farmer I ought not to be. Mr Colville strode on; such things did not exist for him.

Yet one of those, I thought, would look pretty on my farm . . .

A woman attended there, dressed in a garb, which seemed to hesitate between male and female, of a kind of art linen which suggested a direct link with Chelsea. I felt she had once painted animals, in a studio, and was now writing a book on *Pigeons for Pleasure and Profit.*

Next, Mr Colville and I visited the livestock. Pigs, so obese that their legs and faces were mere warts upon their general bulk, lay snoring in their pens, as though each breath was to be their last. If they were not regularly exercised they would never be able to get up. We inspected the cattle, Mr Colville finding in favour of the Red Poll as the best all-purpose breed; for, as he said, if one will not breed, or is past breeding, she can always be easily fattened for the butcher, 'whereas these Friesians – well, their bull calves aren't worth having.' We passed some black cattle. 'They are no farmers' cattle – they never appear to "do". I call them gentlemen's cattle – you always seem to see them in parks.'

In the poultry-tent there were cockerels looking like the hats of twenty years ago, masses of feathers, spraying plumes, and in the midst the merest glimpse of beak and eyes. There were white turkeys that would have graced a caliph's garden, and bantams neat as robins, crimson and gold. The sunshine was subdued to an aura through the canvas, which they seemed to herald as a Paradisal dawn, for the noise of their crowing was deafening.

At last we had tea, blessed tea, in the enclosure of a seed merchant. We sat at a bamboo table surrounded by high sample sheaves of corn and some early oats of that season, just pulled, green and seven feet high.

Here I reflected further on that dovecote. I saw it standing near my farmhouse, the white birds fluttering to and fro. It was an appealing vision, but with misgiving in it. It was not the thing itself, but what it stood for in me, that made me pause. I feared (the sherry was wearing off) that I was still far from being the complete farmer. Mr Colville had once remarked at sight of some doves on a house-roof, 'You'd never believe the damage they do; stop up gutterings, pick out the mortar, and muck all over everything. I wouldn't have them about my place.'

I treasured his sayings: his point of view I regarded as law in practical farming; he was such an example of success himself. Could I be a success if I let my mind be beguiled by dovecotes? That was the pretty-pretty touch, the amateur's symbol. It went with tame rabbit breeding, and all those kinds of petty and polite rurality of which the Suffolk yeoman took no account. Even poultry (until recently) he regarded as a feminine pastime.

I had learned enough by now to reject most of the things that constituted the townsman's golden dream. I had found farming most unexpectedly different from that.

I revived my self-confidence with more virile memories of how the local hounds had galloped full cry round the ring, horn sounding, audience hallooing. That had been, perhaps, the most popular event. Of the jumping, and how the riders had seemed glued to their saddles. It had looked simple really. Yes, in time the anxious hiatus I felt when taking a fence would be no more, and I should jump like that. Then there had been a parade of four-in-hands which my Tory self applauded, and a display of trotting-horses, the control of whom seemed as delicate as violin-playing. They had glided round, their legs like flickering shadows, leaning inwards as they took to a curving course, with the true poetry of motion.

By evening the annual fair, pitched close to the show, came into its own, with gleam of spiral brass and florid decoration embodying the yokel's dream of royal furnishings. From twirling panoplies issued music, and golden horses cantered aerially. We left the show and passed through the fair towards our car. The young men looked hot in their stiff collars, shying for coconuts or trying to ring the bell at the top of the pole. Some tried houp-la, or went into the mystic bower of Madame Valerie, the World's Premier Palmist, patronised by Royalty, or strolled bearing greenish-yellow vases, the hard-earned 'valuable prizes' of the evening, while their girls, clad in diaphanous pink and blue, were collapsed upon their arms in aftermaths of mirth.

The first day of the show was nearly over. We were part of a stream of people coming away. Cars hummed. There were handshakes between friends, wavings, final shouted pleasantries. I took a last glance back at the show as we mounted a hill; its flags, variegated as confetti, fluttered an adieu. It seemed like the ghost of some mediaeval Utopia,

this city of white pavilions with its classic beasts and saunter-
ing crowds. Like a ghost in its transience, too; for whoever
returned in a few days' time would find here only a bare
meadow, and larks singing in solitude.

10

Things had now reached their climax of growth. The corn stood high in the fields, green yet, but with emerging ears, and the grass was deep in the meadows left for hay, and shimmered in the breeze. Every corner by wall or barn had its growth of grass and nettles. Nothing was yet cut down, but blades were being prepared. Scythes were brought from dusty retirement and weighed in the hands. No golfer is more exacting over the balance of his clubs than the countryman over the set of his scythe. Groups of two or three would be seen taking a scythe in turn by the handles, standing in the mowing position and pronouncing on the hang of it.

Bob's scythe-blade was worn as thin almost as the carving-knives of the Three Tuns Inn at Stambury. 'A rare blade that is,' he said. 'Some of these you get nowadays won't keep the edge on 'em not for a minute hardly: you wholly have to keep rub, rub, rub.'

It had been set on a new handle, and Bob was trying how it suited his reach and swing. It is difficult to set a scythe well; it is a blacksmith's job, after which niceties of adjustment are made by the owner with leather pads and iron wedges. The whole matter is a harmony of curves and angles – the sinuous long handle (snath), the angle of the encompassing blade to that, and the positions of the two short handles whereby one holds it, on the long handle.

Sainfoin was mown for the horses, as the summer of 1921 was memorable for heat and drought, and already the grazing-meadows were becoming bare. Green beans were mown for the pigs. The grass machines were brought out and oiled and adjusted, their knives sharpened and fitted with new blades where needed. It was time to cut the hay.

The scythe has the traditional reaping motion, but the modern grass machine cuts on the scissors principle. A row of triangular blades on a stem run between sharp guards, to and fro very swiftly, which rips the grass off as fast as the horses walk. The knife of a grass-mower works more swiftly than that of a corn-reaper, as the grass is much thicker and tougher, being in mass, and only speed prevents the knife from choking. In regard to this Bob spoke aptly to me, telling me of an attempt he once made to cut flax with a reaper and binder.

'It were too thick,' he said; 'the knife didn't "multiply" fast enough.' The word caused me to comprehend exactly.

Now there are some farmers who do not think about grass-cutting until the day they decide to start 'haysel'. They find then that the machine needs a new part, or a new knife, and so are delayed. Mr Colville always had his machines examined a fortnight before he needed them, and in the case of his reapers and binders a month. His bugbear was delay. In contrast to King Ethelred, his title might have been 'Colville the never-caught-napping'. He always told me that a good farmer has to farm looking seven years ahead in order to keep his crops justly proportioned with the due amount of fallow.

There are general rules and advisabilities within which the farmer's judgment has play. Wheat after beans, oats after wheat or barley, then clover, trefoil, or roots. Wheat after clover, too; but not so advisedly after a fallow where the ground is loose. Plough shallow for wheat, etc. But influencing this there is the quality of the land, for one field varies from another surprisingly, even on five hundred acres. A light and a heavy field sometimes lie side by side.

The farmer, too, must be a lightning organiser. Fifteen minutes' rainfall may alter the whole scheme of work – it will stop the rolling of land, as the earth will clog on the roller; it will stop horse-hoeing in corn; but it may be still possible to harrow a field where the corn is not yet showing, or hoe between the ridges of the root crop. Therefore he has to direct men and horses to different jobs with the least possible delay.

The farmer has a certain number of horses. Now, different implements need one, two, three or four horses. The jobs to be done are of varying urgency. One, two, or three men are needed to handle the different implements, so the farmer must arrange to be doing the things that are of greatest moment in a way that employs all the horses and men. To have a horse standing in the stable on a fine day implies mismanagement, or, for that matter, a man doing a job that he could do equally well if it rained. The farmer's brain must be as elastic as the weather.

Say you possess a farm of two hundred acres and keep six horses. You send one horse-hoeing, three drilling barley, and two harrowing. Just as you have got them all off and foreseen a good day's work, the boy comes and tells you that he is out of pig-meal and needs a horse to fetch some from the mill. Probably a man who was doing an unimportant job the afternoon before could have fetched some meal with a horse not employed then. It is the elimination of situations such as this that makes a successful farmer. All this I was to learn in time.

Mr Colville was a first-class organiser. He had a way of marching out in the morning and giving orders bustlingly, hardly stopping in his stride, which lent an air of urgency to the occasion and made the man bestir himself. In addition to seeing seven years ahead, he had a faculty of immediate observation that made me feel a Johnny-head-in-air. A whipple-tree or a harrow buried in corn he would note, and stand up against the hedge, and have carted home. He would notice boughs likely to impede wagons at harvest, and send a man to lop them so that they did not cause delay at a pressing time. A cast shoe he would pick up and examine, saying, 'Nearly a new shoe,' and give it to Bob to have put on again when next the horse to whom it belonged went to the blacksmith.

July was very hot. The grass machines hummed in the meadows, and as an undertone there was a monotonous zip-zip as a man in each field sharpened a spare knife with a file, tying it on to the top bar of the gate for the purpose if he had not a special stool. The farm worker is an adept at substitutes, or at patching things up and making them go with string, wire, and bits of iron.

Bob, a few acres being cut, gazed at the first swathes already shrinking in the sun.

'This'll have to be put on the cock to-morrow or it'll be all parched up to tinder,' he said, bearing out the calendar writer's advice in the farm account-book.

Grey moths flew out of the grass as it was cut, and pollen glorified our boots. When the sun had withered it, it was raked into rows and cocked. There is art even in making a haycock. It is easy enough to bundle hay into a heap, but I found that was not to the point. One must build it a forkful at a time, shaking the wads so that it all lies lightly and the air can draw through the cock.

'There's more hay spoilt in a dry time than in a wet,' Mr Colville said to me. He meant, not that the goodness was parched out of it, but that farmers, being over-anxious and fearing such fine weather could not last, cut it before it was really fit, and the stack heated.

If a stack heats, it can, if taken in time, be turned over, i.e. rebuilt in another place. It is often so hot that the men can hardly stand and work on it; but this lets the heat out. If it is beyond this point of heat it is fatal to open it to the air, as it immediately catches fire, and probably catches other stacks or buildings. Many an anxious week some too headstrong farmers spend watching a stack smoulder and smoulder, wondering if it is going to burst into flames. Even if it does not, it is found to be all charred inside and black, like ashes.

About the time we were carting the hay the ponds on the farm dried up altogether, and it was now necessary to cart water from a well a mile and half away for all the stock. Three times a day, and twice on Sundays, Jack went to and fro with the water-cart.

'Never knew such a time in my life,' said Mr Colville; but he was not dismayed. 'There's an old saying that it pays heavy-land farmers to cart water.'

This meant that in a dry summer the crops on the heavy land were so good that they quite outweighed the inconvenience and expense of water famine. So, while the light-land farmers moaned together in groups in the market over crops six inches high, the heavy-land farmers strutted about with their hands in their breeches pockets saying, 'Aha! this is the weather for us.'

The trefoil had bloomed and seeded. It was very difficult to gather without loss, as the seed only clung round the stems and in the heat of the day a shake would scatter it. We rose one morning at three o'clock to turn it while it was still moist with dew and the seed less inclined to fall.

One of the farthest fields was of white clover. For some

time this had been a white sheet of blossom in the distance; then the pure white grew soiled, and faded to brown. A friend, meeting Mr Colville in the market, said, 'I reckon you've got a small fortune in that white clover seed; I looked at it as I was passing in the road.' And that evening Mr Colville said to me, 'Perhaps I have. We'll go and have a look.'

I wondered at his tone, calm almost to indifference, with a possible heap of money waiting in the form of valuable clover seed in the field afar. But I learnt that, although he organised in advance, he never counted on anything before it was his, and clover seed in the field was even less certain than chickens before they are hatched. So much depended on the season that he never congratulated himself till it was safely under thatch. In any case, white clover seed is always regarded as heaven-sent. Every year the farmer sets a piece of white clover, and once in twenty years he gets a crop of seed safely harvested.

We stood in the field and rubbed out the heads, between thumb and palm, blew away the chaff, and pale golden seeds remained in our hands.

'There's five hundred pounds' worth here,' said Mr Colville, 'and if we get a few showers after it's cut it won't be worth anything.'

But it seemed as though the sun could never be dimmed now. Day after day dawned clear, still, almost dewless; and the sun sank without the attendant pomp of clouds, and died away in starlit afterglow. It happened that, when the trefoil was ready to cart, Mr Colville's father was not engaged upon carting anything, so he lent his aid at Farley Hall, and all his wagons and half his men came trooping into the field that morning, where we already were with our wagons. Three stacks were built, and the wagons unloaded on both sides of the stacks simultaneously. People passing in the road paused to gaze at such a crowd of men and horses at work on one farm. By evening all was cleared and safely stacked.

One day, when I was in the hayfield, Midden came down from the farm saying that a telegram had come for Mr Colville about the delivery of some wheat, and as he was not at home, would I take it to him? Mr Colville was a member of the local Board of Guardians, and was at present in council 'at the Union'.

'Where is that?' I asked.

'At Enston,' Midden replied.

'How do I get to Enston?'

'You turn to the left at the four-a-lete half-way to Share.'

I set off on my motor-cycle with his instructions in my mind, trusting to find the place without difficulty. I turned to the left at the cross-roads. I looked at the signpost, but it gave me no help, pointing only to a place called Hanardiston two miles along the road. When I had proceeded about two miles beyond, and still found no mention of Enston on the sign-posts dotted about that road of many turnings, I enquired my way and learnt that I had come too far. I had only to retrace my steps and I should find it without difficulty. I went back, carefully noting every turning, passed through Hanardiston and almost to the cross-roads again.

Once more I asked, 'Can you tell me the way to Enston Union?'

'Oh, you must go back and turn to the left in the village there.'

I reached the village again and took the left-hand turning, and continued for another two miles without coming to Enston or any indication of it. 'Well,' thought I, 'everybody seems to know this place quite well, yet it has vanished off the map.'

I asked again. 'Why,' said the labourer, 'you want to go right in the opposite direction to what you're going. You can't miss it. Anybody in Enston will tell you where the Union is.'

Once more I returned, rather hopelessly this time, and stopped and asked at Hanardiston.

'You're in Enston,' said a young woman.

'But I thought this was Hanardiston.'

'So 'tis. It's called Enston for short.'

The Union was indeed down the road indicated, but standing behind trees, so that I had not noticed it, thinking Enston miles ahead. I was relieved, after these John Gilpin exploits, at last to deliver up my telegram.

So shone the sun that hardly had the hay been carted and a few fallows cross-ploughed before the corn harvest was in sight. The crop promised to be exceptional. The wheat ears were long and well filled; each field was a level expanse of them; they were heavy, and swayed pendulously on their slim stalks. On his evening walks Mr Colville would pluck an ear and squeeze the grain in his fingers. At first a milky juice oozed forth, but later this became tough, a fibre, and a tinge of gold was seen upon the grain. Then Mr Colville said, 'It won't be long now before it's fit to cut; you'll see, harvest will be on to us all of a sudden, such weather as we are having.'

The bearded barley ears showed also above the leaves, and gave those fields a hazy look. The oat stalk, however, spread its ear in a fountain shape, and a delicate thing it was, with the long grains drooping from branching tendrils. The bean-leaves were growing black and beginning to fall, and the beans becoming, as they said, 'corny', and those fed to the pigs were no longer green food, but strong nourishment, heating and thirst-begetting, so that Mr Colville would say to Jack, 'Mind them pigs have plenty of water always,' and order him to pull some mangolds and throw to them also.

Our farming walk after tea was a daily function in summer. Mr Colville liked to look round after the men had gone and the fields lay quiet, as he could think better then, he said.

We observed young game about the hedgerows. A leveret would go bounding away from us across the clover hay, the retriever Donald eyeing it all the way, his habit of obedience overcoming, at his master's loud 'No!' the natural instinct to pursue. On one occasion, earlier in the summer, we were walking along a cart-path beside a field of roots when I was amazed to see a partridge attack the dog, jumping up at him, fluttering its wings, and crying. It had some young ones near, and was prepared to bar the way to the end. The dog could have snapped it up in his jaws with ease, but he stopped, baffled by the unexpectedness of the assault, then turned and made a careful detour, like a rustic avoiding a scolding wife. I had seen hens with chicks make for him; he was chary of them when thus accompanied, but I hardly believed a partridge would be equal to it.

Our walk usually inclined towards the wood. Mr Colville had had a rustic seat made in a clearing, and here he liked to rest perfectly still, watching the rabbits come round and the pigeons settle into the trees above. The seat commanded a vista down a ride-way, and sometimes a fox passed across at quite close quarters. The sight of a fox to Mr Colville was like a cocktail: it stimulated him for an hour or more, and he told of it to all he met. A glimpse of cubs was the heaven of his eyes. One Sunday, Horace Colville told us where such might be had; there was a certain sandpit (this was whispered news: a general curiosity would drive them away) where evidences at the mouth of a hole of life within had at last been proved by the creatures peeping forth. There was a hedge, too, at some distance, commanding that spot and offering cover. Here, the next evening and for several evenings when the wind was not blowing scent of us to the lair, we set ourselves in ambush in vain. But on the fifth evening there they were, three cubs playing by the hole and the vixen sitting near, intensely watchful. They stood up and hugged one another, and rolled over in mock combat. We scanned them with field-glasses. 'Pretty as paint,' Mr Colville whispered excitedly. Then the dog fox made his appearance, coming over a rise with a dead chicken. Whose? Mr Colville cared not, and wouldn't have robbed him of it for worlds. The cubs bounded to meet their sire, and ran alongside jumping up at him.

As we walked home, Mr Colville stopped at a hollow tree and said, 'We ran a fox into that once, and they lit a fire in it and tried to smoke him out.' Then he pointed to a small hole near the top. 'But he stuck his head out of that hole into the clear air and stayed looking at us as comfortable as could be. They had to leave him. I was glad, too, because he'd given us a long run. It may be silly of me, but I hate to see the fox killed when he's given us a good run. No more ought they to dig him out of an earth they've run him to. People write to the papers about it sometimes. But you see,' he confided, 'if they didn't, then these little farmers would begin to grumble. They'd say, "It's all very well, you run a fox to earth on our land, then leave him there to eat our chickens!"'

Sometimes we would meet Bob (whose cottage adjoined the farm) out surveying the prospect, and he would accompany us for a way. As horsekeeper he had a keen eye for a wasps' nest, and one evening we found him plugging one with a paraffin-soaked rag.

'There's nothing will make horses bolt quicker,' Mr Colville said to me.

Said Bob, 'These oats wholly begin to gape in the middle of the day.' He meant that the husks which enclosed the grain parted in the heat of the sun and the black oat peeped out, a sign of ripeness.

The oats were cut first, as the straw is coarse and the sap takes a long time to dry up. Oats must remain stooked for over a fortnight before being carted – or, as Mr Colville said, 'must see three Sundays in the field.' Next the wheat was cut, the first while almost green, because, Mr Colville told me, if we waited till it was all ripe in a year such as this we would not be able to cope with it before it began to fall out from the ears.

We were now officially 'in harvest', but it was not attended with the jovial ceremonial of the past. The war seemed definitely to have cut away what remained of old custom. Even the bargaining between master and men as to the harvest wage was superseded by the Agricultural Wages Board, with its tabulations of harvest bonus per man per so many hours' work, hung in all the post-offices. The picturesque election of a lord of the harvest – one who should be their chief among the men – was also no more. The price of beer (a really unkind cut, this) and the restrictions upon home brewing had done away with the old bacchic welcome to Ceres in her bounty. It had been like this, Mr Colville said.

A farmer in those days never expected any work of his men on the first day of harvest. He sent them to mow round the first field of corn ready to admit the self-binder.

They took with them scythes and a cask of beer. The lord of the harvest wielded the first scythe, and the only one to be wielded that day. As he mowed, the others tied the corn into sheaves, and when there were enough for a stook they stooked them and called a halt. By that sign harvest was begun. They then tapped the cask and drank to it, and somebody started up with a song. They continued drinking and carousing in the corn for the rest of the day. But on the next day they really set to work.

Appertaining to this, there was a gap in the hedge at Farley Hall which put those who passed it in mind of a certain Walter Pettifer – a strange memorial, I thought, till I knew the story. As the inauguration day of a certain harvest drew to its close the harvesters rose from their roystering and made unsteadily homeward. But Walter Pettifer was left behind, forgotten. He lay in the ditch, drunk beyond rising unaided. At intervals through the night he grasped at the hedge. But instead of pulling himself up, he pulled the hedge out, being a heavy man, root and all, and by morning lay beneath a canopy of briar. Walter lies now in a battleship at the bottom of the North Sea, but a gap in a Suffolk hedge remembers him.

But those days, and those of the 'trooped keg and friendly cooling horn', are done – the days of low wages and free harvest ale. To-day, no doubt, brings its own advantages. 'But,' say the farmers of Benfield, 'although the men receive three times the wages, they aren't half as content. Then they used to work longer, but more happily and quickly. Why?' they ask one another. Where there is hard work and beer there is apt to be good cheer, and I have found in an evening pint in the harvest field that which really seemed to justify God's way to man. For, as a man remarked to me, 'Sixpence isn't the same as a pint of beer when you're needing it.'

That was a chance acquaintance, a wagoner, on the subject of the young labourer of to-day, and his infrequent patronage of the inn. One farmer, as a gesture of appreciation to his men of an urgent job well done, bade them call at the inn on their way home and drink a pint on his score. Whereupon one said, 'If it's all the same to you, master, I'd rather have the sixpence.'

'Bah!' The wagoner spat at the memory.

We slipped into the lengthened harvest working-days. Two new meals were introduced into the routine. One, a snack, was called 'elevenses', though it took place nearer twelve. The men paused by their horses for fifteen minutes and ate a mouthful of bread and cheese, took a swig of cold tea, and smoked. The other was 'fourses', which took place at 5 p.m. – a meal of half an hour. Wives and daughters used to bring this to the men in baskets or wrapped in cloths, and lingered sometimes among them as they worked on, the daughters notably with seemingly nonchalant glances towards the younger men, some of whom bantered, while others became silent and shy.

Often, if we were carting, Mr Colville would send out beer to the men at seven. 'A pint of beer about seven makes a wonderful difference to a man what's been working all day,' said Bob as he drained the mug. A new vivacity was noticeable even at the first glimpse of the stone jar in the offing. I am sure the evening pint was good business for Mr Colville, as well as hospitality.

There had been tennis-parties throughout the summer. All the young married farmers of the district had tennis lawns. We gave parties at Farley Hall, and then were invited by the others in turn. Mr Colville played a good, hard-hitting game; the tennis-court seemed to restore to him the fire of his youth. But there was a curious convention among the Colvilles – a Victorian remnant again – that it was unchivalrous to serve a swift ball to the ladies. In a men's set the game waxed hot and exciting, but a mixed double was more of a polite exercise. One sent a gentle lob to the lady, who responded with a like return, but when the point was made and it was her masculine partner who faced one, a demon serve was quite in order. I did not realise this at first, and sent my fair opponent a scorcher. She said just 'Oh!' and there was a heavy silence among the others. I soon learned, and did not offend again.

But the tennis-parties were over for a time; all such things halted at harvest eve. It was difficult even to spare anyone to mow the lawn, and sometimes Mr Colville and I used to do it by turns after supper.

Never had there been such weather, Mr Colville assured me. I had purchased drill shorts and breeches; by the end of the summer the sun had rotted them. The farmer saw little of his friends now, each staying on his farm in his shirt-sleeves among his men, day after day. There was no hesitation, no wondering, 'Is this fit to cart?' It was. But, though such weather made swift work of harvest, it imposed a considerable strain on men and horses, for a showery day or two here and there comes not amiss as a respite, and can be counted on in a usual year.

Stooks began to stand in the fields in place of level seas of corn. The whir of self-binders droned in the bright, breathless air like giant grasshoppers, and tractors hummed. There, and there, and there, one saw them in the valley vista trailing round diminishing patches of corn that still retained the contours of the fields. There was no sky save at morning and evening, only a pale, misty vacuity above.

Now, Mr Colville, in order to take full advantage of the weather, had bought an extra-large binder with a seven-foot cut, and hired a tractor and driver to cut his corn with it, thus leaving the horses free for carting. I was put in charge of this binder, immaculate in blue paint and as intricate in its workings as a woman's mind. Before its arrival I had followed Bob round and round the oat-field as he drove one of the old ones. I puzzled over its chains and rollers and packers, its levers and shafts all working in and around and about one another, not to mention the needle and knotter which tied the sheaf up and cut the string, handing it out in as neat and expeditious a manner as the shop assistant your old hat done up in a parcel when you have bought a new one. It seemed the most illogical machine, the dream of a mad inventor working as it would only in his dream. It seemed to function by a divine chance, dropping sheaf after sheaf as some say day follows day. As complex at least as Nature. But I was interested to observe that Bob was perfectly familiar with every part and its duty, making small adjustments here and there that at first meant nothing to me. This, and other machines, might have been as traditional as the scythe, for the handling of which heredity had prepared them, the labourers so took them for granted, and received them into their life and speech. Indeed, to speak of a man swinging his arms like the sails of a binder was now more apt than the sails of a windmill.

My mind becomes suddenly logical when faced with machinery, and by the time the new binder arrived I had mastered the principle of the thing. I perched upon the binder with a cord in my hand attached to the foot of the man on the tractor; if anything went wrong with the binder, I pulled the cord as a sign for him to stop. With complicated processes going on beneath me I had to keep a sharp look-out. I had heard by chance words spoken about me by Mr Colville to his wife: 'Quick in the uptake', which brought a sudden zest of self-confidence. I was no longer a cipher, then, on the farm (or, even less, a danger, as are the ignorant), but a thing of use. I was anxious to justify his opinion; the urgent spirit of the hour entered into me. Swiftly, when the twine broke, I grovelled under the binder, re-threading it, careless of the tractor exhaust belching in my face; swiftly I freed the choked canvases, that not more than a minute of golden weather might be wasted – for who could tell when it would cease?

The first time I pulled the cord attached to the driver's foot it nearly caused a mishap, for he had made a mistake in tying it to the foot which worked the clutch. As he didn't stop, I continued to pull, and the more I pulled the less able was he to push down the clutch pedal. Knowing nothing of that, I was surprised to see him stretch his leg out behind him as though about to vault from his seat. The cord thus slipped from his foot and he pulled up. After that he tied it to his arm.

On another occasion the coupling broke. I suddenly found the back of the binder tipping high into the air, which so surprised me that the cord slipped from my hand and the tractor went pounding up the field without me. It was a long field. Of course, the man did not hear my shout above the noise of the engine, so there I sat, perched high, and watched him receding.

It was not until he turned at the corner that he realised that the binder was not behind.

We were on a field far from anywhere. It was very hot, especially sitting on a tractor. He had exhausted his bottle of cold tea.

'Is there any water hereabout?'

I looked round. I felt thirsty too. Had there been an inn . . .

'None fit to drink,' I said, 'nearer than the farm.'

He asked, 'Isn't there a pond?'

There happened to be a small pond in some trees, too remote for farm purposes.

'But it's green,' I told him.

He skimmed off the scum and dipped his bottle, then looked at it in the light. He lived in a district badly off for water. 'Why, I've drunk a lot worse water than this at home,' he said, and put the bottle to his lips. He is still alive.

Towards evening it got round that we were likely to finish cutting that piece of corn by nightfall, and children appeared, and the men who had come into the field to start stooking it cut sticks from the hedge and gathered round the last acre yet standing. Occasionally I saw the corn quiver violently, indicating life huddled there in ever more precarious concealment. All of a sudden the rabbits made up their minds, it seemed, to dash for it. They ran in all directions and everybody shouted and gave chase. The rabbits were baulked by the sheaves, which gave the men a chance. The squat Midden, Mr Colville even, took to their heels and lumbered after the creatures bouncing this way and that. Hats flew off. Midden caught his foot in a bramble and fell headlong. It was a sight as unusual as plough-horses galloping. The dog seized a rabbit, and, true to the fable of the reflected bone, dropped it to pursue another, ending, since he was soft-mouthed, with none. Half of them escaped. Mr Colville had the dead ones brought before him and divided them, giving the single men one each and the married ones two.

This was a time of plenty for the birds. Pheasants and partridges were welcome, and the hares, if they gnawed the young roots here and there, were not counted despoilers. But rooks robbed the oats as they stood in the field, crowding upon the stooks and flattening their tops so that, had it rained, the wet would have penetrated them. Nothing is so exasperating to the farmer as the sight of a crowd of them settled on his cornfields. Mr Colville was moved even to take down his gun on a Sunday against them, a thing otherwise undreamed of and illegal. Pigeons plundered the peas also.

The possibility of rain was almost forgotten. Never had harvest progressed so rapidly. Half-finished stacks were allowed to remain uncovered all night, and latterly sheaves were not stooked, but lay flat in the fields as cut. Sometimes I would ask Bob his opinion of the weather, and he would reply 'Rain? It can't rain.' But his tone changed somewhat a day or two afterwards. He looked about him dubiously, but decided, 'It won't rain, not without we get thunder.'

We were carting a large field of barley. I was in the stack-yard on the stack.

'Seems as though they'll get it all on this load,' Bob said, shading his eyes and gazing over the field where minute figures moved. Simmons stacked. I passed the sheaves to him one by one as they came up on the elevator. He did not use a fork but put the sheaves in place with his hands, crouching and pouncing about on the edge of the stack like a monkey. Sometimes for a joke the men would fling sheaves to him much more quickly than he could cope with them.

'Ye'll have me off the stack, blast ye!' he'd swear. He could snap out like a ferret with anger. He was clever beyond most; he could carpenter, stack, thatch, make hurdles, lay a meadow hedge, so he was allowed a temperament. I have never seen a man drive in a five-inch nail truer than he.

Suddenly somebody said, 'Look at the sky.' Instead of its white haze it had become leaden. There was no cloud visible, only this ominous change of light. Then came a wind, skimming straw from the stacks, sending men's hats bowling along the yard. Said Bob, 'We're goin' to cop, chaps.'

Cold drops fell on our faces and rustled on the sheaves. Grasses trembled. A flash of lightning flickered twice; thunder rumbled like barrels rolling over a wooden floor above us. As though that had been its signal, the rain hissed down, hazing everything.

The first surprise over, there was a great running to and fro. Coats? Some had left theirs far off, others had forgotten where they had laid them, and others had left home without coats at all. I thought they would all take shelter. But no; they knew this was the moment for redoubled action. Flinging sacks, cloths, or anything that lay handy round them, they ran to new work, losing suddenly their leisured stride as only on the occasion of the rabbit chasing before.

Four lifted a stack-cover on to the unfinished stack, the top of which was so flat that the rain would have soaked half the sheaves in ten minutes. When it was unrolled, the wind got under it and would have wrenched it off, but others below hung upon the cords and fastened them to logs of wood. Another group was forking straw on to a second stack for which there was no cloth. Meanwhile, Bob and his sons had run into the meadows to fetch in some mares with foals at grass. They came through the yard at the trot, whinnying loudly, their foals prancing excitedly behind.

Puddles now stood in the yards; the wheel-tracks became streams. The men in the field were seen working energetically to complete the last load there. This they did, and urged a single horse home with it, not waiting for the trace-horse. Only when all this had been done did the men seek shelter under a Dutch barn, and stand wringing out their wet clothes.

'Blasted if my face don't stream as though I sweat pourin',' said Bob, mopping dews from his cheeks.

'Who'd ever have thought a half-hour ago 'twas goin' to rain pouring like this?' said another above the din of the rain upon the tin roof of the Dutch barn.

'Pourin',' pronounced with an onomatopoeic slur, from its obvious application to rain, has become a general superlative in Suffolk. Thus we get Bob's remark of 'sweat pourin',' and from that Simmons's even less salubrious, as he struggled to dislodge barley spikes from his neck, 'I itch pourin'.'

The rain did not last long. It softened, becoming just a delicate gauze over shadowy places, and ceased, leaving a verdurous smell in the air. Clear sky approached again from the horizon, and the sun gleamed out upon the retreating storm, lighting trees and fields against a background of gloom.

By the morrow the earth had forgotten the shower and harvest continued. On that day two horses ran away with a wagon. It was on its way to the field empty when the trace-horse jerked his bridle up and caught a glimpse of the wheels behind him, which started him off, and the shaft-horse had perforce to follow, and was in a moment as uncontrollable as the other. Bob's son was riding in the wagon. Bob witnessed the whole scene from the barn, which we were filling then; he said nothing, but just watched and waited. The horses were quite out of hand, and making roughly in the direction of the gateway. As they reached it, his son leaped out into the hedge. The wagon got through, dipping a wheel into the ditch, and the horses galloped twice round a twenty-acre field before coming to a halt.

The boy picked himself out of the hedge, scratched but otherwise not hurt. As for the wagon, it was seventy years old, but finished the harvest.

In the afternoon I went to the inn and ordered some beer for the men. Two men were tarring the road, and they came into the bar as I was there. I asked them what they would have, as I was just ordering a pint for myself there and then, that being none too much for me now, and the day when I had poured some away seeming distant almost to disbelief.

It was three pints of 'old and mild,' and as they gave me 'Good health' I suggested that their job must be as hot a one as could be devised for summer days, dabbling with boiling pitch. They said I was right, and envied me my harvest work. The fumes of the tar made their throats 'dry fit to crack,' they said. Their hands were black, and they reeked of it.

Stebling paused in passing on his way home from market. I asked him, were there many farmers there? He said the markets had been very thin of late owing to this grand harvest weather. 'But there's always several chaps hang about there, wet or fine, dressed up and with nothing to do seemingly.' He deplored modern dress tendencies. 'Why, you can't tell the master from his chaps; they are all collar-and-tie men nowadays.'

When the beer arrived in the field, we drank to Bob's son's lucky escape. He was seventeen but at harvest-time I have seen loaded wagons in charge of boys of twelve. They manoeuvred them through gateways and round corners with the utmost assurance. Driving a wagon through a gateway or into a barn is not easy. One is at first inclined to discountenance the length of the thing. Nor can the front wheels be locked round too sharply or they catch on the undercarriage, and the wagon is likely to be tipped over.

I was speaking to Bob about a certain field of barley, recently cut, wondering whether it was to be carried next: but he said, 'No, it wants more "bright Phoebe" on it yet.' Where he got his corruption of old mythology from I could not tell.

So we worked. The fork-handles bent and shone, occasionally snapped, and were replaced by white straight new ones. Even fork-sticks, according to Bob, were not what they used to be. There was individuality in forks. Bob would have none but his own. He could tell it with his eyes shut by its weight and the feel of the stick. There were discriminations. 'That's a good fork for straw-carting, now, but the tines take hold too much for sheaves. But that there [taking it in his hands], I reckon that's a nice weight for a sheaf-fork.' Of one, particularly light and small, that a certain dilettante young labourer affected, Bob remarked, 'I reckon he uses that to take the dumplings out of the pot.'

There was one big labourer among them that prided himself on his strength, lifting two and three sheaves at a time from the wagon, even when we were unloading in the barn where the elevator could not be used, and the stack was so high that he had to lift them, causing me embarrassment as I stood on the edge taking them from him. When his back was turned, the boy Jack tied a couple of the sheaves to the side of the wagon. When he came to them in unloading, he stuck his fork deep in as usual, and strained and strove, his fork bending, and the very wagon creaking and wringing, while those on the stack shouted encouragement: 'Pull, Bert, don't be beat.'

All day the loaded wagons come rumbling into the barn. Again and again they are unloaded and the sheaves stacked in the bays mount gradually higher, till the men can rest, between loads, against the cobwebbed cross-beams. All morning they talk and laugh. They become expansive and reminiscent at harvest-time. The older men speak of harvests that have been, of men they have worked with that are dead, of times and places – of particular crops in particular fields. It is always, 'Do you remember that time when . . . ?' or 'Do you know what became of So-and-so?' As they rise higher, and the country seen through the open doors is spread at their feet, old horizons give place to new, more distant ones, where buildings show faintly, churches or farms, and discussion turns to them, whose or of what village they may be.

Towards evening talk languishes; the intervals between question and answer lengthen. Laughter is peremptory, short-breathed. A grimness then steals over the scene – arms and bodies swaying, forks sweeping to and fro, eyes cast down and little said. Only the rustle of sheaves is heard in the settling gloom. I take my turn at unloading with the rest. At first it is distress, for one must unbuild a load as a stack, taking always the top sheaf, and always that seems the one I am standing on. There is no room to move about on the load of sheaves; they are uneven, slippery. My feet fall into crevices, and I stumble. Uncertain foothold makes double labour of it. Yet the men, unwieldy-figured, balance easily, and bend and thrust up, rhythmically. I watch them to learn their ease; the motion that saves the most energy is also the most graceful.

I stand on the stack catching the sheaves as they swing up from below and passing them across. As my fork comes back empty, I find almost automatically another sheaf on its tines. I can labour thus rhythmically, I feel, for ever, but when the rhythm is lost then labour is despair. Comes one sheaf a second – there is a moment when it has left the unloader's fork and not yet reached mine, and pauses in a last sun-ray that transmutes it to a fiery symbol. The next moment it is on my fork, the rich light past, a sheaf of corn again.

My shirt, open to the waist, reveals to me my body at work, the flesh rippling, tightening, and subsiding. What a rare machine this is, able to balance on two feet on a shifting surface and wield weights.

Outside the moon is up – the harvest moon over harvest fields. It casts a sheen upon the empty stubbles, the bare rounding slopes, so altered from the close-crowded landscape of standing corn. It has glimmering secrets among the trees, and pierces into every entanglement of foliage, and lays faint shadows across the paths. Each finds a ghost of himself beside him on the ground. An elusive radiance haunts the country; the distances have a sense of shining mist. The men move homeward from the field; the last load creaking up the hill behind them, the hoofs of the horses thudding, their breath sounding short. Peace comes, a vision in the fairy armour of moonlight, the peace of 'man goeth forth unto his work until the evening.'

The last load is drawn into the barn to be unloaded in the morning. The horses stand with foam on their bridles, their flanks heaving after the long pull; struggle is in their attitude. It is quite dark in the barn. There is a rattle of chains as the horses are unhitched and led away, the voices of men helping the load into position, a clatter of wood as a block is kicked under a wheel, the music of steel on steel as forks are laid together.

The men straggle out into the moonlight and pause in a group on the roadway, gazing at the sky, at the moon in her glory. (When the men pause in their work they always look at the sky.)

'Don't look much like wet,' says one. 'Don't want neither till that barley's out of the way.'

'Looks like the colour of money to me,' says another. Bob comes down from the stable. 'Ho, she's regular showing off to-night,' is his tribute. 'Well, I'm goin' to see about some supper,' he says. There is a murmur of considered assent, as though there was something original in the idea. With gruff 'Good nights' the group disperses, some going up the road, some down, and some across the fields.

The last footfall dies into silence. The stillness tingles with the aftermath of noise. All around stand the new cornstacks, unfamiliar shadows, ramparts thrown up suddenly round the yard. An owl detaches itself silently from the darkness of a beam, swoops down into the moonlight and away, now white against a shadow, now black against the moon. A mouse scuttles somewhere in the straw. The gaunt shape of a binder stands in a corner, angular as a skeleton under its cloth. Its work is over until next year.

Harvest was over, and Mr and Mrs Colville and I were off to the seaside for the week-end. We passed the farm of Mr Depden, Mrs Colville's father, on the way, and he was in shirt-sleeves and bowler hat, bending over a binder in an uncut field of wheat, with a labourer beside him, while the horses stood swishing their tails.

'I see you've started harvest,' said Mr Colville, pulling up.

I found this was literally true; he had just started. All around were fields of standing corn, some still green.

Mr Depden turned. 'Good morning,' and 'Good morning to you, my dear,' he said to his daughter in the precise sing-song voice he affected.

'You'll be done by Christmas, I expect,' Mr Colville said with mock solemnity.

Mr Depden bore the jest. 'I shall be done in time, never fear. I'm in no hurry.'

'Something broken?' Mr Colville asked.

'Just a little hitch,' the old man replied.

'Not the first one, I'll be bound.' The binder certainly looked more fit for the scrap-heap than the field.

'I thought perhaps you might be coming to the seaside with us.' Mr Colville laughed.

Mr Depden shook his head. 'Ah, no. I find that as soon as you set foot outside your farm you are apt to be spending money. They are always inventing something to get your money nowadays.'

As we pushed on, Mr Colville remarked, 'You can't say nothing to him that he'll take notice of. He just goes on in his own way. He doesn't care when he finishes harvest; nothing puts him out. But he's got plenty of money; he can afford to do as he likes.'

Mr Depden was a man who chose rather to lose a pound than spend a shilling.

'I don't reckon he's bought a new implement since he was a young man,' said Mr Colville. His cartsheds were like lumber-dumps; he was always buying lots of old iron at sales, in the hope of finding therein wherewithal to patch up his dilapidated machines and carriages. Thus his farming was beset with delays, men and horses standing idle in the field while he fumbled about replacing a broken part with one from a machine still older. He set his barley in June and harvested it in October. He has set corn even later that never came to harvest at all.

He had an old steam-engine, a rusty monster, and a threshing-drum sprouting grass and corn at every crevice, an elevator all awry. It was a fearsome sight to see him getting up steam for threshing. The engine spurted vapour like a dragon with fifty nostrils. Said Mr Colville, 'I durstn't be within half a mile of it – it would blow up any moment.'

If he couldn't make just the price he asked for his wheat, Mr Depden would not sell it, and it would lie for months in the barn till in May the weevil got into it, and a heap of one hundred coombs would be seen moving, every grain, like an army. The wheat crept everywhere, even into the house, and Mrs Colville told me that when a girl she had found it in her bedroom.

Mr Depden's agriculture was eccentric in this also that one year he would fallow the whole farm, another year grow only beans. Yet he had strange luck. The year he fallowed his farm turned out a very bad harvest; one year he set every field with oats, and oats happened to make unusually good price.

But luck like that was not sufficient to make him rich, and I asked Mr Colville how long he had practised these disastrous methods; they surely were the whimsies of old age, for an ordinary man would long ago have been ruined by them.

'Well, he had two wonderfully good foremen,' Mr Colville began. The first one had started as what they call in Suffolk a back-house boy, at the age of fourteen. He chopped wood, pumped water, etc., and lived in. He had the peculiarity of buttering his bread on both sides. Mr Depden scolded him for this extravagant habit, but nothing would break him of it. The boy was ambitious, and raised himself to the position of foreman. He 'managed' Mr Depden and practically ran the farm. Thus, if a machine needed repair and Mr Depden refused to have it done, the foreman sent the machine to the blacksmith on his own account. Now, to Mr Depden, when a thing was done it was done and no more to be worried about, so when the machine returned repaired he just said, 'Dear, dear, you'll ruin me,' and there was an end of it.

Nine out of ten men in that foreman's position would have made capital for themselves out of Mr Depden, but that one was the tenth. Mr Depden had also, by his curious luck, a like foreman on another farm he owned some miles away.

Some years ago the first foreman died, and since then he had practised farming in his own odd way on his home farm. He had given each of his daughters a substantial marriage portion and still had plenty for himself. But buy a new harvest-binder he would not; he preferred to hammer away at the old one and let the harvest wait.

Another curious thing was that, despite his eccentricities and care over pence, despite the fact that he imposed long hours, none of his men ever complained of him or wished to leave him. He had a fatherly and easy manner, and criticism of his methods was not criticism of the man.

On our way to the sea we passed through the town where brother Arnold lived and traded. It consisted chiefly of one long main street and a hill beyond, which had just been attacked by villa-itis.

Arnold's shop had not an imposing exterior, but within it was as murmurous as a hive, and good Saturday afternoon business was being done. The labourer had just received his harvest bonus, and the shopkeepers were now devising how they might get it from him. Temptations stood in every window, or even on the pavement outside. Bicycles glistened: '£1 down and 6 monthly payments,' etc. Clothiers announced, 'Great Harvest Sale: Unique Opportunity', with goods largely labelled and the 'old price' most ruthlessly cancelled with red strokes. In the old days barrels of beer had stood behind the counters, and it had been free drinks to all, under the influence of which the unsteady yokel had seen that the goods were in truth remarkably cheap, and that he had need of them. But the shopkeeper's beer was now illegal. Those days had been known as 'Harvest Saturdays'.

There were gramophones, furniture, all for such a small sum down and such interminable credit.

Arnold was there, keen-eyed and full of bustle, unrolling oilcloth, not for covering his floor, which was bare, but to tempt his customers. The shop, indeed, was singularly unadorned, for, Arnold said, if he put a covering on the floor and made it look a bit sophisticated, the people would

215

murmur among themselves that he must be making large profits out of them, and view his prices with suspicion; these country folk being shrewder in this respect than the London citizen, who, the deeper his foot sinks in a carpet, the more flattered he is and hypnotised.

Arnold did not confine his activities to what he sold in his shop; anything he could turn to good account he dealt in – wine, antique furniture, cars. The average person passing that shop would think, 'Some threadbare fellow just scraping a living.' He would not connect it with a large house in the genteel quarter. Here Arnold lived, and we had tea with his wife. It had been 'bought cheap' at a moment when by chance nobody else had been looking. It was filled with elaborate furniture 'bought cheap' also. Palms reared themselves with lazy grace in the conservatory, and lilies glimmered. And Arnold, financial pillar of the family, had said, 'Anything up to ten thousand pounds I can lend you if you should want.'

As we continued on our way, we came into the main road between the coast resort we were making for and London. An immediate change was apparent. The farm cart, the occasional cattle, the rustic with his pails from the well, and such-like, that had been our only encounters, were here lost in the traffic of fast cars to and fro. Here were hatless heads, flannels, bare legs, flying scarves. And the laughter on the people's faces seemed one with the swiftness of their vehicles, even as were the countryman's quizzical looks with the slowness of his. Here they were elbow to elbow, England's two races – the one whose work the fields were, the other whose holiday.

I tried to imagine Mrs Colville going about without stockings in Benfield or Mr Colville without a hat!

Even the fields beside the road were sprouting a pink

and white fungus of bungalows and tea-houses. Agriculture became a secondary consideration.

And later, as I lay on my back rocked gently in the warm September sea, and gazed at the hotels, piers, promenade, and all the characteristics of that town built for those who did not live in it, and at the crowds sitting on the shore that had gathered from all parts to be its citizens for three weeks or so, I could not banish a feeling of strangeness that the vale of Benfield, with its timeless scenes, should be less than an hour by car from here. About a year ago I had been one of those people on the shore, and their route of London to the sea my route, and all between just 'the country.'

Surely, I thought, as I lay luxuriously among the waves after toil, and watched the fluttering flags and the *Seamouth Belle*, all white and stately, putting off from the pier – surely this town, with its modern architecture and music and shrubbery gardens, is a world away from ploughing, stacking, threshing? But there, just beyond the golf-links for which this place was famous, I saw a Suffolk mangold-field.

Now, harvest being over, I heard talk of farms changing hands. 'So-and-so is giving up his place this Michaelmas; he's bought Such-and-such farm.' 'Has anybody taken— yet?' Rumours of sales and hirings flew about during Sunday evening discussion in old Mr Colville's parlour.

I began, therefore, to consider again my own project of a farm. The idea at home was, I think, that I should spend another year with Mr Colville, and then – well, we should see. I had grown rough-handed and round-faced, was in such robust health that I felt positively oafish in certain tense drawing-rooms of London friends. That was, to my parents' eyes, ample recompense for the present. The country as a career could be considered later.

I had not so far mentioned my secret hope that, despite my mere smattering, Michaelmas should see me in a farm of my own. I have ever been one to try to run before I could walk.

Passing a small farm one day in the car, Mr Colville said to me, 'That chap is getting out of there in October; he has taken a bigger place.'

'Has anyone bought it?' I asked, all alert.

'He only hired it. The owner lives in Stambury. He's a shopkeeper. But he wants to sell it, I believe.'

I asked so many questions about the quality of the land, the acreage and probable price, that Mr Colville, guessing the trend of my thoughts, said, 'It would just about suit you for a start, if you wanted a place of your own.'

I confessed that that was what I did want, remote as the prospect at present seemed. But did he think I should be capable of managing one? I asked.

He laughed. 'There's only fifty acres of that place. Besides, anything you wanted to know I could tell you: it's not far across the fields from Farley Hall.'

He saw that I was taken with the idea, and did what he could to help me. We went to Stambury one day, and interviewed the owner in his shop, whom Mr Colville knew, as he knew everybody. We did not enter full of eager enquiry, as I alone might have done, but strolled in and bought some wire nails (the man was an ironmonger). Then, as though by way of conversation, Mr Colville asked, 'Got a tenant for that little farm of yours, Mr Pyke?'

'No,' replied the man. 'There's a chap would like to hire it, but I want to sell it really.'

'What sort of price do you expect to make of it?'

'Well, I reckon it ought to be worth £25 an acre, seeing it's a small place.'

Mr Colville said 'Hm!' dubiously. 'Things don't look too bright at the moment; there aren't so many buyers for farms as there used to be.'

'I reckon he'd sell it for £20 an acre,' he said as we drove home.

Mr Colville knew the outgoing tenant, and he was pleased enough to show us over the place.

I admit I did not view it in a strictly agricultural light. I found myself attending as much to the decorative aspect of the thatched house as to the quality of the pigsties, and the state of the gutterings. Mr Colville gave the house one glance.

'The roof looks sound enough,' he said, and 'the roof is the thing you want to look at; if that's all right, the house is.'

The walls were ivy-clad. He remarked in passing, 'How the old place is cumbered up with that stuff. I should have it off; it ruins the walls.'

'Yes,' I said, knowing that I should do no such thing.

I saw a space, too, where it occurred to me a dovecote might stand very prettily. Mr Colville was also looking about him here. But he said to the tenant, 'I don't see how the water gets off this bit of ground; looks to me as though there ought to be a grip dug along by that wall.'

I erased the dovecote vision hurriedly, and attended to this more important matter.

We looked over the fields. Mr Colville knew well the quality of the land of this as he did of most farms in the district. His glance to-day was for the state of the stubbles, his questions to elicit how closely the land had been cropped by the tenant during his last years, and whether there was any 'heart' left in it. He had an eye, on our return, to the depth of manure in the cattleyard, and the size of the haystacks, as an indication of the amount of valuation I should have to pay if I came there.

We were strolling back to our car.

'Would you care to see into the house?' the tenant asked.

'I don't think that matters,' Mr Colville replied, and my heart sank. He paused, however, and asked me, 'Would you care to?'

'Well –' I began, irresolute, trying to be the severely practical farmer, yet longing, in spite of that, to see what was behind those casement windows. 'I don't want to disturb your wife,' I said to the man; 'perhaps another time –'

'That's all right; she'd be pleased to show you over,' he replied.

'We might just look, then,' said Mr Colville, and we went in and were met by the farmer's spouse, who looked as though she had worked all the days of her life without ceasing, as she had. (They were an ageing couple, but blithe this day I met them, despite their tooth-and-nail existence since youth. For they had succeeded; they were going up, were getting on; and, though themselves nearly worn out, had two sons to leave to continue the work of family betterment.)

The cottage was as cosy as it looked from outside. There were two living-rooms and three bedrooms with attic ceilings. They led out of one another, so that the earliest riser must have the one nearest the stairs. There was a tiled hall, with an interior window of diamond panes looking into the dairy, which took my fancy, I remember; and an open hearth.

'It would just do for you nicely, that little place,' was Mr Colville's opinion of the farm as we drove away.

I had been beginning to feel that it was already mine,

but now woke up to the fact that I had not yet even told them at home that I was ambitious of owning a farm. I was mostly silent on the way back to Farley Hall, for the possibility of my taking possession of Silverly Farm seemed very remote. Even if in the end they were persuaded in Chelsea to take a sympathetic view, this particular farm would probably be already sold. That should not have worried me in my character of practical farmer (there were other farms): but that character was still liable to desert me suddenly at times. I desired, above all, that particular farm.

I spent a week-end at home. I approached the question diplomatically. I spoke first of the present season in agriculture, and the work which was being done on Farley Hall. Then I mentioned that this was an unsettled time in the country, as Michaelmas was the date when people took farms or gave them up, or changed from one to another, and that date was approaching. From that I went on to remark that several farms were changing hands in our vicinity. There was one, I said, quite near Farley Hall for sale – a little place. Mr Colville had said that it would suit me nicely if I wanted one.

Silence followed this remark. I hastily flung in a few rosy prospects to propitiate it, adding that Mr Colville had said that one never learned farming really till one had experience of managing a place of one's own. (If he hadn't said it, he might have done.)

But the subject was at once shelved with 'Ah, well; one day perhaps.'

I returned to the attack later; generalising mostly, particularising sparingly. My parents had no respite from agricultural topics that week-end. But I returned to Farley Hall without much hope.

Mr Colville suggested, let my parents come to Farley

Hall for a week-end then perhaps they would at all events have a look at Silverly Farm.

My mother came. I led her in the desired direction in the course of a walk.

'What a pretty place,' she said, when the thatched and ivy cottage came in view.

'That happens to be the farm I was speaking of,' I told her, in an off-hand tone.

The farmer appeared opportunely, and, before my mother quite realised what was happening, she was being shown over the place.

I used my tongue as effectively as I could. In the fields I kicked the earth up with my toe and spoke technically of its quality. But in the neighbourhood of the house I dropped the professional for the decorative point of view. I let her see it, not only as it was, but as it *could* be.

'And here,' I said, 'a dovecote; can't you see it, just in that space?'

My mother, as I have mentioned, had been an artist, and she saw it there, just in that space. I had already noted the effect of the interior diamond paned window on her, and the old open hearth, and the old red tiles in the hall.

She came away quite in love with the place. But on the way back she awoke to practical possibilities, as I had done before. 'But your father, I am afraid, would never – never –'

She was on my side, though, now. Somehow, I shall never know how, she got my father used to the idea; infused it in the form of a potion in his tea, perhaps. At any rate, there came a day when I was sitting with Mr Colville and Mr Pyke in that man's parlour behind the ironmongery shop, having handed him a cheque for the deposit on the purchase money of Silverly Farm, and received from him a signed receipt and preliminary agreement, drinking the first whisky and soda of my life, and thanking Mr Pyke for his wish of 'Good luck.'

October; and the signs of October again in the land; ladders in orchards, sheep and fowls on stubbles; new thatch; notices of farm sales plastered upon walls; the first scattering of leaves; and the spirit of ocean in the trees.

I went through the ceremony of valuation on my farm, an auctioneer acting between the outgoing tenant and me. Among other things, I was liable for the ploughing of fallows during the past summer and the setting of clover seed in the corn, the benefit of which I should have the next year. Another rule was that the new owner must thresh the outgoing tenant's corn for him, for which he received the straw.

I was to take possession on October the eleventh, Michaelmas Day, which was the usual date on which farms changed hands. It was a day of General Post in the countryside. Everywhere vans and lorries stacked with furniture went to and fro, for foremen, stockmen, milkmen, horsekeepers, often moved with their masters. The evening of that day saw many settling into new homes, for better or worse.

It was already October, so I made haste to procure implements and horses. I went with Mr Colville to a sale of farming stock near by, whose owner had the reputation of keeping the best.

Cars lined the country road, and tethered ponies in gigs stood against a meadow fence. Auctioneers' men in linen coats bustled about the buildings. The coachhouse had a cardboard notice, 'Office', pinned to the door, and within sat a clerk at a table. The implements were set out in rows in a large meadow, and here also was a roped-in ring with a wagon standing by it, from which the auctioneer should sell the horses.

The farm was a large one, and there were many lots, so the sale had been fixed for eleven o'clock, which meant eleven-thirty, the equivalent of punctuality for a farm sale.

Mr Colville, as usual, was greeted by many. 'Hullo, Colville, how are you?'

'Fairly, thanks.'

'Ah, yes, I can see you're well alive.'

The farm sale, the first shoot, the early morning cubbing – these were the farmers' reunions after harvest.

We received catalogues from the office. As we came out, we met the late occupier of the farm who was retiring on his war-time gains, and was pleased to make a lavish gesture of the occasion by providing luncheon in the barn for the chief farmers of the neighbourhood who should attend the sale. He invited us to partake when we felt inclined. It was a usual thing to provide a barn luncheon in the old days of agriculture, as it was also, at a sale of stock, for the owner to distribute glasses of port round the ring.

We took our catalogues and proceeded to inspect the implements. Some of them shone, newly painted, which Mr Colville said meant precisely nothing, or even less, for such were to be viewed with suspicion as having been 'got up for sale', and their blemishes varnished over. He stuck his penknife into the wheels of carts, testing the soundness of the wood, and with his stick (that invaluable stick) ascertained the play of wheels on axles; poked deep into things, trying the firmness of vital cogs. Of every machine he knew the part which received most wear, and went to that to learn the age of the whole.

He looked at the two corn-drills. 'I reckon they'll be dear,' was his opinion. 'You see, they are what everybody wants this time of year. If they are, don't buy one. I'll lend you my drill to put your corn in with. But I expect the binders will go fairly cheap; it's a long way to harvest.'

A bell rang, and a group collected at the far end of the field round what looked from here like a corpse. The sale had begun. I turned to my catalogue and read:

'Lot 1. Old Tree.
Lot 2. Wagon Wheel.
Lot 3. Quantity of old Iron.
Lot 4. Ditto.'

Lot 5 was 'Sundry Casks' while Lot 6, subtly different, was 'Sundry Tubs', and Lot 7, amplifying the tree motif, was 'Sundry Timber.'

Lot 8 was more definite: 'Pair of Iron Wheels.' Lot 9 struck an imaginative note: 'Ale Stool and Sawing-Horse.' Lot 10 was a generous one: 'Sundry Gate Irons and Rabbit Traps.'

A policeman hovered on the outskirts of the group, observing that all was conducted in an orderly manner. Had he had a catalogue, he would probably have retired tactfully a little distance before the next lot. The auctioneer's man announced in a loud voice: 'Old Copper.' A laugh went round, and the law was a little less majestic in our eyes. Lot 12 had the good taste not quite to repeat the joke – 'Ditto.' Lot 13 had a threatening echo: 'Cart Jack and Knife-sharpening Stand.' Lot 14 was inquisitorial: 'Three Tar Brushes and Pots and 12 long Iron Hooks.' Not just iron hooks, but long. The next lot was a return to the idyllic: 'Pigeon-cote and 2 Milking Stools.' But the devil had not done yet; he was only in ambush. Lot 20: 'Butcher's Block.'

In set-out the catalogue had the appearance of an ode in free verse. Had it come into my possession before I lost interest in free verse I should have copied out a section and sent it to a coterie magazine; and probably it would have been accepted as a piece of inspired exuberance. Perhaps that portion where, after the brusque opening lines ('Old Tree' seemed to me a splendid start), the metre lengthens out and becomes more undulating:

> *Muck crome, two pitchforks, and two 4-tine forks.*
> *Two 4-tine forks, two pitchforks, and two rakes.*
> *Two pitchforks, two spades, fold drift, and stable hoe.*
> *Granary steps and four stable lanterns.*
> *Barn shovel, fold drift, and scythe.*

And then, with just pause for an odd lot, continuing:

> *Two dutfins.*
> *Cob collar.*
> *Two pairs steel hames and chains . . .*

The group round the auctioneer, as it proceeded, gathered to itself those waiting near the things they desired to bid for who had not considered the earlier scrap-lots worth their attention, but left behind it also a trail of those who had bought and were examining those lots and were comparing their money's worths.

There was Jerry Hogbooth, a lusty higgler. He had bought the tubs, and banged each with his hand as though to accentuate his ownership; and held them up to the light, squinting into them to see whether they leaked. The man who had bought the old tree was still standing over it (it was indeed like a corpse whose arms had stiffened while stretching for help), determining how and where he should cut it to cart it home.

Over Lot 3, 'Quantity of old Iron', stooped none other than Mr Depden, and drew forth, and held up triumphant to a friend, what looked like a petrified starfish – the very part he needed to urge on his halting harvest. Such a heap was a mine of possible treasure to Mr Depden, and for a long time he bent over it, sorting and holding things up to the light.

But when the sale reached the lots headed, 'Machines, etc.', beginning: 'Bean Drill, Fiddle Drill, Hay Toppler', it really became of interest to the large farmer. I bought a plough, price £3 10s., two tumbrils, one costing £20, a good one, and another not so good, but serviceable, for £8. I bought harrows, pig troughs, and other necessaries.

Then we had lunch in the barn previous to the selling of the horses. Here stood scrubbed trestle-tables furnished with knives, forks, glasses, ale jugs, loaves, and cheese. At a side-table a matron was carving cold joints of beef and ham, and behind her stood two barrels of beer. A number of people were there, some sitting eating, and others standing in the middle-tree of the barn and round the doorway with mugs in their hands. The lofty gloom of the place, and the tables and food, gave it the appearance of a mediaeval hall. A man recognised Mr Colville. 'Going to have something to eat, sir? Come and sit here'; and to me, 'Here you are, sir; plenty of room here.' He shifted up, and we sat beside him.

He addressed me. 'Ah, sir, you've taken Dobson's farm, I hear. Well, that's a rare good little farm; a sound bit of dirt that is, sir, and if you do it as well as he did it you won't take any harm. I've seen some master crops there, some master crops. You've bought one or two things here, I noticed.' Then he became confidential. 'If you want any horses here, I can put you on to the ones to buy.'

Mr Colville became interested, and said, 'Ah, I was going to ask you, seeing you have to do with them; the horsekeepers, of course, won't tell a likely buyer if there's anything wrong, except he's the incoming farmer who's going to employ them.'

We had gone the round of the stables beforehand, in each of which the huge buttocks of six horses confronted us, with straw-knotted tails; and in each stable stood a horsekeeper in his best clothes, very stiff and solemn, looking upon his horses for the last time, many of them, and prepared to answer questions about them. Mr Colville was indefatigable on my behalf. We examined mouths, feet, legs. Once he whispered to me, 'Grease. I never thought Simpling had grease in his stables.' Of another he said, 'I don't like her; she's too swamp-backed.' Of another, 'Nice clunchy [i.e. compact] little mare.'

The horsekeepers were very reticent, and did not mention faults unless Mr Colville spoke first of them; having found them out. The most one could get the horsekeepers to admit was that two years must be added on to the horses' ages as catalogued.

But the man beside whom we were lunching, and who was just emptying his second pint pot, was the man employed for plaiting up horses' tails and manes with straw in preparation for sale. This, combined with a little subsidiary dealing, was his chief business, and, besides his fee, a hair from each horse's tail was his perquisite. As he practised his trade every day during this season, he garnered a quantity of valuable horsehair, which augmented his income.

Now, as he was not a buyer, and was at work in the

stables before the buyers arrived, the horsekeepers talked freely to him about the merits and demerits of the horses. So he had truly inside information, and imparted it to us marking on our catalogues the horses to bid for.

The horsekeepers were the only employees on the farm who had duties to-day; they alone were 'on edge', the others lounging about, husky and rosy with beer. Even the foreman was more or less bibulous, and his bowler had got askew and was allowed to stay so. Just outside the barn, two of the younger men stood with pint mugs, becoming exhilarated with quite a small expenditure of wit.

As we came out of the barn, an old open carriage known as a Victoria was being sold. It was not by any means outworn, looking glossy and graceful, dreaming a dream of parasols in the Park, but long, long ago outmoded. It was sold for £1. The buyer, who had a milk round, was chaffed. 'Are you going to take the milk round in it, Samuel?' And, 'Now you'll want a coachman.' What he was going to do with it, nobody knew. He did not know himself.

A man with watery eyes approached me, dressed in an old green overcoat. 'You'll be wanting me, I daresay, sir; just send me a card. I do Mr Colville's work.' He was a castrator of pigs, a 'sow-gelder'.

Now people were closing round the horse-ring, and the auctioneer's man in white coat was taking the first horse from the horsekeeper, and the next was standing at a distance, ears cocked and restless.

The horse was trotted up and down the ring, allowed to stand while the bidding began. Half-way through the sale of him, when the bidding lagged, the auctioneer commanded another showing of his paces. 'See how he moves, gentlemen, see how he moves.' Another employee of the auctioneer, posted at the entrance of the ring with a whip to see that they did move, cracked it at the horse's heels as he passed, which made him move a good deal too much for the man leading him, who was embarrassingly trying to check while the other urged, and made savage remarks *sotto voce* to the whiphand as he passed again.

I turned to my catalogue: 'Horses. All Active and Good Workers.'

1. 'Oak.' Pedigree Suffolk Gelding. 6 years.
2. 'Violet.' Pedigree Suffolk Mare. 7 years.
3. 'Beauty.' Bay Mare. Aged.
4. 'Darky.' Black Mare. 9 years.
5. 'Dewdrop.' Suffolk Mare. 6 years.
   Etc., etc.

The next one reared as it was brought forward, and the crowd gave it good space, crying, 'Whoa, my beauty.' The auctioneer turned the incident to good account, saying, 'Plenty of spirit, gentlemen, plenty of spirit.'

I bid for Darky. To-day was the first time I had ever bid at an auction sale, and it was exciting; the business of catching the auctioneer's eye as it swept to and fro over the people, the wondering whether it really was my bid he had taken and not somebody's behind me, the tense pause waiting to see whether my bid would be topped before the auctioneer's drone of, 'Going at forty-five, going at . . .' finally ceased at the hammer-stroke, an interval filled with the thought, 'That animal there is nearly mine.'

When there were only two of us left in the bidding, the auctioneer's eyes reverted immediately to me after the other had bid. 'Against you, there, against you at forty-six . . .'

I bought Darky and Dewdrop for forty-seven and forty-five guineas respectively. The auctioneer remembered my name from the things I had bought earlier in the sale. 'Mr Bell, isn't it? Yes.' It was a recognition of me as member of the agricultural community, a farmer; no longer a youth looking at farming. Had I not received a circular that morning addressed to Mr Bell, Farmer, Benfield St George, desiring to interest me in pig meal of a patent kind? Here, too, I had been approached by makers of poultry huts, purveyors of artificial manures, all smiling, all confident they could serve me to our mutual advantage.

At the end of this sale there were some lots of household furniture, and here and at other sales I collected a few things wherewith temporarily to furnish my house – a bed, a sinuous-backed sofa, an easy chair, a table, etc. There was a choice of two tables, a Pembroke single pedestal of good design, and a light-coloured oval one with bulbous legs. Mr Colville pointed out that the latter was the better, as it had four legs to the other's one. But I bought the Pembroke.

I gathered my things within my gate, and on October 11th took possession.

October 12th was the golden anniversary of old Mr and Mrs Colville's wedding. I went early to tender my congratulations. The church bells were ringing, for it was at that hour they had rung for their marriage fifty years ago. Moreover, the oldest bellringer ringing now had helped ring the bells then.

It was a great family reunion. Many were already there – Arnold, Dick, their wives and children. The old servant was jogging about in a fluster of preparation, the coachman was scheming how to fit all the cars into the yard. Daughters-in-law busied themselves about the house, while the old lady hovered to and fro among them with frail tentative hands. Sometimes one cried, 'Now you sit down and rest, Mrs Colville. You don't need to do anything to-day.' But the old lady was perturbed at so much bustle, liking to do things in her own quiet, drifting way. She was sure something would get broken – in her heart she would be glad when it was all over and she and the old servant Emily were alone again to sort out the things that these well-meaning people had put tidily away in the wrong places.

In the parlour the old man sat for a while in thought; his grandchildren were hanging paper chains across the low ceiling, standing on chairs and chattering. Occasionally, one fell and wreathed him, but he did not take account of it. The table was covered with letters, telegrams, presents. A silver sugar-bowl presented by the villagers stood there; an old sporting-print from Mr Maglin, whom, the first strangeness over, the Colvilles had greatly taken to. Then Arnold and Dick came into the room, and their father went out with them to show them the latest doings on the farm.

That evening all the lights and fires were lit. The lamps with the frosted globes were lit in the dining-room, and the brass standard lamps with the pink silk shades in the drawing-room, and lanterns were hung about the yard that people might see their way after switching off the lights of their cars.

More Colvilles were crowded into the house than I had ever met before. The drawing-room was full of little tables, and the evening began with a whist-drive which was also a conversazione, the party having mastered the art of playing and talking at the same time, in which I was deficient. I drifted from one table to another, dazed by the buzz of conversation. Always some new face would be before me, my partner – now an old woman in a shawl, now a young married woman, now a girl of sixteen. Beside me, as my opponent, would be perhaps one of the brothers, his great hands dealing heavily with the cards, eyes bright to see what pictures he held this time. Arnold would always have his moment of triumph; he might be badly down, but he would contrive to trump on his opponent's ace with, 'There, got you that time.'

Little dishes of chocolates were passed round. One came to the corner of my table. I offered the dish to the girl of sixteen, my partner, and she took a gold-wrapped chocolate, smiling acknowledgment and wondering who I was, and I wondering who she was. Dick's daughter was here too, in a too sophisticated frock. Her teeth halved a chocolate fastidiously, and she gazed enquiringly at the segment in her fingers – pink cream; she approved; the second half followed the first.

Mr Depden was here, stroking his chin as he considered his next lead; he was wearing his lavender waistcoat with the lapels and a grey silk tie. I chanced beside Mr Colville – John, my agricultural guide – at a table, and he asked me how my first day of farming had gone, continued with some advice as to harrowing a certain field destined for wheat. His sister was here, who had married a man who rather fancied himself as a dandy horseman among farmers, distinguished, as he sat here, by a horseshoe pin, a higher collar than most, and a rose in his buttonhole with a little receptacle peeping from beneath his coat-lapel which held water and kept it fresh.

Another Colville brother was here whom I had not met before. He had to do with a distillery, and went all over the country. He told me the best hotels to stay at, and, remembering a name he had mentioned to me when, years since, I chanced to seek a night's rest at Plymouth, I went there, and it was as he said. Uncles conferred together as to how quickly the years do pass, to be sure, and young cousins vied for the favour of Dick's daughter.

The whist-drive ended, and we counted up scores. The prizes were presented amid clapping of hands, the booby prize, an eccentric sawdust-stuffed dog, with laughter; I escaped it by one only.

Then we crushed into the dining-room to a great meal, old Mr and Mrs Colville sitting side by side at the head of the broad table. Mr Maglin arrived for this, having been detained before by parish business, and said grace. Towards the end, Mr Depden stood up and in his best voice said, 'I cannot let an occasion like this go by without expressing what I am sure are the wishes of all – to congratulate our host and hostess on the fiftieth anniversary of their marriage, and to wish them many more years of health and prosperity, and to thank them' – he indicated the table with a gesture, and plunged into the superlative – 'for the magnificent repast they have here provided. I am sure you will agree with me – will agree with me that none have more thoroughly earned the respect of all. They are an example to the young, and to the old – to the old . . .' He could not find a phrase to express exactly what they meant to the old, but left it and proposed their health. This Mr Maglin seconded with a well-turned phrase or two, and we lifted our glasses and drank.

Old Mr Colville then rose and said, 'Well, I'm not anything of a speechmaker and I won't try. All I can say is, I thank you very much, all of you, and I hope you are enjoying it as much as I am seeing you here.'

After the supper we returned, some of us, to the drawing-room where music sounded. The room had been cleared in our absence, and two men played, one the piano and the other a violin. We danced. The Colville brothers seized their wives, who protested their dancing days were over, and pushed them round. They clasped each other by the elbows and jogged along with a kind of shuffle and hop, shuffle and hop. Was that how they had danced in the upper room of the inn in the good old days? I wondered. I steered Dick's daughter through the maze in a fox-trot.

She said, 'Uncle John said, "I don't understand how you dance these modern dances," and I said, "I don't understand how you dance those old ones." I mean, just look at father now.' Dick had definitely abandoned his attempt at the fox-trot and was revolving riotously in a polka.

Mr Depden stood watching in a corner, tapping to the rhythm with his foot. The grandchildren were pulling crackers on the hearthrug. Old Mr Colville sat there rather thoughtful, gazing at the dancers, then at the fire. I joined him, one of the cousins having seized my partner at the first opportunity. A grandchild crowned the man with a paper hat, a bonnet; I received one of a martial kind. On the mantelpiece stood war-time photographs of his two youngest sons in khaki.

I remarked that it was a very happy reunion.

'Yes,' he replied, looking to me from the fire, 'I am glad I have lived to see this day, and my boys all alive and well, what with the war and all, and their children too.'

'It must be almost a record,' I suggested.

'Indeed, I thank God for the mercies He has bestowed on me,' said the old man. And we went on to talk about wheat-sowing, I in my martial hat, he in his bonnet.

Towards midnight we sang 'Auld Lang Syne.' I looked well upon that great circle of crossed clasped hands – father, mother, sons, daughters, sons' sons, and daughters' daughters – for it seemed to me that it had remained unbroken longer than Fate usually allows, and soon somebody must fall out, and, times being what they were, I might never again see such a family thus gathered in their home.

I walked with a lantern to my small farm across the fields. Darky and Dewdrop peered at me over the wall of the yard. The night air refreshed me, and I felt far from sleep. I lit my lamp and opened my new account-book at the first page.

THE END